MW01137777

This is a work of fiction. Names, characters, places, and incidents are products of the author's imagination or are used fictitiously and are not to be assumed as real. Any resemblance to actual events, locales, organizations, or persons, living or dead, is entirely coincidental.

Kyle

Thank so much

for the Support!

Enjoy!

Sada Pearl

DEDICATION

This book is dedicated to my love for music, and especially to the ones who have made my "insane" moments – SANE. Nathan M, Shawn S, Wanya M, Brian M, Sheléa F and all the R& B, Gospel and Jazz Artists who rock my world with their lyrics.

ACKNOWLEDGEMENTS

The art of teaching I have learned now is ongoing. There have been ups and downs in this writing journey of mine and guess what, it is only BEGINNING!! So let's get this rolling, First and Foremost, I am thanking GOD, his will is always my motivation to write. Without him, none of this would ever be possible. I would also like to shout out my family and friends, especially my legacies. Quentein and Alvin Jr., the dash I am creating is for both of you!!

Next my family: Auntie Gloria K, father, Ernest, my sisters Meco, Tricia, Darenda, Ta-Nisha, Tina W, Jay, Dani, Sonia, Joy, Latonya, Monique. My nieces' To-Nesha, Tyra, Ashley, Octavia, Jordyn, Camryn, and Lauryn, I love you all to pieces and all the rest of my huge family & friends that consists of blood, ties, and strength. I can't say enough how you all have encouraged me. A special thank you to my muse, for being my personal sunshine!

Thank you, thank you, thank you: Lovey, N'icola, Jessica Watkins, JWP Authors, and all my current supporters, and future supporters. I wouldn't be here if it weren't for your belief in me. Finally to the best Promotion Team ever, Indie Love Promotions, for stepping in and showing out- Round 2!!

PROLOGUE

Two and a half years ago

Shontell tried to keep her eyes on the road since she wasn't used to the California streets. She still couldn't believe the turn of events that even had her driving here. Usually, she was always with Jesse, and he never drove. He always had a driver.

It had been three weeks since she had heard from or even seen her fiancé. They were supposed to be getting married in a month. She wasn't even sure that was going to happen. Sitting at a red light, she replayed his last visit. She remembered being upset because of a tabloid picture of him and some woman at a party.

"This is what you do now?" she screamed at him, throwing the paper in his face.

"What?! Why are you so mad? It was just a party. You are the one who doesn't like going to these events. You can't expect me to miss everything because you don't like being in the spotlight."

"Wow, that's not fair," she retorted back, quickly wiping the tears on her face away. She stood up in her living room and paced the floor, trying to control her anger. So this is what this was about…because she didn't want to be in the public eye? Why did they always have to talk about this? He always said he understood but then, on the flip side, threw it up in her face when it suited him. His footsteps across her hardwood floor broke into her thoughts as she felt him standing behind her. His breath was on her neck and tickled her skin. She knew what he was doing, and it wouldn't work this time. Slowly he turned her around to him, but she folded her arms and kept her eyes on the floor.

"Listen, I don't want to fight about this. I was going to tell you. You know I didn't want you to see it like this. We are getting married in two months. Are you still going to take this same stand? I mean…think about it…no one even knows we are getting married outside of our families because that is how you wanted it. I've gone along with this for the last three years because I needed you to see how serious I was. But don't you think I have proven that with this?" he said as he took her hand and put the ring he bought her in her face. She glared at him and snatched her hand away.

"Jesse, you knew what my cards looked like going into this game. I get so tired of this back and forth crap when it suits you. All I am saying is if that is what you were going to do, don't you think you should have at least given me the courtesy of a heads up?"

"I didn't have the time. Rodge called me three hours before the event with my tickets, and he said me bringing someone was more favorable than not. And it was not like I could have you flown to California to go. This is not that much of a big deal," Jesse said while he headed to her bar and poured a drink. He watched her stand there over the rim of his glass. She glared back at him and remained quiet. This was what she didn't want. It was just too damn much. Jesse stood at six-foot-two, brown skin, broad shoulders, and a nice body…not great, but nice. He had the kind of eyes that made you want to swim in them. That is what got her when they met, and she was lost after that. She wanted to believe what he was telling her. But she had her suspicions about his manager, Rodge. He covered for him too much.

"I just bet he did," she finally spoke, rolling her eyes at him. Jesse slammed down his glass, and it made her jump.

"Shontell, are you really going to do this? What do you have against Rodge?"

"Outside of that fact that he is a liar and doesn't respect our relationship…oh, nothing. You should be asking yourself; what does he have against me."

"What is that supposed to mean?"

"Please, don't make me laugh. He is the one who told you to get me to sign a prenup."

"He is just protecting my best interests."

"More like protecting his pockets. You know what…I am done talking about this. I am tired, and I have an event in the morning," she told him, finally leaving her spot by the fireplace. She picked up her uneaten dinner and walked into the kitchen. She was about to return to the living room to get Jesse's plate when she almost ran right into him because he was standing right behind her. She didn't hear him this time walk up to her.

"Damn it, Jesse," she told him, clutching her chest.

"I'm sorry. I thought you heard me."

"No, I didn't. Now, excuse me, I want to finish cleaning this kitchen."

"So how long is this going to last, Shon?"

"Until you decide if my needs are greater than your wants. You could have easily told Rodge 'no' about the date request. It's like you are ok with blatantly allowing the disrespect. If I can't trust you, I damn sure can't marry you," she told him as she walked around him to finish what she was doing.

She heard him curse under his breath. When she walked back into the kitchen, he had his coat on. She didn't even care, she was so mentally tired. She stopped what she was doing and looked at him. Jesse smiled slightly at her. That was his usual "step one" of making sure she didn't stay mad at him, but this time it wasn't going to be as easy as it used to be.

"I think I am going to go over to the studio for a while to give you some time to cool off," he explained to her. He walked over to her and tried to hug and kiss her. She didn't reciprocate. He pulled back and gave her a look she hadn't seen on him unless they were talking about her best friend, Sandy. He was getting irritated that for once he couldn't get her to do what he wanted. He let her go and headed to the door. He turned around when she called out his name.

"Jesse, maybe we need to take a little break before we walk down the aisle. We both need to see if we can take one another, flaws and all."

"Is that really what you want?" he asked her with a look of shock on his face.

"Yes. Yes, it is," she said, shuffling her feet and looking at the floor again. That was one of her bad habits she was always trying to break. She needed that moment to completely convince herself of her own request. She looked up when she heard the door slam. That was the last time she had heard from him.

When she pulled down Jesse's street, she had to let the window down. She was nervous and had started to sweat. The warm California air was so much different than Detroit's this time of year. She began to see landmarks that were familiar to her. Slowing down and pulling the car up to the entrance, she pulled her phone out. After searching for the entry code, she located it and punched it in. The gate jerked open and she checked her appearance in the rearview mirror. She pulled all the way in and parked right at the front door. She didn't see Jesse's car. If he wasn't home, she would just wait for him. Maybe she would surprise him with dinner. Using her key, she walked into the foyer, set her purse down, and headed into the main area. She could tell his cleaning lady had been there recently.

Jesse wasn't a slob. But for an entertainer, he always had his stuff everywhere. The house was quiet, and she started to call out his name when she heard a noise from upstairs. Taking the stairs slowly, she listened more closely. She felt her breathing quicken as she stood outside the door. Her legs felt like jelly, and she thought if she tried to move she would fall for sure. The sounds in the room were getting louder. It was definitely the sounds of a woman moaning. Her hands were shaking as she finally willed her legs to move. Maybe Jesse let someone use his house. For his sake, that's what it had better be. As the door slowly opened, she felt the bile rising in her mouth at what she was seeing. A Black woman was sitting on Jesse's face. He was lying on his back. She was sitting sideways, which kept Shontell from seeing both of their faces. But she knew it was Jesse by the tattoo that was on the arm that was grabbing hold of a Latina woman who was riding him; her long hair cascading over his legs as her head was thrown back in passion.

Shontell walked backwards in disbelief until she felt her back hit the edge of the wall hard. She didn't even care about her pain. She didn't even realize she made a sound, but the room suddenly got quiet as they all stopped to see what the noise was. Jesse's eyes bucked when he saw her. He quickly pushed both women off him as he got out the bed and grabbed his shorts. She didn't know when she gathered her strength, but she finally reached her car. When she started it up, she looked in the rearview mirror and saw Jesse chasing behind the car and yelling. She never saw the gate until it was too late. Then she kept screaming until everything went black.

Jessica Watkins Presents

Dreams Do Come True

by Jada Pearl

DIVINE ATTRACTION

Shontell

Shontell has been an events and meeting planner for close to ten years, so why was she so nervous about her new clients? Maybe it's because she completely loved their music and had been a fan since they started. She tapped her heels at the hotel's entrance, glancing at her watch every few minutes. They were running late and would be even later to the new album release party that she was in charge of this evening. Just then, she spotted the limo coming around the corner.

She checked her nerves. Fixing her clothes, she waited until the men stepped out the limo; all four of the members of Divine Attraction were fine. She let out a slow breath. Nico Baker, who was about six-feet tall, was known for his caramel complexion and a shy smile. He wore fashion glasses most of the time. John Dell was about five-foot-eight; he had a dark chocolate complexion, deep dimples, and a stocky build. David and Dennis Roberts were brothers. Both stood tall at six-foot-two and had the same milk chocolate complexion, but only one wore glasses. They weren't twins, but they closely resembled one another. The men came toward her and all smiled in greeting. She had met them backstage each time they came into town, but it had never been this formal. She wasn't surprised when Nico asked if they had met before. She laughed slightly and replied, "Something like that."

Nico tilted his head to the side and gave her a strange look. He didn't say anything back to her comment, but she felt him watching her.

She escorted them to check in and then up to their rooms. Shontell told them they had about an hour to get ready. She informed them that she would be in the hospitality suite off of the lobby area, waiting for them. The group's business manager, Martin, touched her shoulder and asked to speak with her before she went down the hall. Martin Downs was an older man and very thorough. He contacted her shortly after he attended a birthday party she had planned for his sister, and he told her that night that he loved her spirit and professionalism.

"I just wanted to speak with you briefly to make sure that everything was planned as we last spoke," he stated.

"Oh yes, Mr. Downs. Everything is just as you wanted it. I called the location right before you pulled up. They are expecting us by 10:45 p.m. The group will perform two songs, and then they will do autographs and pictures. The radio stations did an excellent job of promoting the event. I heard that it's standing room only, so we should be all set. Three radio station interviews are set up for tomorrow, and then you have the rest of the evening to yourself. Your tour bus has been prepared as requested. It is scheduled to be here at 9:30 a.m. so that you can make it to your next destination on time."

Once they finished with the business conversation, she left to run to her own room and change quickly. On her way back down, she stopped to speak with the hotel manager about the arrangements she had requested. Then she headed into the hospitality suite.

Nico

Nico watched Shontell walk away with a smile of appreciation. He wasn't expecting her as the planner. He instantly liked her flair and professionalism. They usually had a man or an older woman. She kind of threw him for a loop when they stepped out the limo. She had a milk chocolate smooth complexion; he guessed she was around five-foot-five. She wasn't really short, but she was shorter than he was. Her hair hit just under her shoulder. Her smile was amazing, and her eyes lit up in the sunlight.

David shook his head and looked at him. Without even asking him, he already could see that he was immersed in some deep thought. He had been Nico's best friend for thirty years. The bond the guys had was much more than just being in a group, they were brothers. It was a direct brotherhood and they shared everything, so David could tell that his friend had something on his mind.

"What's up with that look? I saw you watching her downstairs. She looks familiar, but we do so many shows here that doesn't surprise me."

David patted Nico on the back as they stopped at the doors of their rooms.

"I'm going to call the wife before we head down," David said as they both opened their separate doors at the same time. Since they were running behind, he knew they needed to hurry and get ready. Nico dropped his bag and looked over the room. He was impressed with the colors and the room setup itself. He walked over to the balcony door, opening it and stepping into the late evening wind. The balcony overlooked the Detroit River. It was a magical night sky of dancing lights. The breathtaking backdrop of the downtown Detroit skyline was a bonus. The stars were twinkling brightly, and the moon was almost full. It seemed like the man in the moon was close enough to say hello.

Suddenly he remembered why Shontell looked so familiar. His heart nearly skipped a beat. He had to know if it was her. He quickly went to shower and change. After getting ready, he took the elevator down to the suite. She was already seated at the bar having a drink. He realized that he was the first one to come down. He was glad of that. He was hoping to get a chance to talk to her before everyone else joined them. She had changed into a skirt and blouse.

She had pulled her hair back with Chinese sticks. Her natural beauty was striking. She only wore lip-gloss…she didn't need any makeup. He nervously rubbed his hands on his pants. It occurred to him that he hadn't felt like this about talking to a woman in a long time. He walked toward her and stood next to her.

Shontell

Shontell didn't see Nico walk in as she sipped her glass of wine. Fighting her exhaustion, she rubbed her neck to get some of the stiffness out.

She had just closed her eyes, briefly, when she heard a deep male voice behind her causing her to jump. "I guess I am the first one ready, huh?"

Turning, she saw Nico. He was wearing brown slacks and a yellow shirt with a light brown vest. Shontell thought to herself, *this man is just too fine.* He had a soft sophistication about him. There was something about him that made him stand out. She could remember when they first came out on the scene. She was instantly hooked on their sound and looks. She was a teenager then, and they were teen sensations. She figured that they were probably around the same age.

"Yes, I guess you are," she replied, as she motioned to the seat next to her. He asked the bartender for a cup of tea with lemon. He explained that was his usual regimen before singing.

"So how was your flight?" she asked, making small talk to hide her nervousness.

"It was pretty decent," he said as he began to stir his tea. Taking a sip, he paused and looked her directly in the face. "I have a question, if you don't mind."

Shontell noted that he looked a little uncomfortable as he spoke. She wondered what he wanted to ask her.

"Sure, go ahead."

"I asked earlier if we had met before, and when I was dressing I remembered something."

"What's that?" She hoped her sudden nervousness didn't show as she shifted in her seat, taking a quick sip of her wine.

"I know I've seen you at concerts before. Even with the lights, I saw your smile because you were always front and center. But the last time you came to the VIP meet and greet after the concert, you asked for a piece of gum and gave each of us a card. Am I right? Was that you?" Nico questioned.

Shontell blushed. *Now how in the heck could he have remembered that? I'm sure they saw a hundred, or at least a few hundred, women that night. And each year it was always the same,* she thought to herself.

Yes, she did ask him for a piece of gum. She was being flirty. That night was one of the best pictures she had with them. She had been to every Detroit show — close to maybe thirty or forty shows — and it always felt like the first time. The guys were all still full of energy, and it showed as they interacted with each other backstage. It was such a rare occasion. One of the things she remembered the most was his cologne as she stood between him and John that night. It had the scent of sage and musk. It was so intoxicating.

Before she could answer him, Martin and the rest of the group came into the suite. The rest of the group was dressed similar to Nico, with John having on the same color shirt as he did. David and Dennis wore oatmeal colored shirts with yellow vests. The band members filtered in, and everyone mingled for about twenty minutes. Time passed so quickly and, before she knew it, they were heading to the club in the limo.

They arrived at the club and entered through the back. She watched as the guys got themselves ready to greet their fans. Within minutes, they were introduced and hit the stage in full energy. The crowd went absolutely wild. An hour into the night, Shontell was glad the night was going good. She had slightly prepared herself to deal with some of the normal issues—like the sound system failing or overcrowding—but tonight everything went as planned. Throughout the club, the ladies were dressed to impress, baring their cleavage and legs. The bouncer informed her that the line outside was still wrapped around the corner.

Shontell noticed how the women flaunted themselves in the presence of the guys. She laughed to herself, wondering if she would be just like them if she wasn't working. Pulling her schedule from her purse, she double checked the time. She caught Mr. Downs's attention and nodded to him. He gave her the signal back and motioned for one of the band members. The group had forty-five minutes or so to continue mingling. She noticed Dennis dancing with two women. The rest of the guys were still out posing for pictures as they were approached. She scanned the room and locked eyes with Nico. He was watching her. After a few seconds, she broke the eye contact. Blushing, she looking down momentarily. When she glanced back up, Nico was gone.

The DJ played one of the groups' songs, and the crowd began to cheer. She was humming along and tapping her foot in sync with the slow music when she noticed Nico coming in her direction. She stood up in her place, trying not to look as nervous as she felt.

Holding his hand out to her, he asked, "Would you like to dance?"

Shontell looked around as she silently thought over his request. She took his hand, and they walked to the dance floor. He spun her around as she easily went into his arms and followed his lead. She loved formal social dancing, although it wasn't done much anymore. Being in his arms felt so good…better than she actually wanted to admit. Just as she thought she would be able to handle dancing with him, he did the unthinkable. He started to sing to her softly. Shontell had to hold back her tears. She was shaking and hoped he didn't feel it, but he did. He stopped singing.

"Are you ok?" he asked.

"Um, yes. I guess I am getting a little bit emotional being so close to you while you sing." She felt embarrassed and said, "I'm sorry."

Nico smiled but didn't say anything. She was hoping he didn't think that she was a lunatic for showing her emotions. When the song ended, she started to walk away. But Nico was still holding her. She stepped back a little and looked at him. He was staring at her intently.

"Thank you for the dance, Ms. Shontell. And, by the way, you never answered my question," he reminded her as he finally let go of her. She stepped away from him but turned back in his direction. Giving into a nervous habit, she twirled her hair before she finally gave him his answer.

"Yes, that was me," she smiled shyly. She motioned for the group to follow her as she headed up to the stage. "Good evening everyone! On behalf of Divine Attraction and the sponsoring organization, Precious Timing Events, we would like to say thank you for being such a great audience tonight. Let's give Divine Attraction a huge round of applause!" The crowd erupted in cheers and applause as the group bowed and waved to everyone. "Now let's all get home safely," she added. They exited the stage to the back.

As they waited for the limo to pull back around, they headed out into the night air.

DOES THE NIGHT HAVE TO END?

Nico

Nico regarded Shontell as she spoke to the club goers. He still was in some shock at his forwardness. He wasn't one who could openly meet women, but he felt something pulling him to her spirit. He was glad he asked her to dance. He didn't regret it one bit. He could still smell whatever scent she was wearing. It reminded him of coconut and berries.

Nico heard his name being called as his thoughts were interrupted. He turned his attention to John.

"Bro, I saw you dancing with Shontell? How was it?" John inquired, speaking low enough just for Nico to hear. He hesitated before answering, trying to find a word that described how it felt to have her in his arms.

"It was amazing," he replied. John smiled, giving him a thumbs up as he joined in the conversation that was going on in the limo. Nico went back to his thoughts, replaying what she had told him when he felt her trembling.

Shontell telling him that his singing affected her completely caught him off guard. That was definitely a first for him. He had met a lot of women, but none had made such an impression on him. Nico almost laughed out loud, recalling how happy he had felt when she told him it was her, confirming what he knew. His search was over. He never told anyone in the group how he had kept all the cards she gave them. Her words affected him on a sincere level, because he could feel they were genuine.

Pulling up to the hotel, they all piled out. The others were still talking animatedly about the club scene. He could have bet ten bucks on what was about to be suggested next.

"We are going to the casino, Nico. You coming?" Dennis asked him. Nico laughed to himself. He just paid himself that ten dollars because, as usual, they were predictable. Shaking his head, he told them to go ahead without him. Nico wasn't in the mood to gamble, although he wasn't ready for his night to end. He wanted to find a way to spend more time with Shontell.

Shontell had observed the atmosphere in the limo. The conversation was very vivid as the men discussed the women. She kept her thoughts to herself. She loved her city, but the club scene was one she did not venture out into much.

She was seated near the far end, closest to the door. She could see Nico, but he couldn't see her unless he leaned forward. This gave her an advantage at this moment, and she took it to watch his body language. He wasn't as talkative as the rest of them, but it seemed they tried to make him talk. She did notice him and John whispering and knew that it was more than likely about her.

Usually, when she had artists come in town, she stayed at the same hotel. She was available if they needed anything from her. She waved to the guys and Martin while making her way up to her room. The hallways were filled with people coming in from the other downtown events. She couldn't wait to lie across her bed

Shontell was just about to get undressed when her phone rang. Glancing at the glowing screen, she saw it was her best friend, Sandy.

"Ok, so give me the digs. Are they really hot up close and more personal?"

"OMG, yes! It has taken so much for me to be professional being as big of a fan as I am, but I did okay. But guess what? Remember when I asked Nico for his gum last year when we took pictures with them? He actually remembered that. Can you freaking believe it?"

"WHAT! Are you serious?" her best friend screamed into her ear. She took the phone away from her ear and started laughing.

"Yep," she said as she crossed her legs and made herself comfortable. They talked about the rest of the evening, including the dance. While they were talking, she heard a knock on her door. She told Sandy to hold on and she got up and went to look out the peephole. When she discovered it was Nico, she quickly checked her clothes and patted her hair down. She slowly opened the door.

Nico

Nico had stood outside her door for a few minutes before actually getting up the nerve to knock. He kept glancing around and was glad that the hallway was clear. When the guys decided to run over to the casino, he convinced himself that this idea was a good one. He couldn't believe how anxious he was. When he knocked, he hoped that she would be okay with this. He didn't want her to think he was crazy.

"Is something wrong?" Shontell asked, clearly concerned.

"Actually, no. I was just wondering if you were up for a nightcap." He held up a bottle of wine and two glasses.

Hesitating for a moment, she opened the door wider. He walked in. He noticed that she was on a call as she went to grab her phone. She picked it up and spoke briefly to end the call. Maybe he was crazy for coming to her room; he didn't know if she had a boyfriend or not. For a moment, he felt uneasy. Taking a breath, he said to himself, "*Oh well, here goes nothing.*"

"I hope you don't mind my being bold," he said as he gestured toward the wine. He pulled the cork opener from his pocket and set the bottle down to open it. "Sometimes it's hard for me to sleep after we perform, and for some reason I'm very wired." They sat on the couch in the sitting area.

"It's okay. I was just up talking to my best friend anyway," Shontell told him, helping him with what he was doing. She held her glass as he poured. "So after tomorrow, where are you headed?" she inquired.

"Well, we have one show in Indiana, then we go for media promotions in Miami, then we are on our cruise for five day, and then we have a week off before we go overseas for about six weeks," Nico explained as he noticed her smile. His heartbeat sped up. He wished at that moment that he had the ability to read minds. "What's that smile for?" he asked her. When she wasn't quick to reply, he thought it was better not to press her. "So what about you? What fascinating things do you have set up?"

"Well, I have two corporate meetings early next week. Then, I am on vacation for two weeks while my business partner handles the smaller events we have planned."

"Vacation! Now *that's* a word I rarely use. Do you have any plans?" Nico leaned over and refilled her glass, then his.

Shontell laughed, and he looked at her quizzically. He felt like he was missing something. He took a sip of his wine, tasting the bitterness on his tongue as he admired her. She played with her hair. The action intrigued him.

"Actually, I signed up for your twenty-fifth anniversary cruise; I'm so excited. I love the water, but I've never been on a cruise before. So I am really looking forward to this." Her face lit up with the admission.

"Wow, you really are a dedicated fan. But I think that is a great thing. I hope you enjoy yourself. Are you going alone?" Nico was hoping her answer was yes. He still didn't know if she had someone in her life.

"No, my best friend Sandy is going too. It's her birthday, so it was my gift to her."

"Nice friend," he said with an impressed expression.

"I try. We have been best friends since we were in fourth grade."

"Wow. Those kind of friends are hard to come by. David and I are the same way. We met in the seventh grade and have always been close. Can I make a toast?"

"Be my guest," she told him as she grabbed her glass from the table.

"To a new friendship that I hope lasts a long time."

"To new friendships," she replied. They clinked glasses. Surprisingly, they finished the bottle. They talked a little more, and their conversation flowed easily. They discussed some of their experiences working in the entertainment industry. Once the conversation seemed like it was about to end, Shontell suggested a movie. Somewhere in the middle of the film, they both fell asleep.

Nico felt someone jostling him, and it took him a minute to remember where he was. He opened his eyes and adjusted his glasses. He looked into the smiling face of Shontell. He didn't remember falling asleep. It must have been the wine. He wasn't usually a heavy drinker. He scooted back and stretched. Standing up, he started picking up their wine glasses from a few hours ago. A part of him still didn't want to leave her presence.

She watched Nico sleep for a few minutes, telling herself that the man was beautiful. Turning the television off, she gently shook him.

"Guess we fell asleep watching the movie. My phone just went off. It was my wake up call. You have to be at the radio station in an hour, so you might want to go get ready," she informed him, standing up.

"Will do," he told her. She watched his movements and tried not to stare. She started to clean up, and he reached down to assist.

"Oh, don't worry about that, I will take care of it. I'll see you in the suite in forty-five minutes." He nodded and headed toward the door. He stopped and came back to where she was standing.

"Thanks for giving me one of the best nights I have had in a long time." He kissed her cheek and hugged her. He quickly walked out the room, and Shontell touched her cheek where he had kissed her. Her face felt flush from her blushing. She snapped out of her reverie. She cleaned up the sitting area and headed to the shower. She kept shaking her head to make sure that she wasn't dreaming. It was nothing new for Shontell to be around celebrities or even date them for that matter. Nico made her very nervous for some reason...very nervous.

Nico

Nico grinned at his thoughts of Shontell. He was proud of himself for taking this chance; it usually wasn't in his nature to really go after a woman. Shontell was like a breath of fresh air. He didn't have to worry about her only being interested in him for what he had in his bank account. Her personality showed that she was her own woman. She liked him for who he was, and she was easy to talk to...unlike his ex, Tina.

He thought she was different until she proved him wrong. She had only wanted him for the lifestyle he had and not for what they shared. Tina loved to shop when she traveled with them. Yet she rarely interacted with him on more personal levels outside of the bedroom. He always felt like she was just fulfilling her end of the relationship. Did he love her? Yes. When the relationship ended, it hit him hard. It took him some time to realize that she loved his stardom, not him. His mother taught him to never let one bad experience keep him from trying again. Nico kept her words in his mind. Nico backed away from love, put it in a box, and threw away the key. It led him to work on his music, like he always had. Maybe that would change now. Nico had almost hit his door when his thoughts were interrupted.

"Um, bro, what are you doing coming out of *her* room at this hour?" Nico heard someone say behind him. He silently cursed himself for being caught. When he turned around, he saw that it was Dennis who was looking at him with one eyebrow raised. He could tell that his friend was waiting for him to answer. Dennis was like the mother hen of the group. He had been burned by a few groupies. He was always making sure they stayed on the straight and narrow, or his version of it anyway.

"Well, if you must know, I went by last night. We talked and watched a movie. She is a very nice lady," Nico told him, trying not to get irritated by the sudden interrogation. He squinted his eyes at Dennis.

"Mmm hmm, guess that is why you didn't come to the casino with us. Well, I hope you know what you are doing," Dennis said with a frown.

"What? Making a friend? Didn't know there was a law against that. You know at some point you will need to get over the things that happened to you. You just seem to keep picking the wrong ones," he told his friend as he headed into his room. He left him standing there. Nico stood in his foyer, shaking his head. He didn't know why he always let Dennis get to him. He grabbed his suitcase. Taking his clothes out for the day, he prepared to get dressed. He needed to make some calls before he went downstairs. He put his phone on speaker as he brushed his teeth and handled his calls. When he finished, he smiled at the mere idea of what he just did. It was done, and he was happy about it. He only hoped Shontell would feel the same way.

BLAST FROM THE PAST

Dennis

Dennis knew he was right. He just wanted to look out for them. David was the only married one in the group, so he had to make sure John, Nico, and himself were cautious. He had very bad experiences with women, but he wasn't sure what it was about Shontell that bothered him. She looked familiar, and he really couldn't place where he had seen her. He let that thought go as he thought about what Nico had said to him. It took him a long time to get over some of the things that the women who he messed around with did. It wasn't like he had low self-esteem, but he just didn't pick them right. He had never been in love or even smitten by a woman. Did that make him strange? When David found Felecia and he saw the love he had for her, he was jealous and envious. Why couldn't he have that kind of love? Now Nico? It just wasn't fair, he thought. Maybe it was time he changed his outlook on women and his life.

Dennis started walking back to his room when his cell phone buzzed. Retrieving the text, he saw it was Jesse asking him what was up for tonight. Dennis stopped in his tracks.

"Oh, snap! That's why she looks familiar," Dennis spoke out loud. One day when he was visiting Jesse, he had seen a picture of them together on his fireplace mantel. She had lost some weight and cut her hair, but he was pretty sure that it was her. They must not be together anymore. He replied to Jesse's text and headed out of his room. David greeted him in the hallway.

"Hey man, what's with that look?" Dennis started to tell him but decided against it. He wasn't sure if it was his place to say anything. If he did, would it even matter? He didn't have any proof it was her. He was just going off a hunch. So he just told him 'nothing.' He was interested in hearing David's response to Nico being in Shontell's room, though. "So I ran into Nico coming out of Shontell's room this morning," he told him.

"Really? Was he dressed?" David inquired, smiling in anticipation of the answer.

"Yes, he was dressed. You're silly. But I did ask him what he was doing, and he just said he was just getting to know her."

"Wow, you asked him that? Why does it matter to you anyway?" David quizzed him.

"I guess it doesn't. I was just asking him. I mean, you know how these women can be sometimes. He has already been hurt once. I guess we can't all be like you. You just lucked out with a good one."

""Yeah, I did. But that almost didn't happen, if you recall. You almost made me lose her. But anyway, how do you know that Shontell isn't a good one?" Before Dennis could answer, the elevator door opened and the rest of the group was standing there waiting for them. He gave David a look but still didn't answer his question. He chided himself. He needed to learn to keep his mouth closed. He followed the rest of the group to the waiting limo, where Shontell was already seated. She was giving directions to the driver. He stared at her, trying to recall the picture to determine if it was her. When she smiled at Nico, who was sitting next to him, it was confirmed. Her smile verified her identity. Now he wondered if he should mention it to Nico. For now, he would just sit back and be quiet.

It was nearly one in the afternoon, with all the radio promotions done. It was time to eat. She was starving. She hadn't been able to eat anything that morning but some fruit. She had just been served her food, when a group of six women walked up to the table and asked the group for autographs and pictures. The group obliged. One woman stood off to the side and waited until the others got what they came for. She had seen the woman earlier that morning as they were getting into the limo. She had been watching them, but she didn't seem like she was a typical fan, like the others. She stood out, just by the way she was sharply dressed. She was wearing a black dress that snugly fitted her body, and her makeup was flawless. If she didn't know better, she would have thought she was a model. Once the others left, she walked over to Nico and spoke softly. She could feel the air in the room change at that moment. The woman looked up and addressed everyone at the table but her; the woman made sure not to even turn her way. They all seemed uncomfortable…especially Nico.

Shontell suddenly had an uneasy feeling in her stomach. He must have sensed that she was looking at them and turned toward her. She quickly turned her head. She was glad that her cell phone rang at that moment. It served as a distraction for her as she excused herself to take the call. When she returned a few moments later, Nico wasn't at the table. She excused herself and told Martin she had to take care of some last minute loose ends for the group. She assured him that she would meet them in the hotel hospitality suite in the evening for dinner. As she was walking through the lobby, she saw Nico and the woman in deep conversation. Neither of them looked happy. She tried not to let it bother her as she proceeded through the lobby to the elevator.

Once she reached her room, she called her assistant. She had her fax over the final contract and bus company details for Martin and the group. She stood near the balcony door, allowing the warm air to come into her room. A part of her was mad at herself for reacting the way she had. She wasn't a jealous person. The woman's presence just threw her, as well as the way Nico and the others responded to her. Something was up with that, but she wouldn't ask…that's for sure.

She rubbed the back of her neck as she felt that old tension creep up into her body. She didn't know what to think about them, but what she didn't want to do was to assume. She needed to do something. Getting up, she picked up a file and walked over to the balcony. Shontell had just opened the file when her phone buzzed, scaring the mess out of her. She laughed at herself and peeked at the screen. It was her partner, Ebony, texting her with a question about a client. She sent her a reply and then set the phone down on the table. After everything that had transpired, it would be impossible for her to concentrate on work. She closed the file after making one small note for later. Then she stood up and leaned over the railing, letting her mind wander. What was she thinking to even imagine that Nico saw her as anything other than the event planner? Still, if that were the case, he wouldn't have been in her room this morning. She shook her head and was getting mad at herself for putting herself down. That was something she worked hard on. She beat up on herself so much after Jesse. She had wondered why she wasn't good enough for him, when the truth was that *he* wasn't good enough for himself. She didn't have anything to do with his cheating. She was a good woman. Jesse had messed up…not her.

She rubbed her hands up and down her arms and felt the goose bumps on her skin.

She also knew that she still struggled with trust. Why did she have to trust him now, anyways? It was too soon. She didn't want to repeat her past mistakes…that was for sure. Having to trust Jesse, so early in their relationship, is how she got her heart broken. She wouldn't do that this time. She was going to hold on to some good feelings about Nico until she felt or saw otherwise, but Nico was going to have to earn her trust.

Nico

Nico couldn't believe his eyes. What the hell was Tina doing here? She leaned over and gave him a soft kiss on the cheek. He felt nothing. He could feel everybody watching them. When he turned around and saw Shontell watching them, he gave her a side smile. He needed to get Tina away from this table and see what she wanted.

"Let's walk," he told her, as he took her away from the table. The surprised and uncomfortable looks that were present at the table increased his uneasiness. Tina noticed it, but she still needed to make her presence known. She had cut her hair and was wearing a bob cut. Her makeup and clothes were flawless as always. He wondered who the sucker of the month was now. Then he quickly thought about how much he didn't even care.

"Ouch, do you have to be so rough?" she scolded as she pulled away from the hold he had on her arm. She stood still, and then her face transformed. She smiled and touched his shirt collar. He stopped her hand as it was heading toward his face. He stood there waiting on her to tell him why she even spoke.

"So what's up, Tina! What are you doing here?"

"Last I heard, this is a hotel. Why do you think I'm here?"

"I don't know, and I couldn't really care less." He saw Shontell walking their way. She glanced in their direction, but kept going. The look of confusion on her face almost made him run after her. Tina noticed him watching her.

She guffawed, "So that's your squeeze now?"

Nico glared at her with a look that was meant to send daggers. He decided it was best to just diffuse this and walk away. Tina was someone else's problem now. He needed some air. He started to walk away when Tina touched his arm.

"Nico, wait for a second please," she said to him, as she leaned against the wall and blocked his path.

"What is it Tina? I am not in the mood for this. I have nothing against you and we said all we needed to say. You told me you were leaving me for someone else with more money than I have."

"Is that what I said?" she asked, him giving him a look of shock.

"You sure you want to put me in that place, Tina?"

"Wow, I...I didn't realize you had so much anger towards me," she said sincerely for the first time since they began talking. She looked like she had been hit with some revelation. Regaining herself, she looked at Nico and saw what she had destroyed with him. He was the only man who had treated her like a woman and not an arm piece.

"I just wanted to say that I am sorry. You deserved better than me." Nico's eyes almost bucked out in complete surprise by her statement. He put his finger into his ear to make sure he heard her correctly. He looked her up and down. He needed to make sure he was standing in front of the same shallow person he used to be in love with. Finally, he spoke to her, smirking.

"Really? Is that what you wanted to say to me? You're sorry?"

"Yes, I mean, I saw you this morning. I was pretty shocked. I know that we don't run in the same circles. Detroit was not a place I thought we would cross paths."

Nico half listened to her. He knew she had something else up her sleeve. He just didn't feel up to entertaining it. He was ready to end this conversation. He knew the fellows were all watching them without even turning around. Tina had him sprung back in the day. She was what every man wanted: smart, sexy, and beautiful. By the time he saw who she really was, it was too late. He had already fallen in love with her. Her cheating and leaving him was something he didn't expect. In the end, he knew he was better off. She was selfish and self-centered but, most of all, just money hungry. Right now, he knew she couldn't hold a candle to Shontell.

"Tina, if it makes you happy, I forgave you a long time ago. It was nice seeing you, but I have to go."

"You're going after your friend, I am sure. Thank you for taking time to hear my apology. I will see you later...I mean on the anniversary cruise." Glaring at him, she strolled away before he could say anything. Nico stood there watching her walk away. He knew the extra sway in her hips was for him. She was one of a kind and at that moment he wasn't impressed.

Instantly his thoughts went back to Shontell. When he looked around and didn't see her, he thought that she must have headed to the elevators. She was probably going up to her room. He headed back over to the table to get his things. The guys all watched him; they were waiting for him to say something. When he didn't, Martin cleared his throat. He looked up and saw Martin and his brothers with expectant looks on their faces.

"Son, are you okay?"

"Oh, um...yes, I am okay. She claimed she saw us this morning and wanted to catch up and talk."

"And why would she think you would even want to talk to her?" David said, getting mad. He didn't like her then, and he liked her even less now. He didn't want Nico to go backwards with her. He twisted his face, waiting for Nico to finish.

"Beats me, man. Get this...she actually apologized for the way things ended with us."

"What?!" all three men chorused in unison. They were completely shocked by what he just told them. He almost laughed. That is all he could do anyways since he didn't want to put much thought into it. He picked up his phone and told them he would be back in a few minutes. He started in the direction of the hallway and was stopped in mid-stride by his name being called by Dennis. He exhaled hard and tried to keep a straight face because he didn't want to start this conversation with him again. He waited for what he already knew was coming next.

"Nico, do you really think that you should be going to her room? I mean your ex just walked in here after four years, and you act like it's not bothering you. Maybe you should just let this thing with Shontell go," he told him as he gripped his arm. Nico looked at where he had just touched him. He took a few steps in his original direction but then stopped in his tracks and looked at Dennis, realizing what he said to him a few seconds ago.

"Excuse me? What do you mean let her go? Why in the hell should I care about seeing Tina? We have been over for several years now. That's not a road I would ever travel again. So I'm going to ask you again; why am I letting her go?" Dennis saw the look on his face. At that moment, he regretted saying anything. He had never seen him give him that look before. He cleared his throat and then began to explain.

"I am just saying...I may be out of line...but don't you think it's too much of a coincidence that she just happened to be in the same hotel where we are staying? Maybe it's a sign you are moving too fast with Shontell. I think you are doing too much already when it comes to her. You don't even know her, man," he told him. Nico stood there for a minute trying to understand Dennis' comments before he addressed him.

"Doing too much? I am curious about what you think I am doing. I thought our conversation was clear earlier. Stop confusing my wanting a friendship with Shontell with the women you have come across. This doesn't even come close...and if we have to discuss this again, I won't be as nice," Nico told him. He began to walk away once again. He didn't even bother to turn around when he heard Dennis calling after him. He stared Dennis down as the doors closed. Nico wondered why Dennis cared so much about him talking to Shontell. Dennis was being a little extra intense, and even with his crazy ways, it was out of his character. He needed to find out what was going on. But for the moment, his immediate concern was with Shontell. Walking down the long hallway, he reached her door and knocked.

Dennis

Dennis turned around as John walked over to where he was. "Man, what was that all about?" he asked him softly. He was the only one who had noticed the heated conversation between him and Nico. Dennis hesitated because he knew that the guys often got on him about his critical ways. When he still didn't say anything, John gave him a look that told him to tread lightly. He didn't want this to be an issue with him and Nico. Dennis was a mother hen, and they all knew it. He was the worst of them all when it came to the ladies. John was always being the peacemaker, so he turned back to Dennis to give him a little warning.

"Dennis, if this is about what I think it is...whatever Nico told you...you may want to take heed. It's a battle you don't want to fight. Nico hasn't dated a woman in years, and it doesn't matter if Tina so happened to be here. If he is showing interest in Shontell, let him. You don't have a right or a reason to try and stop him from getting to know her," he told him, patting him on the shoulder.

John left him there with his thoughts.

"Humph, if you knew what I know," Dennis mumbled, putting his hands in his pockets. He was glad that no one heard him.

Dennis wanted to be mad, but he couldn't. He walked over to the table and sat back down, trying to pay attention to what was going on around him. Everyone was making plans for the evening. Dennis knew how much they were a unit. They were more than just a group. They have become more like brothers than lifelong friends. Maybe he was wrong about them, but he just couldn't help it. He just had a gut feeling. He decided to stop focusing on it and joined the others in talking. They made plans for the rest of the day, but he watched the elevator doors in spite of himself.

ALWAYS FOLLOW YOUR INSTINCT

Shontell

Shontell pulled her sweater from the back of the chair and put it around her shoulders. It was a nice afternoon, but the wind from the water was making her feel chilled. She could hear people talking, and she was getting a little restless. She didn't know what time it was. Sighing, she wondered if she should call Sandy. Sometimes she just needed to hear a voice of reason. She hated that Jesse took away her trust because this was so unlike her character; she always gave people the benefit of the doubt. She made up her mind to call Sandy. Standing up, Shontell's sweater fell to the floor. She reached down and picked it up. She was about to turn around when she was startled by someone touching her shoulder.

"How...how did you get in here?" she asked Nico, surprised to see him standing there.

"You left the door slightly open. Guess you didn't close it all the way. I knocked, but you didn't answer. I apologize for scaring you."

She twisted her hair, which was one of the bad habits she used to overcome her shyness. Realizing what she was doing, she stopped.

"I saw you head up here, and I thought we needed to talk."

"Talk? Because of what, Nico? You don't owe me an explanation for anything. I am not your girl. You have the right to talk to anyone you want," she said, not looking at him.

Nico put his hand under her chin and made her look at him. She tried to turn, but he held her firm.

"Shontell, that woman is not anyone I would want to be with...at least not anymore. That was my ex, Tina. We broke up nearly four years ago. I haven't seen her since she left. She claimed she just saw me this morning and didn't know we were staying here."

"Do you believe her?"

"I don't know yet. But the thing you need to understand is that I don't care. She's in my past. I don't go backwards...ever," he told her, never breaking the eye contact they shared.

Shontell didn't say anything, but inside she let the breath go that she was holding. Her insides were doing flips. Shontell watched his expression. At that moment, it was a little amusing. Maybe he could see her turning inside out. She shifted her weight to her other foot. She was completely caught off guard by what happened next. Nico leaned in toward her and kissed her slowly at first. Shontell felt his tongue part her lips and she stepped in closer to him; they kissed deeply. Shontell was the first to break the kiss and move away. She needed to regain her thoughts quickly.

"I'm not so sure you should have done that," she said, looking at him, "As good as it felt." She touched her lips with the back of her hand. Nico laughed, and she wanted to fall through the floor because she knew he heard what she said.

"Listen, I don't know what it is about you that has me so drawn to you. I would like to find out if you will let me. Please don't let what happened earlier stop that. I can more than guarantee that Tina will never be an issue. Just hear me out first. Even when you did the meet and greets, I wanted to say something. I didn't want you to think I wanted you as the fan of the night. I still have every last one of your cards. I always wished you had left a number or something. The words in your cards told me that you weren't that type of person. I know this might be a lot to take in, so I will give you some time to give me an answer. I'll see you at dinner," Nico said. He walked the few steps that separated them and kissed her softly on the forehead. He then left her room.

Once again, Shontell was left floored by his actions. She could still feel the imprint of his lips on hers. She wanted to jump up and down for joy. This had never happened to her before; it had never been even close with Jesse. She twirled around the room and landed on her bed. She pinched herself to make sure she wasn't dreaming. She had to tell Sandy. She grabbed her phone, sending her friend a video message instead of a long text. Her hands were still shaking from the excitement.

Nico

Nico closed the door behind him and leaned against it. He chuckled at his bravado. This woman had him spinning, and her kiss was just like he thought it would be. It was soft, sweet, and mind blowing. He took a deep breath and knew that everything was in her hands now. He went to his room to get his gym bag and head to the work-out room for a bit, but he was sidetracked by David. It looked like he had been waiting on him. He wasn't surprised when he wanted to talk. He got him through those days after his break up with Tina.

"Hey, man, got a minute?" David asked.

"Sure, what's up?"

"I just wanted to come check on you. That scene with Tina blew my mind. I didn't think she would be bold enough to even speak."

"Yeah, I am still trying to understand that for real. I know she is up to something, but I don't even care. Shontell is the total opposite of what I had with Tina."

"Speaking of Shontell, Dennis told me he saw you coming out of her room this morning. That's not usually your style."

"Glad to know I am the water cooler topic. Is something so wrong with me wanting to get to know her?" He wasn't upset, but he was unsure where all this concern was coming from. David gave him a condescending *you know better than that* look, but he continued with what he was saying. "But I will tell you this, I am not going to entertain whatever it is Tina has cooking. I don't trust her as long as that short ass dress she was wearing." They both laughed at his joke. He wanted to change the subject on her, anyway. She didn't deserve the attention they were giving her. Besides, he had been wanting to get David alone so that he could tell him what he had learned about Shontell.

"Do you remember the cards we always got with the poems? I told you how the words had always hit me. It was her...Shontell. She was the one who gave those to us. Now that I have found her and have been able to have conversations with her, I am not ready to just let it go that easy."

"I hear you...believe me, I do. I just want you to know I got your back. You know I can put myself in your shoes. You haven't been with anyone in a long time. Just take it slow. If she's the one, it won't matter."

"Okay, bro. I needed to hear that. Thank you for understanding." He looked at his watch and saw he wouldn't have time for a workout. They had been talking longer than he thought, and now they were late for their meeting. He patted David on the back, closing the room door behind him.

"Come on, let's get to this meeting before Martin sends the guards out for us." Both men laughed again as they headed to Martin's room.

Shontell

Shontell finished her message and lay her head on the pillow, looking at the ceiling. She wished she hadn't broken the kiss. She closed her eyes to reminisce. She could still feel him holding her. The smell of him lingered. It was like his cologne was on her clothes, the scent was so strong. Maybe it was just in her mind, but she still loved it. She sat up and looked around her room. She still had a few minutes before she had to call Ebony. They were to discuss new clients, in addition to the paperwork she needed to finalize. She grabbed her tablet and hit the meeting conference app. The tablet beeped, and she was in the virtual conference room waiting on Ebony. They always did virtual face meetings when she had out of town business. She was lucky to have met Ebony at a networking event two years ago.

Her business had been in trouble. She was losing capital due to a bad supplier, and she was deep in the red. If it were not for Ebony offering to be a partner and putting up some capital, she would have had to close her business.

But after merging their resources, they were making more than projected. They were actually making so much that she had been thinking she had enough of her own money to buy Ebony out and continue comfortably.

Ebony was a bright young woman, but she didn't understand the vision for PTE. She would go days, and sometimes weeks, without coming into the office. Shontell still did more than half of the networking for new business and worked eighty percent of the events. She had her assistant place an ad for two managers. She would need the help when she made the changes. She pulled herself out of her thoughts as Ebony's face appeared on her screen. They greeted one another.

"Good afternoon, Ebony. Are you working at the office or home?" she asked her. They normally didn't hold Saturday hours, but sometimes the workload of clients called for it. Ebony looked a little distracted and took some time before she answered. She thought maybe she couldn't hear her. "Ebony, can you hear me?"

"Oh, yes. I'm sorry. I was in the middle of something when the tablet beeped. I guess the time just got away from me. How are things going there?"

"Everything here is going good. Are you ready to go over the new client list? Dez sent me the contracts and I looked them over," Shontell said. She began to flip through the paperwork. She made sure her tone was professional so that Ebony would know this was strictly about their business projects.

"Yes, I looked them over too. I see that everything is in order. Are we still having a staff roundup tomorrow? I can sign these tonight and then bring them with me." Ebony grabbed her pen and made a note on the document she had in front of her.

"Yes, I think we need to cover the upcoming schedule of events and parties," she told her. She was just about to say something else when she heard a man's voice. It sounded familiar, she thought, but how could that be? She didn't even know Ebony was seeing anyone…guess that would explain her lack of appearance at the office and store. She crossed her legs and set her tablet on the stand, hitting the volume button so that she could hear her background more. "Oh, I didn't know you had company. We can finish this tomorrow," she told her.

Ebony's eyes got big at her comment, and Shontell wondered why. Suddenly the screen went black, but she could hear muffled voices. A few seconds went by, and then Ebony's face came back onto the screen. She looked upset.

"Everything okay?"

"Oh, yes. Okay, I will see you tomorrow," she told her hurriedly and ended the call before Shontell could say anything else. Closing the conference call app, Shontell hit the side button to turn the tablet screen off. She thought about how odd that was. She dismissed it as she checked her watch and saw she had some time to kill. She decided to listen to some music to gather her thoughts. She thought about Nico's visit and smiled. She hoped she was making the right choice because she knew her last relationship ended badly. She had been single for close to two and a half years now. She told herself that the next time it would be with a normal guy. She caught herself from laughing out loud. Voicing her thought to the empty room, *"Hell who determines what a normal guy is these days."* Industry men, as she called them, were normal too; she just happened to fall for one back then that wasn't.

She took her iPod out of her purse and then set it in the radio. She let the music take over her. She was asleep before she knew it. She dreamt of her and Nico as they were on the cruise, watching the sunset together. They were just holding one another. Then she heard ringing in the distance, and she slowly opened her eyes. She realized her cell phone was ringing. She reached over and accidentally knocked the phone off the nightstand. She picked it up and spoke softly, "Hello."

"Girl, that video was something else. What were you doing? I know you aren't sleeping when you have all those fine men around you…especially the one that kissed your behind," Sandy rattled off non-stop.

Shontell took the phone from her ear, still listening to Sandy ramble on. She was a bit confused and looked around, halfway thinking Nico would be lying next to her. The dream had seemed so real. "What time is it?" she asked her friend, hoping she would just answer and stop what she was saying.

"It's 4:45," Sandy told her.

Shontell jumped up, looking around for her shoes. She dropped the phone again. Yelling, she told Sandy to hold on. She picked her phone up and put her on speaker. Shontell went around the room, getting her clothes while she continued their conversation. "Damn, I didn't realize I fell asleep and especially not for this long. I was only trying to power nap...Dinner is supposed to be served in fifteen minutes, and I am not even ready. I'll call you back when I come back to the room. They have a free night so, depending on what they want to do, it may be late." They said goodbyes and ended the call.

Shontell quickly took a shower and then put on a flowing dress and heels. She did her makeup and glanced at the clock. She was fifteen minutes late as she headed out the door. She stopped at the front desk to make sure that everyone was set to be checked out in the morning and that the luggage would be brought down with no issues. She didn't know what made her look over at the bar-lounge. When she did, she saw Tina surrounded by three men. She was definitely the center of attention. The woman was model beautiful with her Halle Berry cut and red lipstick. She could see how Nico fell for her. What man wouldn't want her? She was just about to turn her attention to the desk when their eyes met. Tina nodded and smirked.

Shontell nodded in return and continued her conversation. She let the young lady know she would clear the bill in the morning at breakfast.

She headed into the suite and found that everyone was there. They were all milling around and talking. Shontell shifted her mood. She was not going to let that woman get under her skin. She knew how to handle her kind. She stopped one of the servers and quickly spoke with him about starting dinner now and gave instructions on the early breakfast.

"Sorry I'm late, everyone. Dinner is going to be served in a few minutes, but I wanted to make a small toast," she told them. On cue, she was handed a wine glass and waited until everyone had a glass. Once everyone was ready, she proceeded.

"Thank you all for allowing Precious Timing Events to take care of you for your album release party. I hope we left a good impression. This has truly been a dream come true for me. I am not only a representative of my company but also a huge fan of the group. Your music has gotten me through some rough times in my life. I just want to thank you for blessing me and the rest of the world with your music. Happy twenty-fifth anniversary, guys. You deserve it and much more!"

Everyone in the room clapped, and it was filled with the sound of clinking glasses. Shontell walked toward the bar area and set her glass down. She noticed Nico's eyes on her and tried not to look at him. She also heard Dennis say, *"I told you that was her."* Soon after, they were all seated for dinner. Nico sat on her left while John sat on her right.

"So, I made a bet with Dennis and lost," John said to her.

"Oh really, and what exactly did you bet on?" she asked, turning in his direction. She was giving him her full attention as she took her a sip from her wine glass.

"Well, Dennis said that it was you that always came to the meet and greets when we came here, but I told him that he was wrong. Your speech proved he was right, so I lost." He laughed and shrugged his shoulders. He went into his pocket and then handed some money over to Dennis. She looked at Dennis, who she noticed was already staring at her. She didn't understand his look and quickly looked back at John to finish their conversation.

"Yeah, it's me. I haven't missed a concert here in fifteen years. I've even traveled to see you guys a few times. I absolutely love your music and what you all represent to the community. I am a lifelong fan," Shontell admitted.

"Wow, that's deep," replied Dennis, out of the blue. Even though she felt uneasy because of his tone, the comment made her blush. She tried to steer the conversation away from her, but didn't have much luck. She noticed that Nico wasn't saying much. Did he see Tina at the lounge like she had? That would explain why he was so quiet. She didn't want to believe that was the reason, but the guys ribbed him on his silence. She watched his every emotion play across his face.

NOT LIKE THE EX

Nico

Nico kept his head down and focused on his food. He wasn't really hungry, but was making himself eat so the guys wouldn't rib him. He knew it was coming, though. "So, Nico, why you so quiet man? You're usually more talkative at events like this," David said.

"Yes, Nico, why you so quiet? I ran into Tina when I was coming in here," Dennis said. The table got quiet for a few minutes. Nico shot Dennis a look. John kicked him under the table. "Ouch, what the hell," he exclaimed raising his voice as he glared at John. Nico looked over at Shontell, but he couldn't read the expression she had on her face. She picked up her glass and didn't look at him or Dennis. Nico hoped Dennis' comment didn't upset her. Out of the blue, she gave off a slight awkward laugh. He watched her pick up her fork and glance down at her plate.

"You have to excuse Mr. Tack-less over here," John said to Nico and Shontell.

Observing the activity at the table, Martin took that as a cue to make an announcement. "Okay, everyone. I just got word that Divine Attraction's new album, *Dedicated To You,* is number two on the billboard charts." The room erupted in cheers. Martin sat back down and, within a few minutes, the room was back to its normal chatter. David leaned back and tapped Nico to let him know he was sorry for Dennis' behavior. Nico nodded and let him know he was cool. They both knew Dennis had a way about him sometimes. But Shontell wouldn't know that, and he didn't want to cause her to feel uncomfortable around them.

Nico pushed his plate back and leaned back in his chair. He wished he could rewind to the moment she walked in. This wasn't how he wanted the evening to begin. He was glad to see that Shontell's mood had changed. Nico smiled at Shontell as she was making jibes with their drummer, Vince. She was so different from Tina. Tina would have never interacted with everyone as she was. He knew then he had made the right choice. He noticed that David had been watching Shontell too. Although he was sure his reasons were way different from his, it probably stemmed from their earlier conversation. He observed how she handled the room with ease. Although the group was comprised of mostly men, she mastered the situation elegantly.

David spotted Shontell as she was talking to John, laughing at something he said to her. She was enjoying herself, despite his brother's comments. That put him somewhat at ease. He had been worried that Dennis was going to damage any beginning Nico and Shontell had. He then quickly looked over to where Nico was seated. He was glad that, for once, Nico had an interest in a woman again. Nico was the one that had always kept his distance. He may have gone out and indulged every now and then, but for the most part, he was the groups' serious one.

Nico looked up as the room erupted in cheers and music. Shontell was dancing with John. They were doing old school dances. They were going back and forth, competing with each other. He laughed, watching them. Martin came over and sat in the chair next to him. They both watched in silence. Nico's thought was that he wanted what David had. He knew if anyone understood his emotions it would be him. David met Felecia, his wife, at one of their concerts. He felt a sudden tap on his knee as Martin was laughing extremely hard at the impromptu dance contest. Nico continued watching them.

Martin was like a father to them. He had been their manager since the beginning. Martin had wanted to snatch that Tina girl up earlier. If he found out who it was that told her they were there, he would give them hell. He didn't like his boys hurt, and he knew that she was just plain trouble. Now that Shontell, she was what Nico needed. The look he had on his face said he knew that too. Martin scooted his chair closer and got Nico's attention. "I see you watching her, son. You like her?" he asked. Nico nodded his head as they both continued watching them dance for a second. Shontell was dancing against David and Vince at the same time.

"Well, I think that one is worth it. Go for it."

"Thank you, Martin. That means a lot to me...your approval, that is. But if she gives me the go ahead, I definitely will," he told him. Shontell looked up at that moment and their eyes locked. She smiled at him, and he returned her smile. He knew he would never get tired of seeing the way her face lit up when she smiled.

The music stopped, and they all clapped. She hugged Vince, David, and John and then grabbed a water bottle. Heading in his direction, she sat down in the chair that Martin had just vacated.

"Why didn't you come save me?" she joked with him. She put the bottle to her mouth and chugged the entire contents in two seconds. He watched her, chuckling.

"Thirsty?"

"Heck, yeah. I haven't danced like that since I decided to lose weight. It's great cardio. You guys have too much energy for me," she told him, laughing and still trying to catch her breath. After a few minutes, Shontell turned towards him. She took his hand and kissed the back of it. "Before they all come back over, my answer is yes. I will give this a shot; let's see where this friendship will take us." Nico looked at her. He wanted to kiss her right then, but refrained.

"Thank you!" he told her, smiling from ear to ear.

"For what? I should be thanking you for choosing me," she told him, winking. They both scooted to the table as they were served dessert. It was vanilla bean cheesecake, she told him as she took her fork and dug into it. She closed her eyes and moaned slightly at its taste. Nico stared at her because that simple act had him squirming. Nico has never seen anything so sensual and sexy on a woman. She took another forkful and pointed the fork in his direction. He opened his mouth and accepted the cheesecake. The taste was divine. He closed his eyes the same way she did, but hoped he didn't moan the way she did. "This is one of my favorite desserts," she told him.

"I can see why. It just became my all-time favorite," he responded as they both smiled. Neither of them even saw Dennis watching them.

Nico and Shontell finished off both pieces of the cheesecake. She excused herself to go to the restroom, and Nico felt like he had just won the lottery. He was so glad that he didn't mess things up with her. He really thought he blew it. When he left her earlier, he pulled out the cards she had given him. He didn't even remember when he started bringing them with him when they traveled. Some days they gave him the boost he needed. She had a way with words, which always left him in deep thought. If she knew how many songs they produced, it would probably blow her mind. When he first started getting them, they all would swap and read what they said. He knew after the first few words they were just for him, as they were never duplicated. It was as if the words from her cards had hit him all at once. He didn't know how he would have handled it…if she had said no. Nico knew she was the one and wanted to make sure that she knew it as well.

Earlier that day, Nico found a florist. He had wanted to get something special for when she got home. He ordered a dozen lilies and orchids for Shontell to be delivered tomorrow. He heard her tell one of the fellas they were her favorite. Nico wanted the week to go by fast. Their concert tomorrow in Indiana was going to be a good one. He felt it. Being an entertainer had its advantages and its disadvantages when it came to relationships. His mother was always telling him that he would find the one when he least expected it. He thought, for once, that she was spot on. He was looking forward to getting to know Shontell.

Shontell

Shontell pulled her gloss out of her clutch and applied it to her lips. She was closing the cap as Tina walked out of the stall. As they were washing their hands, they looked at one another through their reflection. This woman thought she had the upper hand. She was way too much of a good person to even give her the satisfaction. Tina dried her hands and pulled her dress down. The dress was so tight and short…it didn't move an inch. She watched her in amusement. Hoping her facial expression didn't give away her thoughts, she glanced over her outfit again. Back in the day, the dress was referred to as a move-something dress. She wasn't aware that they were back in style. They both walked out together, but headed in opposite directions. Shontell shook her head as she heard Tina say, "Let the best woman win." *Guess there went Nico's guarantee.* As she headed back into the hospitality suite, she saw that she had a voicemail. She listened to the message and started smiling.

She had forgotten her friend was performing tonight. She had an idea.

The dessert was being cleared away when she sat back down. The guys were talking about what they had chosen to do with their free evening. They were hitting the other two casinos downtown. The band members and the others were all talking in a group. She, Nico, and Martin were all still sitting at the table. She turned to Nico and smiled, "Are you up for a walk?"

"Yes! I think I need to walk off that dessert. I can meet you in the lobby in ten minutes?"

"Okay, that's fine," she told him, as he got up and went to where the others were. She heard Martin call her name, and gave him her undivided attention. He asked her to follow him. "You are doing a great job so far this weekend. I will be sending a ton of work your way. I hope you are ready for it," he told her as he grabbed one of the last desserts from another passing server. Spooning a hefty piece into his mouth, he shook his head in response to the taste.

"This dessert is plain sinful," he told her, finishing it off and setting the plate on the pickup tray. Shontell nodded her head in agreement. He returned his attention back to her, wiping his mouth.

"Thank you so much." Shontell responded. "I am sure I will be. I can't thank you enough for this opportunity." She hugged Martin, and he laughed.

I can't thank you enough for making Nico smile, because his smile had been lost for a while. You seem to have found a way to bring it back. You are just what he needs. Just wait. You two will be great together. Just remember to not let outsiders and the industry tear down what you two are starting to build. Communication is the ultimate key."

"Thank you for the advice. I will keep it close to heart," she told him. She admired Martin very much. She kissed his cheek and then headed out of the suite. Quickly entering her room, she grabbed her jacket and returned her missed call. Calling her dad, she told him she wanted to stop by. He said it was okay. She ended her call. She smiled as her idea was coming to life. She hoped Nico liked it. She grabbed her purse and headed back downstairs. When she got on the elevator, she was joined by Dennis. He didn't say much as they rode down, but she felt him watching her.

"Is something wrong?" she asked him, just as they were getting to the first floor.

"Don't hurt him," was all Dennis said as he got off the elevator with her. Shontell was completely perplexed by his words and just stood there for a moment. Dennis looked back at her, not with hatred but with sincerity. She realized he was looking out for his friend, the same as Sandy would do for her. As she walked toward Nico, she saw he wasn't alone. Tina was standing there with another woman talking to him. The other woman had her arms around Nico as they took pictures. Shontell just stood back and watched. Tina looked her way, and Shontell knew it was time to interrupt. She walked over to the group, smiling the whole time. Nico saw her and reached for her hand as she stood by his side. The look on Tina's face was priceless.

"Okay, ladies, it's time to get my evening started. It was nice meeting you, Diane. Now both of you enjoy your evening," he told them. They walked toward the lobby exit still hand in hand. The night air greeted them as they walked out into the street. "So where are we headed?" he asked.

She loved the fact that he treated them like the fans they were, and kept it moving. It may not have been something he saw as a big deal...but for her, it was. He got two points for that. "I have a little surprise for you."

"Oh really?" he said, enjoying the gleam in her eyes.

Dennis

Dennis was standing against the wall. He watched the exchange between Tina, her friend, Nico and Shontell. Tina may make this easier than he imagined it would be. But, would it be more interesting to stir the pot a little more. He thought for a moment about what he had done. He had paid Tina a good amount of money to show up at this hotel. Nico would never go back to her, but he knew her demeanor would at least cause some ruffles. Now it was time to add some waves. He knew he probably shouldn't be doing this, but he couldn't let Nico fall in love with Shontell. He didn't want to let that side of his friend go again. Nico became a different person when he was with a woman. First it happened when he was with Tina, and now Dennis saw it happening with Shontell. He didn't think that Shontell was bad for Nico, but he had already noticed a change in him. He didn't want a woman to shake up their equilibrium. That was what his brother did with Felecia in the beginning. Dennis wasn't saying they all had to be single, but why did love have to make them change? He couldn't explain it. John would always be the carefree one. He just liked to have fun. It didn't always include partying, or a woman, and he was cool with that. Dennis would never admit that he was being selfish. He shrugged his shoulders and made up his mind. He watched Tina in action from his view of the lounge and was glad she wasn't in the mix anymore. She was useful for what he needed. He took his cell out of his back pocket and dialed a number. He diverted his attention elsewhere as he watched Nico and Shontell walk out the lobby doors. Dennis put his foot on the wall and listened to the ringing on the line. Jesse answered on the fourth ring.

"Hey, what was the name of the lady you used to be engaged to? Really? Okay, so have you talked with her lately? Maybe it's time you do! Oh, and you are confirmed for the cruise." Dennis continued his conversation with Jesse until John signaled that they were ready. He gave their destination to him and ended his call. He smiled and headed out behind the group.

MORE THAN A CRUSH

Shontell

Shontell and Nico walked for about ten minutes, but they didn't really talk. The silence wasn't uncomfortable, and they just held hands like long time lovers. They were enjoying each other's company. She stopped where there was a beautiful boat docked right in front of them. She had always loved this boat. Nico looked from her to the boat and then back to her again.

"We are here," she told him. She laughed as Nico twirled her around. It was a feeling she thought she had forgotten. She was smitten with a person that she never thought she had a chance with. There were a few other couples out enjoying a nice walk as well. He stood behind her, holding her. Looking up, he admired the beauty of the boat.

"She is a beauty. Are we going aboard?"

"Yes, in about ten minutes or so. The captain is doing me a favor. They just finished a concert cruise. They are going to get her ready, and then he is going to take us out for about two hours. I hope you enjoy it. It always relaxes me." As she was telling him that, the captain waved them aboard. They walked up the plank and were greeted by the captain.

"Good evening, Shon. And who is this young man?" he said, motioning at Nico and smiling at them both. Nico stepped up to him and extended his hand.

"I am, Nico, sir. Nico Baker."

"Well, nice to meet you, Nico. Welcome aboard! Her name is the Mystic, but I call her the S. A. Lydia. And I'm Captain Banner. Enjoy the tour."

"It's nice to meet you, sir. Thank you, and I am sure I will."

"You guys will be served a light supper and dessert in about thirty to forty-five minutes. Oh, and your friend, the singer, has agreed to stay on board with you two. She did an excellent job with her performance. We will have her back again for sure. The photographer is also at your disposal." The captain gave his only daughter a stern look and then spoke. "Before we take off, Shon, may I speak to you for a moment?"

"Sure, Captain Darnell," Shontell said, knowing she was about to get into trouble. He raised his eyebrow at her.

"Young lady, you want to tell that man who I am before we get going? I have decided that I will be extra nice tonight and give you both some extra boat time. You have to promise to close up and call the car for your friend when we dock again."

"Yes, Daddy, I will. And come on and let me reintroduce you," she said, kissing her dad on the cheek and laughing.

"Nico, come here for a second!" Nico walked to where she and her father were standing. Shontell took his hand as she tried not to laugh out loud. Nico gave her a strange look of complete confusion.

Nico

Nico watched Shontell walk away. He wondered how she knew the older man, although he did look a little familiar. He watched the exchange between them as he saw a few of the crew members notice him. He heard one of the girls say his name. Shontell motioned him over and took his hand. He immediately felt warm.

"Nico, I just got scolded by the captain here," she told him, smiling. Looking confused, he looked from Shontell to the captain.

"For what, may I ask?" He looked from one to the other.

"Well, the reason why I was able to get this huge favor is because this grand man here is my dad, Captain Darnell Banner."

Nico laughed. He suddenly realized why he looked familiar to him. The resemblance was very clear now. He shook his hand again, and then her father turned and began walking into the ship's foyer. They walked behind him until Captain Darnell turned around.

"Young man, you take care of my baby girl. Treat her better than the last one did, or I will come looking for you," he said with a straight face.

His comment shocked them both. Shontell was embarrassed, "Dad!"

"Baby girl, don't you *dad* me. You know that man nearly destroyed your spirit. I am not going to let that happen again. So Nico, I hope you heard me loud and clear," he said as he tipped his hat, and gave him a serious look.

"Sir, I heard you. I will take care of her...you have my word. " Nico put up the scouts honor sign. Extending his hand again, they shook. He wanted her father to know he would keep his word to him.

"Enjoy the cruise, Shon. Your mother and I will see you Tuesday for dinner."

"Yes, Daddy, thank you." He waved to them as he went to his helm.

"I am sorry about that. I am so embarrassed!"

"Don't be! He loves you. I hope you will tell me what he was talking about."

"I will tell you soon, I promise. Come on, let's take some pictures before we go upstairs."

"Okay...whenever you are ready, I will be here to listen."

"Thank you. I appreciate it." She reached up to kiss him. She wrapped her arms around him. She only meant to give him a quick peck, but the simple kiss turned into much more. A noise around them caused them to stop.

"You are going to get me in trouble with your dad," he whispered into her neck. She laughed. They headed to the picture area and soon felt the boat in motion.

Nico wrapped his arms around her as they took pictures. He loved the coconut and berries he smelled in her hair. They took a few pictures and then went to the dining area. They took the seats up near the front where a table had been set for them. She noticed the projector was out as she requested. She looked around for her friend and figured she must have still been in the back dressing area. Shontell was just about to inquire when Michael, one of the waiters, came out with a tray. He set it down and began placing their light dinner on the table.

"Michael, is everything ready?" she asked him in a way so as not to give away her little surprise. He nodded and then motioned for her.

"Shon, I hate to ask this, but the crew has been going crazy because of him." He motioned toward Nico. "Do you mind if they come out and say hi and get some pics while you talk to Sheléa?" he whispered. She looked over her shoulder and back at Nico. She wondered if this is what she would have to get used to again. When she was with Jesse, it occurred sometimes. Most of the time he kept her out of view, like she asked. She walked back over to Nico and explained the request to him.

"Nico, do you mind?"

"If you're sure you don't, then it's okay."

"Michael, you guys have ten minutes. Nico, I will be back in a few minutes," she told him. She headed back to the area where Michael had come from. Her father's staff greeted her warmly as they headed out to where Nico was. Shontell stood there and watched as they made a big deal over him. He took it in stride. He was used to this and much more, she was sure. She didn't hear Sheléa come up behind her.

"Are you sure you're ready for that again?" Turning around, she faced her friend and saw the concern that she was wearing.

"I've asked myself that over and over again in the last twenty-four hours. I can't punish him for what Jesse did. I just hope I am not proven wrong," she admitted to her honestly, as the vision of Tina came into mind. "Anyways, it's so good to see you. My dad told me how you *wowed* everyone."

"Girl, I love your dad. He is so sweet. I can't wait to come back," she told her as they hugged.

"Okay, they are almost done. It's up to you how many songs you do, but I want the video to play first. Then you can come on out and do your thing."

"Okay and I got you. I will rest after that until we dock. I am headed to DC when I leave here to perform with Lalah Hathaway."

"Alright now. I am so proud of you." The two women hugged again and promised to catch up later in the week. She walked back out to where Nico was and the lights were dimmed. Nico looked up at the lights and then his glance went to her. He was still standing and smiling. He pulled her into his embrace and kissed her. She was blushing and couldn't do anything but smile.

"What was that for?"

"Just being you."

"Well, I should mention something to you; I don't like being in the limelight. The first quote-un-quote celebrity I dated was awful. He took me to a premiere, and my life after that was an open book. I was always followed by some paparazzi. I ended it because I just couldn't do it. So when I dated the next guy in the industry, I asked him to keep me out of it. He did, and it worked better for the most part. So I hope my asking you about this won't be a problem."

"No, I understand your concerns, and I will do my best to protect you." He held out the chair for her, and the projector screen came to life. Nico pulled his chair next to hers and pulled her body closer to his.

"Movie?"

"Nope, just watch." The music came on over the speaker, and Sheléa's video *Love The Way You Love Me* played. Nico sat up straighter in his seat but didn't release her from his embrace, as they continued to watch. Right before Sheléa walked out, Shontell turned to him and asked, "Can you give me that type of love?"

Nico

Nico couldn't believe how good it felt to spend time with Shontell. He watched the video, and he loved the concept. The couple on the screen looked to be so deeply in love. Again he thought about how much he wanted the same type of love. That's what his parents and David had. So when she asked him that question, he didn't hesitate in giving his answer.

"Yes, yes, and with everything in me, yes," he told her as he leaned in to kiss her. But then he was surprised when he heard a woman singing. He looked up at the screen but was amazed to see the girl from the video standing there in person singing the song. He looked over at Shontell and laughed. He pulled her up and brought her to him. They danced while her friend sang...and she could really sing. She looked familiar, but he didn't know her name.

They danced to one more song and then clapped in appreciation of the personal performance. Bowing, she greeted them both.

"Nico, this is one of my dearest friends, Sheléa Frazier."

"Nico, it's a pleasure meeting you in person finally. I am a fan of the group. Be good to my girl here," she winked at him and smiled.

"That I will do, and thank you. Now you have a fan in me. Didn't you do something on the *Jumping the Broom* soundtrack?"

"Yes, I did."

"Okay, okay. I thought I recalled that voice…absolutely fabulous," he complimented.

"Thank you…I try. I can't hold a candle to your girl's octaves here," she told him, motioning to Shontell. Shontell cleared her throat and placed her fingers to her lips to end the conversation. He saw it but pretended he didn't.

"What do you mean?" he asked her, playing along, not wanting to give what he saw away.

"Um…nothing…nothing. Ms. Frazier needs to go rest before her flight…don't you?" Shontell put her arm around her friend. Her friend caught on and laughed.

"Oh, yes. I do. It was nice meeting you, and I hope to see you again."

"I am sure you will. Why don't you look me up when you are in LA? I am sure we can do some work together." Nico never missed an opportunity to work with talented singers, and she was one of them. She waved to them both and went in the kitchen area.

"So what was that about?" he quizzed.

"What was what about?" Shontell replied, trying to act innocent.

"Okay, I am going to let that go. Do you want to go outside?"

"Sure," she told him as he took her hand. She led the way.

Michael brought out a bottle of wine and glasses. They spent the rest of the ride watching the scenery and making small talk. They docked and, doing as she promised, she called Sheléa's car for her. They both waved to her off the side of the rail as they watched her get in the car. Afterwards, they shared a small dessert. The staff had all left, and it was just the two of them. He helped her clean up as they locked the boat down and headed back to the hotel. It was nearly 1 a.m.

"Do you want to come to my room?" Nico asked her.

"As long as you promise to behave."

He did the cross my heart sign. Then he said, "I promise."

"Okay. Do you mind if I stop in my room for a second? I will meet you at your room in a few minutes." Stepping onto the floor, they walked in opposite directions.

Nico showered quickly and dimmed the lights. He opened a bottle of wine, just in case. He heard the knock and opened his door. His mouth hung open.

Shontell went into her room and sent Sandy a text. She told her to meet her at home in the morning. She showered and put on a silk gown before heading to Nico's room. She knocked on the door and waited for Nico to answer. She smiled when she saw his reaction to her gown. It was a deep-fire red, V-neck, silk charmeuse with a robe. She didn't even know why she had packed it, but she did on impulse. She was glad that she had. He stepped back and let her in the room.

"Wow."

"Thank you."

"Do you want a glass of wine?"

"Sure, this is the most that I've drank in a long time."

After pouring the wine, they reclined on the bed and began watching a movie. It was just like the first night. It seemed different because things had changed some. They cuddled and laughed at the movie. She didn't remember falling asleep, but knew the night could not have ended any more perfectly. Nico gave her something she had been missing in her life. He gave her pure intimacy. She awoke and watched him as he slept, tracing his face with her fingers. He smiled as he opened his eyes and looked at her.

"How long have you been awake?"

"For a little while…did you sleep okay?"

"Thanks to you, it was the best sleep that I've had in a long time." They hugged and he rolled her on top of him. Shontell could feel him rise on her buttocks.

"I thought you were going to behave."

"What? I thought that I was behaving." She scooted back so that now she was on his lap, and she wrapped her arms around his neck.

"Ha, you were until I felt that." She started grinding a little on his erection. He groaned.

"I'll tell you what…if you do that again, I won't be behaving."

"Sorry, I couldn't resist. Good thing it's almost time for you to get ready. Your bus will be here in an hour and a half. Breakfast is in twenty minutes." Nico groaned again as he leaned in to kiss Shontell's shoulder. They straightened up the room. Then Shontell left Nico's to finish packing and head downstairs.

HOOK, LINE, SINKER

Nico

Nico finished packing and ran into the gift shop to grab a few supplies. He groaned when he saw Tina at the register. He cut to the left sharply to avoid her. He got what he went in for. Purposely, he hung around...idling. He wanted her to finish in the shop, so that she wouldn't see him and speak to him. He still felt something wasn't right when it came to her being at the hotel. She should have known he wouldn't be happy to see her. They didn't exactly part as friends.

He decided not to think about this now. Nico finished his transaction and headed into breakfast. All of his friends looked at him. He noticed that Shontell had not come into the room yet. Dennis spoke first.

"So how was your night, bro? Did you two do something I would have done?" he smirked. Nico looked at him and paused. For some reason, his questions sounded more like an interrogation. He decided not to let Dennis' smart attitude ruin his mood. He smirked back at him. He grabbed a glass of orange juice and a bagel.

"We had a great evening. How did you guys fare at the casino?"

"Oh, we had a good night as well."

"That's good." He took his food and headed to the table. John could almost choke on the thickness in the air. It was building between the two, and he thought he needed to intervene. He normally did. He stepped in between them putting, both arms over their shoulders.

"You know *I* was hot on those tables, boy. Got me a mint," John said, laughing. He changed the mood quickly. The room erupted with chatter. Nico took that time to talk to the members about a possible incentive gift for Shontell's service. They all agreed. Even Dennis had to admit she was good at her job. It had only been two days since the release party, and their sales had increased. They were finishing up when Shontell walked in wearing a purple pantsuit with purple and black heels. The whole room became quiet, and Shontell's face turned the color of her suit.

Martin walked over to her, and they began talking. Nico watched her, and John came up behind him. "Man, you got it bad already huh?"

"I don't know what you're talking about," Nico said as he smiled the whole time. He bit into his bagel. Shontell grabbed a cup of coffee. She walked into the room, making sure everyone was ready. Nico and John both watched her do her magic. John nodded. He was clearly impressed by the way she handled things. Moments later, she announced that the bus was waiting out front.

They were getting ready to load up in the bus when Nico pulled her to the side. He gave her a card. He wanted to kiss her, but chose to hug her instead…not wanting them to be watched by the others.

"Shontell, thank you for everything. I will see you in a week, but I will talk to you tonight after we arrive. My contact info is on this card." They hugged again, and he gave her a peck on the cheek. She pulled a medium sized envelope out of her purse and handed it to him. They both must have felt that someone was looking at them. Nico was surprised to see it was Dennis and Tina. They were off to the side. Now he definitely knew something had to be up with the both of them. He was going to find out. Shontell looked back at him, but said nothing. She stepped in closer to him and gave him a hard kiss on the lips. She stepped back as quickly as she had stepped up to him. She gave him a look, and he understood. She took his hand and he squeezed hers. She turned and motioned to the envelope that she had given him a few minutes prior, and she smiled slightly.

"Look at it once you get to the hotel," she told him. She hugged the rest of the group, outside of Dennis. He was still standing near Tina. Martin walked over to them and took Shontell by the hand, whispering something into her ear. She nodded in reply. Turning, Nico waved as he and Martin stepped on the bus. He was trying to understand what was going on. He watched Dennis, as he held a conversation with John. He was silently seething. He could see Shontell at her car as they pulled out of the lobby parking lot. He hoped he was right when he told her Tina would not be a problem for them.

Shontell

Shontell pulled off right after the bus left. Tina was getting into a black town car. She paused as she passed by. Shontell didn't even give her the satisfaction of looking at her. She tried not to think about her. Her woman's intuition told her that she was going to be more trouble than not. Shontell stopped at the store to grab some wine and brunch items for her and Sandy. It was going to be a long day. She had a lot to tell her. Once she got into her condo, she threw her mail on the table and went to change clothes. As she was undressing, Nico's card fell onto the floor. She had completely forgotten about it. She picked it up, opened it, and sat open-mouthed at what it said.

Shontell, usually I am not a person who is at a loss for words. Ask any of the guys and they will tell you, I am always one to say what's on my mind. There are very few people who cross my path that make an impact enough for me to pursue. But like I told you, there was something about you that has had me wanting to know you as a person, even before I knew your name. I have been all over the world, but no one has had me smiling like you.

And speaking of smiles, your smile is amazing, and it just seems to lift my spirit each time I have seen you. This weekend has been a trip for me, but I guess you saved me having to seek you out at our next Detroit concert. Lol. You have a way with words, and I am a little embarrassed to tell you just how many times I have reread your cards, even as recently as this weekend...

I can't believe I just wrote that. But I hope my actions make a deeper impression on you. I am looking forward to getting to know you. Our small amount of time that we've spent together has left a huge impact on me. At this moment, I'm feeling that a week is just too long to go without seeing you. By the way, I took the liberty of upgrading your room on the cruise. You and your friend are now in a grand suite with VIP status for the whole cruise. I hope you don't mind, but this was a bonus from me. The monetary bonus is from me and the guys for the great work you've done this weekend. Use it to get you something special for the cruise.

See you soon. Yours, Nico

Shontell read the card three times. Inside the card were five, one-hundred-dollar bills, which she lay on her bed. She shook her head and quickly put his numbers in her phone. She sent him a text.

Thank you for the card, bonus, the cruise gift, and thank you for just being you, she typed and closed her phone. She went to let Sandy in who was now banging on her door. She didn't even realize she still had the card in her hand until Sandy grabbed it from her.

"What's this?" Sandy started reading it.

"Well nosey, it's a card from, Nico." She handed her a glass of red wine and a plate. When she finished reading, she almost knocked her glass off the counter.

"OMG, OMG...my best friend is dating, Nico!" she screamed.

"Sandy, stop being so dramatic. You act like I have never dated a celebrity before."

"But none has been someone you had a crush on for years, have they?"

"Well, I guess you have a point there. You are making too much of this. This whole thing has me nervous. I mean, you know what happened the last time. That's why I haven't dated anyone since him. I never want to feel that kind of pain again. I didn't get a chance to tell you, but I met Nico's ex-girlfriend, Tina."

"Tina?"

"Yes, and she is everything I am not. But Nico was adamant about her not being an issue. Still, from what I can see, I am not so sure."

"Oh...okay, so do you think he wants to get back with her?" Sandy asked as she finished off her glass of wine and poured another. She grabbed some fruit and started eating it. Sandy looked at her best friend and could see the emotions all across her face. She had hoped that the next man she dated would be a doctor or dentist. For whatever reason, her friend seemed to be a magnet for industry men. The women ate in silence for a few minutes.

"You deserve to be happy. The few times I talked to you these last couple of days I heard it in your voice. It was something I had never heard with Jesse," Sandy offered, breaking the silence in the room. Shontell looked at her best friend and couldn't refute her admission. If she never saw Nico again, their memories definitely would keep a smile on her face.

"What if I do go into this further? What if he breaks my heart?"

"Shontell!"

"I know. I know. So before you even say it, I know I can't judge all men the same way. You know, trust is a huge thing for me."

Sandy looked at her friend and felt her pain. Jesse had left her in shambles when she caught him cheating, plus it took a long time to recover from the accident too. It was a huge deal. She knew it couldn't have been her, because that fool Jesse would have been in the hospital bed next to her. It took her nearly three months before she could even get her friend out the house. It was not a good scene at all. Just as she was about to say something, Shontell's phone chimed. Sandy was being mannish when she grabbed her best friend's phone and read the text. Her mouth flew open, and she handed her the phone.

Nico

Nico remained quiet for the rest of the ride to Indiana. He had his eyes closed so that they would think he was sleeping and not bother him. He listened as they were talking, though. He really started listening when John asked Dennis about him talking to Tina. Dennis claimed he was just making idle chatter with her. He stated that he was trying to get information on her friend. Nico had to force himself not to react. He felt it in his bones that Dennis was lying. Why would he bring Tina around him? Why didn't he want him to date Shontell? He never thought his friend would betray him like this. When the bus pulled up to the hotel, he had already decided he would play his game. Dennis winning was not an option.

Nico picked up the envelope Shontell gave him. It changed his mood immediately. After being given his key, he was about to take the stairs to his room when Martin stopped him.

"Son, come here. Let's talk."

"What's up, Martin?"

"I know you are upset about Tina being at the hotel. I know what you're thinking. I saw Dennis with her. Let me deal with him. Do you hear me?" Nico looked at Martin, but stayed quiet.

"Why would he do that to me?" he asked, trying to contain his emotions and keep his voice low. He kicked his foot outward. He felt like he was about to lose control. Martin put his hand on his shoulder.

"Nico, I said I will handle him. You go hit the gym and blow off some of that anger. You are friends. Don't let this interfere with the group. Here is something to think about...Dennis lost David when he got married. I think he sees that same thing happening to you if you continue with Shontell. He is afraid of that." Martin patted his shoulder. He left him to think about what he'd said.

Nico headed back in his original direction and took the stairs to his room. He flung his bag to the floor. He paced as he replayed the conversation in his mind. It did make sense. Dennis went all crazy when David got engaged and almost broke them up with his antics. He wouldn't let that happen this time. He decided to do what Martin had suggested. He had a couple of hours before they had to be at sound check. He picked his bag up and sat on the bed. He took the envelope out that Shontell had given him. Carefully opening it, he smiled at its content. She had put a set of pictures inside that were taken on her father's boat. He had forgotten all about them. He was so glad that she had given them to him. He looked at them and saw the glow on her face. He sighed because he could not understand how she was affecting him like this. He instantly forgot about the situation with Dennis and Tina as he ran his fingers across her face. His heart skipped a beat. This had never happened to him before. He had never even felt like this as a teenager because he was so focused on singing and music. He had even been accused of being gay back then because he was never seen with girls. He didn't care what they were saying…he was just focused. Being that focused is what got him to where he is now. He was able to help out his parents and his siblings. His mother was the director of the youth academy that they had opened together nearly six years ago. That was his biggest accomplishment.

As he placed the pictures back inside the envelope, his phone went off. He read the text and grinned. He was wondering how long it would take her to read the card. He didn't get her number, so he had to wait until she contacted him. When he reached the gym area, he was alone. He was glad about that. He saved her number and then opened his video messaging. He began talking into the camera, letting her know he saw the pictures and thanked her. He was about to end the video when he decided to sing a little something for her. Hitting stop, he laughed at himself and hoped she didn't think it was too corny. He stretched and started his workout. His anger had already left, so this workout focus was something totally different. He recalled her in that red nightgown. He groaned as he lifted the 150-lb weight with his shoulders, doing presses. He was hoping it would override the sensation elsewhere.

Shontell

Shontell wondered what the sound was on her phone and why Sandy had such a crazy look on her face. She took the phone from her. She sipped her wine and then opened the message. Nico greeted her immediately. He was serenading her. She was floored. How was she going to handle this?

"Oh my, what have I gotten myself into?" She was fanning herself as she said it out loud.

"I am at a loss for words, but all I can say is tread slowly," her best friend replied. She shook her head, agreeing with her. They finished their lunch and decided on some evening plans. They were laughing and enjoying themselves when the doorbell rang. Sandy got up to answer since she was the closest. While they were talking, Shontell couldn't help but think about Nico and the last two days. She had been contemplating if she should send a response to his video message but opted not to. Nico really made her feel things she had not felt in a long time. She decided to write back her thoughts instead, which was one of her favorite pastimes. She finished just as Sandy called her to the door.

Nico

Nico stepped out the shower with steam surrounding him. As he was drying off, his phone went off. He walked over to his nightstand, where he had left his phone charging, and hit the screen. Shontell's name popped up. He grabbed his musk oil and poured it into his hand as he began reading the text:

Thank you for the beautiful message. You are so amazing and any woman would be lucky to even have a deep conversation with you, and yet you want me. I am still in awe. I just wanted to let you in on a little secret. I'm nervous, but I am ready for the journey, even with our disruption. I absolutely can't wait to see you... but for now I will have to settle for hearing your voice. By the way, I hope you're enjoying Indiana. Just in case we don't talk, have a good show tonight.

Nico finished with his oils. He laid back on his bed and closed his eyes. All he saw was Shontell's smile, and he wished she was lying next to him. He got up after he lay there a few minutes more, and picked up his pen and paper. He always kept them near his bed. He had finished three new songs within two hours. He looked at his clock, and it was an hour before rehearsal. He was just about to call Shontell when his phone beeped. The good mood changed as he looked at the message from Tina. He deleted it without even reading it. He decided to close his eyes. He couldn't call Shontell now in this mind frame.

Shontell

Shontell went to where Sandy was and was greeted by the most beautiful arrangement of purple roses, lilies, and orchids. Her eyes instantly began to tear up. How did he know? She finally noticed the delivery guy still standing there and went to get her purse for a tip. Once he left, all she could do was admire the flowers. Her whole kitchen immediately was filled with their scent. She looked for a card and began reading it quickly. The whole time, Sandy just stood there and watched her reaction. She tried not to react, but that was too hard for her. Her face flushed, and she exhaled loudly. She picked up the phone and started to dial. She quickly ended the call. Her hands were sweating. This was so unreal. There was that feeling again. She felt like a young girl again, not a thirty-nine-year-old woman.

"What should I say to him?" she asked Sandy while she paced her kitchen floor, barefooted. She kept moving her toes upward as she walked, which was another one of her nervous habits.

"How about…thank you. That would be a good start. I am impressed though. He does know how to court a woman." She went to get some water for her vase.

"Ha, ha. You're funny. But yes, I guess you are right. Courting seems to be a foreign word to men these days."

"Yes, it does," Sandy said as she played with the arrangement.

"Okay, I can do this. I don't know what is wrong with me," Shontell said, fidgeting.

"I do, but I will keep my comments to myself. Now call him!" Sandy handed her back her phone. Shontell took the phone hesitantly. She flipped it over in her hands a couple of times. She was being silly because he was no different than any other man. She dialed the numbers and waited for him to answer. He answered on the third ring. She could tell she woke him up.

"Good afternoon. I'm sorry. You sound like you were sleeping, and I didn't mean to wake you up. I just wanted to say thank you. The flowers are so beautiful," she told him. She could hear him moving around. He was probably trying to sit up. She waited until he finished and spoke.

"Good afternoon to you as well. It's okay. I didn't realize that I fell asleep. I had just lain down and closed my eyes, I thought. But enough about that...I would have given anything to see that smile I am hearing in your voice."

"Wow, is all I can say about you. You got me feeling some type of way," she admitted.

"I know the feeling...I know the feeling," he told her.

"Well, at least I am not alone. What time is rehearsal?" She twirled her hair and swung her legs on the barstool she was sitting on.

"In about thirty minutes. I think I need to grab some food beforehand, though. I haven't eaten since I left you this morning."

"Ohhh, that's not good. Sandy and I have been eating since noon," she said, as she arranged the cheese that was on her plate. She poured wine into her glass and then into Sandy's glass. She handed it to her as Sandy looked over a magazine.

"Really? I was a little upset on the ride so I didn't have too much of an appetite, but now I am starving."

"Nico, don't let her have that power over you. You said she wouldn't be an issue...so don't allow her to be,"

Shontell scolded him lightly. She was surprised at her words because she herself felt the same way earlier as she was driving home. She had to hang on to some hope. Nico didn't reply. "Nico, you still there?"

""Yes. Yes, I am sorry. I will work on that, I promise. I do have some good news. After I read your message, I was motivated to write. We are starting to work on the new album, so I got an early start...thanks to my new muse. I am glad you liked the flowers. My original intent was to call you before we got to the radio station. After that, we have a sound check for the concert tonight. It's officially time for the countdown to begin. Only five days until I see you again," he told her.

She rocked on her heels as she smiled into the phone. They talked for about another fifteen minutes, until he said his stomach was screaming at him. He needed to go find food, so they ended their call. It was decided that she and Sandy would go down for the cruise a day earlier than planned, and she and Nico would do dinner the night before the cruise.

Shontell asked Sandy to ride down to her office with her. They planned to hit the mall after her staff meeting.

When she reached the office, Shontell took notice immediately that Ebony hadn't arrived. They had talked about her being on time. Looking at the clock, she started the meeting without her because of her other plans. During the meeting, Shontell came up with an idea; she knew Sandy would go along if she asked. Now she was ready to get out the office. Shontell had just finished giving out the assignments and introducing her new two new hires to the staff when Ebony walked in. She ended the meeting. She was more than thirty minutes late. Shontell didn't want to ball her out in front of the staff. It wasn't her style. She waited until everyone had left the building before she spoke to Ebony. She could tell Ebony was hoping she wouldn't say anything, because she was messing with some paperwork and avoiding her. Sandy took notice and told her she would wait in the car.

"So, what's up, Ebony? I thought I stressed to you that I needed you here for the meeting. Does this new boyfriend of yours have anything to do with this?" she wanted to know. The mention of the boyfriend caused Ebony to tense. She looked wide-eyed at her.

"Look, I am sorry about being late. I would have texted you, but I couldn't find my phone. That's one of the reasons I was late."

"And what was the other?"

"What?" Ebony appeared perplexed that she asked her that. "I just lost track of time. I apologize...dang...get off my back," Ebony stated.

"Is that really the stance you're going to take with me? I know that this company doesn't mean shit to you. For me, it has my blood, sweat, and tears for the last ten years. So, if you really don't want to be here, please do us both a favor."

"Hmph, isn't that ironic? Isn't that what I was doing for you two years ago? I did you a favor and saved this place," she retorted back to her, waving her hand around the office. Shontell wanted to smack the smug look off her face. She had her twisted if she thought she was going to do whatever she wanted because she loaned her some money. She was glad she had been planning her next move. She would wait this out. She laughed to herself, and it seemed to make Ebony react.

"What's so funny?" She folded her arms and pouted, trying to understand her partner's change in mood.

"You are. I am going to give you your little rant here, because you are on the defensive when *you* are the one who is wrong. But, let me say this...and, trust me, I won't repeat it...if your passion isn't in PTE, don't fake it...just walk away." She picked up her purse and headed out to her car. She was fuming. What she was thinking, letting this woman help her! All she did was spend what she made. She didn't bring in new clients. She sure played favorites to her so-called friends. Ebony was a socialite. She prided herself on being in public and being seen. It didn't matter, because she still didn't have class. There was no amount of money that could ever afford her that. Shontell got in the car. She hit the steering wheel. Her reaction made Sandy jump. "Sorry. That, that...woman or *girl*, should I say, has pushed my buttons!"

"Yes, so I see. How long are you going to keep this up? Don't you have the money to buy her out?"

"Yes, I do. I could have done it today, but I haven't started interviewing for a manager. After this cruise, things definitely will be changing. Okay, so anyway, I was brainstorming during the meeting. I know we were supposed to hit the mall, but I have an idea."

"Which is?"

"Are you up for a spontaneous road trip?"

"I'm always game to do something. What do you have in mind?"

"Hmmm, maybe taking in a concert?" she said, smiling. All the while, she was dialing a number in her phone. Shontell called Martin as they headed out of the parking lot. She asked him if the concert was sold out. He told her it was. She thought her idea was going to go sour as she waited on Martin to come back onto the phone. She almost screamed when he told her he would have tickets waiting for them, as well as backstage passes. She asked him to keep it a surprise, and he agreed. He knew Nico would be ecstatic, considering what had happened earlier when they got to the hotel.

Shontell and Sandy said their goodbyes as Shontell dropped her off at home. She would be back by her house to get her friend in an hour. She waved to Monica, her daughter, as she sped off. They needed to be on the road fast in order to make it to the concert on time. It was only 2:00

p.m., but they still had a four-hour drive ahead of them. The concert started at 8 p.m.

Nico

After they ended their call, Nico headed to their hospitality suite to grab some food. Dennis was sitting at the bar talking on his cell. He wasn't in the mood to deal with Dennis. He decided to go straight to the food table. He sat at a table in the corner, and he said his grace. He started eating, but was interrupted by Dennis half way through.

"What's up, Nico? You've been quiet since we left Detroit," Dennis said as he grabbed his own plate of food.

"You seem to notice a lot about me lately. You might do better to worry about yourself."

"What's that supposed to mean? I know you're still not mad about what happened with our little tiff?" Nico took a deep breath before he responded. He saw Martin heading in their direction out of the corner of his eye.

"Gentlemen, the car is waiting. I was looking for you both. Let's go," Martin informed them. Martin observed both Nico and Dennis, and decided he needed to keep them separate. Mostly he needed to keep them civil until he could get Dennis alone. Both men followed him in silence. Nico finished his drink and threw the paper cup into a trash can as they walked. He knew Dennis was watching, and he ignored him on purpose.

Somehow the atmosphere in the car was normal, and the group talked all the way to the rehearsal. Nico told the group about the songs he had completed, and shared the concept with them. Dennis gave him a look, and Nico laughed. He wasn't going to give him the power, especially when he remembered Shontell's words. John saw the look that passed between the two and decided to be the one to lighten the mood, as usual. He changed the subject by asking David about one of Felecia's friends she was bringing to the concert. They finished their rehearsal and arrived for the concert. Nico was preparing himself to perform, but he took out his cell and sent a message before it was time to hit the stage. He could feel the adrenaline hitting his body the way it always did when they performed. He knew that whatever the tension was between him and Dennis wouldn't show on stage. That was a pact they always stood by. He was trying to honor what Martin had asked of him. He wanted to shake some answers out of him. He wondered if Dennis was willing to lose their friendship over Shontell. But was the real reason a woman, or the fact that they were getting older and wanted something more than what they currently had? They had been through a lot more than most people would have ever known about. David and Nico met in seventh grade, and then they started hanging out with John in their junior year of high school after hearing him sing on a dare. He had a crazy range. They recruited him, and the rest was history. He snapped out of his thoughts as he could hear the screaming fans outside his room door. His door was opened, and one of the assistants informed him it was time to hit the stage. Nico and his brothers all stood still. He then looked at each of them and the other family and friends they had standing backstage. They had a lot to be thankful for. The guys finished their prayer right as they heard the opening music start. They were on song three when he thought he saw Shontell in the audience. He thought that he was seeing things because he knew that she could not be there. He really had her too much on the brain. He turned back around and looked in that same direction, but he didn't see her again. Yeah, he had been seeing things. He sat on the stool as the group was about to sing the final song.

Shontell picked up her cell phone and read Nico's message out loud. *Hey beautiful, just letting you know I was thinking about you. Getting ready to hit the stage.*

She typed a reply to him. She and Sandy laughed because she couldn't wait to see his face. They made it to their seats right as the group hit the stage. She hoped that he wouldn't notice her in the crowd. When they were singing her favorite song, he looked dead at her. She wanted to wave but didn't. She wondered if he had seen her. She couldn't tell with his glasses on and the lights shining on him. When he stepped to the back of the stage area for a drink, Martin got her attention. He signaled for her and Sandy to come to where he was. He said that they could watch the rest of the concert with him.

While she was backstage, Martin introduced her to David's wife Felecia. There were others back there that she briefly spoke to, whom she assumed they knew from back in the city. She had a clear view of the performance from where she was sitting. She was so excited, like she was every time she watched them in concert. It was always fun. The energy they brought to the stage was phenomenal. They gave the fans what they wanted. They were clearly great entertainers. When they were on the last song, Martin took her by the hand and down to Nico's dressing room. Sandy wanted to watch the end. She decided to stay with Felecia, whom she had instantly liked.

Shontell was nervous, but she sat completely still in a chair off to the side. She wanted him to be surprised, so she made sure he wouldn't be able to see her when he walked in. She could hear them saying goodnight to the crowd. Then the hallway became noisy as the guys were speaking loudly. She heard someone at the door. Nico walked in. He headed straight to his cell phone. That action alone impressed her. He really did like her. She watched him read her reply. Shontell paid attention to his body language. She always thought it showed a lot about a person's true emotions. She sometimes thought that if she would have paid more attention to Jesse, she never would have gotten hurt. He was now water under the bridge, as far as she was concerned. She continued to watch Nico and heard him say, "Wow," as he shook his head. He ran his hand over his head and smiled. Nico looked up towards the ceiling and spoke aloud, "Thank you. I think we got it right this time." Shontell was so touched by his words that she instantly became emotional and had to keep from making a sound. She quickly got herself together. She stood, but stayed hidden. He began undressing, taking off his soaked shirt. She hesitated as she watched him wipe off with a towel. She was still overwhelmed by what she witnessed. He grabbed some cologne, and she saw her moment. She quietly walked up behind him and placed her hands over his eyes. He almost dropped the bottle.

"Guess who?" she whispered. Nico could smell the coconut and berries, and he knew it was her. He grabbed her hands and brought her around to him.

"I knew it. I knew I saw you in the audience," he said as he leaned in and kissed her deeply. They kissed until someone opened his door and said his name.

"Nico, are you ready?" Dennis asked him. He noticed Shontell standing there with him. His facial expression clearly showed his surprise and disappointment at her being with him. Shontell wondered what she did to him for his actions to be the way they were. He tried to cover it up, but it was too late. They both saw it.

"Oh, I'm sorry, Shontell. When did you get here?" he asked her.

Before she could answer, Nico spoke. "Can you guys give me ten minutes, please?" Shontell took notice that Nico never let her go the entire time. It was his way of letting him know she was around to stay. She felt overwhelmed with emotions again.

CAUGHT OFF GUARD

Dennis

Dennis stood there watching the look on his friend's face. This was the first time he had seen Nico like that since they were younger. That time it wasn't even about a girl. It was about passion. He never saw that look on his face with Tina. They all knew that he was head over heels for her, but it never came across like that. He had seen that look another time within their group. It was when David fell for Felecia. He nodded his head and was about to close the door when he heard Shontell call his name.

"Dennis, my best friend, Sandy, is out there. She may be near Felecia. Can you let her know I will be out in a few minutes? She has on orange and white. Thank you."

"Sure," he told her, nodding as he was getting ready to close the door. Dennis looked at them once more as they hugged. She laughed at something Nico said to her. He had a fleeting thought that maybe he was wrong in his assumption about them hooking up. He knew that he didn't want to lose his friend like he had with David. He never got time with his brother anymore. It was different before he was with Felecia. Things were sometimes strained because he tried to break them up, although he apologized for it. The end damage was done. It seemed like he was doing the same thing now. He was about to look for Shontell's friend when his cell phone beeped. He checked the message and saw that it was Tina, telling him that everything was in place for the cruise. He typed in some words and then paused before hitting send. He looked at his words, and he felt conflicted by his own plan. In the end, he knew he had too much invested He closed his phone without sending the message. He continued down the hall to look for her friend, and then he made his way to her. She was gorgeous but, for some reason, he immediately knew she was probably not in his league. She was talking to a couple of the band members. They were cracking jokes as he approached her. "Sandy?"

"Yes, Dennis, right?" she asked.

"Correct. Shontell wanted me to tell you that she will be out in a few minutes."

"Okay, thank you for letting me know. I enjoyed the concert. I can't wait for the cruise at the end of the week."

She moved her hands as she was talking. He thought that was different. Dennis watched her mouth move, and again it amused him. She wore a very red lipstick, which brought out her dimples.

"Thank you. Glad you enjoyed the concert. Oh, you're going on the cruise?" he asked, surprised. Leaning against the wall to get more comfortable, he awaited her response.

"Yes, Shon is treating me. It's my birthday week."

"Oh wow, nice gift. Well let me go meet the others. I'm sure I will see you in a few," Dennis told her. He headed to the meet and greet area. He could feel her watching him. She might not be out of his league as he had originally thought. He pulled out his phone and sent the now drafted message. *It may be a good thing to have them on the cruise.* He laughed to himself. He peeped out at the meet and greet line. He saw two women who would be perfect to cap his evening off with. He sent his usual person to do what was needed. He looked back at Sandy, who was talking to Felecia. They were in deep conversation. He couldn't wait until they were on the water.

In their rehearsal earlier, they were told the cruise had sold out. This cruise was Nico's baby. He was the one who approached them about it. As it always turned out, he brought them another notch of success to their twenty-five years in this business. He spotted John and David as they were coming out of their dressing rooms. He stopped and waited for them to reach him. They were almost to where the meet and greet was being held. John looked back, noticing that Nico wasn't out there.

"Where's Nico?" he asked Dennis.

"Seems as if Shontell surprised him. They are in the dressing room. Her friend Sandy is over there talking to Felecia," he responded. He was hoping that his tone wouldn't change to show his irritation of the whole thing, again.

"Oh, that was sweet of her. I am sure Nico loved that," David said, not even looking at Dennis. "I bet he did," Dennis mumbled. Both of the men looked at him strangely, but neither said anything. Dennis knew he was failing at trying to be nonchalant, and he decided he needed to just shut up. He grabbed a glass and had the bartender add some liquor. He swallowed it quickly before Martin saw him, but when Martin walked up behind him, he knew he was busted. "Dennis, I don't know what you are up to, but please, know that I am on to you. I am sure you haven't forgotten what happened the last time you thought it was your place to interfere in someone's love life. You almost ended this group," Martin told him. He spoke in a low tone so no one else heard their conversation. Dennis was about to say something when Martin put his hand up to stop him. "Let me finish. I want you to think very long and hard. You all deserve a life outside of this group. I say if love is that renewal of life, then go for it. Hear me clearly when I say this. If you pull what you did before, you won't have to worry about the group ending. That won't happen. But you will be out," he told him firmly and walked away.

Dennis never turned around but finished off his drink.

He observed Nico and Shontell as they walked into the room. She let go of his hand. She joined her friend, and they went and sat with Felecia and a few others. He quickly thought back to what he saw in Nico's dressing room. He could see his happiness. Whatever Shontell was giving him, it must be good. He couldn't recall the last time he'd seen Nico into anything outside of music and his parents. He had to admit though, Nico was different...including towards him.

Shontell

"Shontell, I want to ask you how you got here, but it doesn't even matter. I am just glad that you are. Let me get changed," he told her as he stepped over to his clothes rack and grabbed some jeans and a shirt. Shontell walked over to his table and picked up his mic, which was blinged out with green glitter and rhinestones. She knew green was his favorite color. They all had their personal microphones. She had always loved that. She glanced back at Nico, and he had his back to her. Was this real? It had to be. She closed her eyes for a few seconds and started to pinch herself. She was doing too much. She almost laughed out loud at her antics. What was wrong with her? She kept reminding herself that he was a regular person. It didn't matter what he did for a living. That's the way she looked at Jesse, like he was a regular guy. She wanted to give Nico that same image...of him being a regular guy. But her heart was telling her it was something totally different.

Once he was dressed, he took her by the hand and they left the room. She introduced him to Sandy as they all walked down to the meet and greet area. Martin had them go over to where Felecia and a few other people were. She watched as the backstage excitement started. The group greeted women and men for the next hour and a half. She noticed how a few women boldly tried to come at him, but Nico paid them no mind. He looked in her direction more than once to reassure her. His actions made her feel even better. She and Sandy were brought food and drinks by staff as they waited.

"Remind me to tell you something later. But I did want to ask, what's up with, Dennis? He seems like he's really distracted tonight," Sandy said, as she motioned toward Dennis who was looking in their direction but then turned away.

"If I knew, I would surely tell you. I guess it's a good thing that I don't have to worry about him and his behavior," Shontell told her best friend. She watched how he openly flirted with two women in particular. He was single, so it wasn't like what he was doing was wrong. Maybe they were just used to how he behaved. She made a mental note to ask Nico about it later.

"Girl, I can't believe we are here...sitting in the corner and getting special treatment," Sandy said.

"Neither can I."

Felecia turned to them and began asking questions.

"Shontell, do you have a business card? David told me how good you were this weekend. I could use your services soon. I have decided to launch my business nationwide, and I am thinking of having a launch party. Do you travel with your services?" she inquired.

"Yes, we do. Here is my card...and yes...we should definitely talk," she told her as she answered a few more questions. Soon they were down to the last few people. Nico waved them over, and they were introduced to the other people that were there.

"So now does this mean I can't get a meet and greet picture anymore?" she asked him in a voice that only he could hear. He laughed.

"You can have whatever you want, pretty lady."

"Be careful what you say, I just may take you up on that."

"I hope you do!" he said. He gave her a serious look.

She smiled and blushed. They asked the rest of the guys if they could all take some pictures together. She and Sandy took two with the group. Nico had the guy take a few of just him and Shontell. They finished with the pictures, and she turned to him. She looked at the guy who had been taking the pictures. He looked so much like Nico that she did a double take. The only real difference was that he was older.

"Is that your brother?" she asked Nico. He didn't respond quickly, but both of them started to laugh. "I guess you get that a lot. You two could pass for twins. But I can see the older distinction of...Nathan, am I right? She recalled reading about him having a brother in a magazine article.

"Yes, I'm Nathan. It is a pleasure to meet you, Shontell. I have heard a lot about you."

"Have you? I hope it was all good."

"Yes, all good."

"Whew. Okay, now I feel better. It is nice to put a name with a face. I didn't know you worked with the group. I don't remember seeing you with them before," she said as they made small talk.

"I do from time to time. But Nico has asked me to come on-board full-time. So, I am sure you will see a lot more of me." He started putting the cameras away, and she stepped over some photography equipment to get out his way. Nico approached Nathan, and she watched how they interacted. She could see the love between them. She felt envious. Sometimes it was hard being an only child. Sandy was the closest she had ever come to having a sister. Nathan waved to her when he was done, and Nico held out his hand for her. She took it.

"Are you ready?"

"Yes, I am. What's that?" she asked, pointing to what he had in his hand. He handed her the envelope. It was the pictures that were just taken.

"Now, we both will have two different sets of us to look at when we are apart," he told her. She watched as he put his own set in his back pocket. She held on to hers. They all went to the bar in the casino for a drink. She didn't realize how tired she was, or the hour, until she yawned.

"Tired?" Nico asked as he pushed a few strands of her hair behind her ear.

"A little. I have been up since you left the hotel. I had a meeting, then I had to run errands before I came to surprise you. I have been going all day."

"Do you want to go upstairs?" he asked. He never even asked if they were staying the night. He hoped they were not going to try and drive back to Detroit at such a late hour.

"Only if you promise to be good." They both laughed at the continuous joke between the two of them. He leaned over to her and kissed her shoulder. The sensations that went through her almost rocked her soul. She was glad her back was to him. She was blushing hard, and she could feel her face getting warm. She knew her face was telling all of her emotions.

She needed to focus on something else and remembered her question about Dennis. She was about to ask Nico, when she noticed he was sitting at a table nearby. He was with the two women that she saw him flirting with at the meet and greet. She cocked her head to the side slightly.

"Is this the norm?" she asked, motioning with her eyes toward Dennis.

"No. Please believe me that none of us do the things he does. He is definitely in a class all by himself."

"Okay," was all she said. She turned her attention away from Dennis and then looked over at Nico. He stood up from his barstool and leaned up against her.

"To answer your other question before the distraction, I promise," he said, trying to make sure that their mood stayed the same. Shontell took his hand and squeezed. Their road was going to be hard, and she was hoping that her past wouldn't make it harder. She still had some demons that she thought had vanished. She excused herself and got up to head over to Sandy. She was talking to a guy at the far end of the bar. She told her where she was going, and then she gave her friend the room key. She added that if she didn't come back to the room, she would see her in the morning. Shontell thanked her for coming with her, and they hugged. She would be lost without her best friend. Sandy always had her back. She couldn't and wouldn't trade her for anything.

She watched as her friend had the full attention of the guy she had just met. She never had the knack for meeting men like Sandy did. That was something she was always envious of. Shontell said good night to Martin and his wife. She had recently joined him and they were talking to Nico.

She took his arm and put it around her as he finished his conversation. A few moments later, she found herself looking up at him a little. They both realized how much shorter than him she was. He playfully called her shorty.

"Ready?" he asked her as he finished off his drink. She touched his face and nodded. They walked to the elevators, hand in hand.

LET'S TAKE IT SLOW

Nico

Nico was riding on cloud nine. He still couldn't believe that Shontell was there. He watched her on the sly as they rode up in the elevator. He got nervous all of a sudden. He remembered the chemistry that passed through them this morning when he had her on top of him. It had been a long time since he had been with a woman whom he had feelings for. The last woman was Tina, and he knew what he did and didn't want. Tina's lessons made him take a serious look at how he did things. He knew some things were better not said. They all had women that they had played around with on occasion, with the exception of David. It wasn't something that he was proud of. That was part of being a single man. He knew going in that none of them really mattered, but sometimes the need was just there. This was different...way different.

He pulled her to him, and Shontell leaned into his body. She seemed to fit perfectly into him, like they were meant to be. He loved the way they seemed so natural to each other. They say you only get one, or maybe two, soul mates in your lifetime. He never took any real stock in all that. Right now, with everything he was feeling, he was holding on to prove that it did.

They made it to his room, and she walked straight over to the balcony. She opened the door. It was cold out, but he joined her.

"Aren't you cold?"

"Normally I would be, but being around you is like having a hot flash. I just needed some air," she told him. They both looked over the railing, taking in the downtown activity. Not many people were out. He figured it was because it was a work night.

"You have a beautiful view. Do you mind if we grab some blankets and sit out here?" Nico nodded and instantly complied with her request. He would have told her she was crazy if she was any other woman. If she wanted to sit on top of an igloo, he probably would have said yes. It was only in the high 50's. He went in and got the blankets, two glasses, and a bottle of wine. They wrapped up together and laid on the chaise. They sipped the wine in comfortable silence. They got accustomed to one another's body. Shontell took his glass from him and set both of them on the table. Readjusting herself, she leaned her head back on his chest. Looking down, he watched how her cleavage went up and down with her breathing. Trying to stay focused, he tried to look in another direction but failed. His eyes went right back to her cleavage. Wanting to get the thoughts out his head, he nuzzled her neck.

"That tickles," she laughed, squirming a little.

"Oh, so you must be ticklish?" He gave her a devilish look.

"I truly plead the fifth," she said, trying to keep a straight face and not give away the fact that she was truly very ticklish. Nico caught the look and began to try to tickle her again. She screamed, and he continued trying to tickle her for several minutes until she was out of breath. They both laughed as they switched positions on the chaise. It was a good thing it was a nice size. He cupped her chin and lightly kissed her nose, then her eyelids and the side of her face, stopping briefly at her lips. She had her eyes closed in anticipation of his lips touching hers. He wished he could take a picture of her just like this, he thought, as he gave her what she was expecting. The kiss was brief...just enough to tease them both. He intertwined their fingers.

"Thank you," he whispered into her hair. She tried to look up at him, but he held her in place. He heard her intake of breath.

"Thank you," she replied softly.

"Yes, thank you!"

"I want to say you're welcome, but I am kind of confused as to why you are saying it."

"It could be for a lot of things. But if you really want to know why, it's just for you being here."

"Hmmm. Where else should I be?" She pulled the blanket around them more, as she waited for him to answer.

"I'm sure you have men flocking to you in Detroit. Yet you decided to give us a chance. You have made the last couple of days different for me in a very good way."

"Wow. I guess then I would owe you a thank you as well," she told him.

"I can't imagine why." Shontell felt her nervousness coming back. She reached for the wine glass and took a sip.

"Really?" Nico lifted the blanket some, and they were both greeted by the wind. He straightened out the blanket. He laughed as she scooted back into him. That one movement almost sent him over the edge.

"Do you realize what kind of effect you have on me? I have been trying to have self-control when it comes to you, since the first night we were alone. But then you go and do what you just did."

"What *I* just did?"

"Yes, scooting back. So this is how you affect me." He adjusted himself so that she could *feel* the effect. Shontell blushed and tried not to smile.

"Wow. I...I am sorry. I didn't mean to do that."

"I know, but it happens. You are a very sensual woman. That in itself is a rare find. Most women now are aggressive. That is a turn-off to me," he told her. He watched her movements as if they were in slow motion. She reached up to him and kissed him, not even letting him finish his thoughts. She pressed her full lips on his. She tilted her head and opened her mouth slightly as Nico pressed his tongue into her mouth, tasting the wine they had both been sharing. He could feel the electricity go through his body as the kiss deepened. He moaned.

He shifted his body to where they were more sandwiched. He kissed her neck as she lifted his shirt and ran her hands across his abs. Nico sucked in his breath. Her fingers felt like lightning bolts on his flesh. He pushed the straps of her dress down her shoulders, kissing her skin as he made his way to her breasts. She wasn't wearing a bra, so it made it easier to cup her breasts. She arched her back, and he tongued her dark areola. He went from heavy to light pressure on her nipple, as he lightly bit her. He repeated the same thing on her right side, and then went back to her lips. Shontell stopped the kiss to pull her dress over her head. Now she was only in her lace panties. Nico looked at her body and smiled. He kissed her stomach and pulled her on top of him. He was holding the blanket around them, although there was plenty of heat between them. The room could have caught fire. Nico began grinding their bodies together, and he could feel the heat from her core through his pants. Shontell threw her head back and bit her lip. She raked her nails over his chest so hard he knew that there would be marks, but he didn't care. Shontell wrapped her arms around his waist and laid her head partly on his shoulder and back.

He could feel the heat and wetness from her tongue. His whole body was at full attention. When did making out get so intense? He couldn't help thinking about this as she began tonguing his ear. That was his ultimate hotspot. His leg began to shake and he was losing control.

"Shontell? Um, Shontell?" he repeated, barely getting it out of his mouth before she lifted her head and stared into his eyes.

"Ne vous arrêtez pas," she told him in French.

Nico froze. He had never heard anything sound so sexy. He didn't even care that he didn't know what she had said. He couldn't take her body being any closer to him. He quickly picked her up and took her back into the suite.

Nico laid Shontell on the bed, and he lay on top of her. He propped his hands on the bed. He didn't want to have all his weight on her. As he was walking into the room, he knew he had to slow this down. Shontell had him wanting her in ways he only saw in movies. Yes, he needed to cool them off. He wasn't surprised when she opened her eyes and looked at him in confusion.

"What's wrong?" she asked, touching his ear and playing with it. He closed his eyes with her touch and again lost all train of thought. Man, she was making this hard. He was rock hard to prove it. He sighed, and he grabbed her hand gently. He kissed her fingers, distracting himself so that he could think for a few minutes.

"I am probably going to regret this. I think we had better stop now while we still have the chance. I don't want either of us to have regrets after this night."

"Thank you for thinking of me, but I am a big girl. I think I can handle making love to you," she said, pouting.

"Yeah, you can. But I don't think *I* can. I know I will have to watch you walk away from me tomorrow. I am going to have some restraint for the both of us," he told her.

He kissed her lightly and then slowly. She went from kissing him to sucking his tongue. They began kissing again after a few minutes. When they broke apart, they were both breathing hard from the intensity.

"Well, if that's the case, then you need to not kiss me like that again, sir." She was looking him dead in the eye. She gently pushed him off of her. She grabbed the blanket and put his shirt on. He watched her as she wrapped herself back up and then turned back to him. He liked seeing her in his shirt. He loved how such a small thing had a huge effect.

She pulled him up off the bed and took his hand and led him back on the balcony.

"Let's sit back out here and talk. It's almost time for the sun to rise," she said as they got comfortable again. He didn't realize that it was such a late hour. He looked at his watch, and it was 4:30 a.m. They talked and watched the sun come up before they both fell asleep. They were awakened by one of their phones vibrating.

Nico gently shifted her as he went to grab their phones. It was Shontell's. She answered it and spoke to her friend. She told Sandy she would be to the room in a bit and ended their call. She stretched, and she was surprised to see Nico watching her this time. Her hands instantly went to her hair. He wanted to renege on what he said earlier. She looked so sexy like that, but he refrained and smiled at her. "Umm, why are you looking at me like that? You are freaking me out." She ran a hand through her hair again.

"Oh, I am sorry. I didn't mean to make you uncomfortable. I love seeing you in my shirt as you are just waking up. You look radiantly beautiful to me," he said as he kneeled in front of her to kiss her. She moved back. She shook her head and placed a hand between them.

"No…mmm…morning breath," Shontell said through tight lips. She was still shaking her head, and she placed her free hand over her mouth as he reached in again. They both laughed.

"Shontell, I am going to kiss you. Stop moving woman," he said. They shared a brief kiss.

"Okay, I'm going to my room to shower. What time are you guys heading out?"

"I think at eleven. I will meet you downstairs in the breakfast area after I finish getting myself together." She nodded as she grabbed her dress and other things. She bounced out the door.

Uninvited

Shontell

As Shontell walked back to her room, she couldn't believe how giddy she felt. She hoped no one would see her looking like this. She looked down at his shirt and her bare feet. She was holding her clothes and shifted them so she wouldn't drop them. She pulled the shirt to her nose and inhaled. It smelled like him. She would attempt to give it back but hoped he would let her keep it.

It had been a long time since she felt like this. The last time was with Jesse. Jesse Wright, her ex-fiancé, was another R&B singer whom she had dated for three years. He wasn't the sentimental, quiet type like Nico. In fact, he was the complete opposite. The man gave her some serious butterflies when she was with him.

When they dated, she always seemed to be in a whirlwind of emotions. Although she always had his back, Jesse had two major flaws: he had issues with anger and women. The women were what made them split. Hearing her text message tone, she looked at her phone...expecting it to be Nico. Seeing that it was a number she didn't recognize, she realized she must have spoken *him* up. She hated when that happened. She knew it had to be Jesse because every time she blocked him, he would call her from another "new" number. She huffed, reading the message out loud.

Hey beautiful, it's been a minute. I had you on my mind and I wanted to say hello. I hope that all is well with you. -J.

She didn't respond. She reached the door and knocked, since she didn't have a key. She tapped her foot as she waited. She was pissed as she conjured him up. Trust and believe, he wasn't what she wanted to think about right now at all.

She was just about to knock again when the room door swung open. She almost fell into the guy she saw Sandy talking to last night.

"Oh, I'm sorry. Good morning," he smiled as he reached out his hands to break her fall. His deep baritone voice startled her. She stared up at him because the man was gorgeous. He had chocolate skin, abs for days, and a broad chest. His bald head glistened even in the dim hall light.

Shontell lowered her eyes so he wouldn't know she was measuring him up. She smiled back

"No, it's my bad. I wasn't paying attention. Good morning to you, too." He scooted out so she could go into the room. She leaned out the door to look at him from behind, as he walked down the hall. Sandy was standing behind her, as she joined her in watching too.

"My goodness. I might need to move to Indiana," Sandy said, fanning herself with her hands.

"OMG, you are such a freak. What was he doing in here?" she asked her playfully. She went to her overnight bag and grabbed a few things to take out.

"We were...playing cards. He uh...challenged me," Sandy told her, trying to sound innocent.

"Yeah, I bet he did. What kind of cards were you two playing? Was it Strip Poker?" she asked her. She took off Nico's shirt and folded it. She laid it on the bed.

How the hell did you know that? You got cameras in this room?" she asked, looking around the room. She burst out laughing and fell back on the bed.

"You are crazy. I hope you at least won."

"Oh, you know I did." The women high-fived. Once again, she had to admit that she envied Sandy's free spirit and openness on life. You only live once. Shontell grabbed her toothbrush from the pile she took from her bag and headed into the bathroom. She remembered her text as she was brushing. She waited until she finished brushing and then began speaking.

"Guess who texted me?" Shontell said as she spit out the paste and wiped her mouth.

"Who? Please don't say that loser," Sandy said, rolling her eyes. She was never a Jesse fan and she let it be known, but she never interfered unless she needed to.

"Yep. It's been six months since the last time. I figured that he had given up by now."

Sandy shook her head. That man was priceless. He cheats on a woman and then gets mad when she leaves him. She didn't want her best friend hurt, but she didn't want them together. She always felt uncomfortable around him. She had always felt he was up to no good. It must have been the creole in her blood. She would be damned if she let him try and mess up all that she and Shontell's family had rebuilt. "Does that man have a radar that lets him know when you are remotely happy?" she asked to no one in particular.

Shontell could tell Sandy was upset by what she told her. That's why she hadn't mentioned the flowers and gifts he sent her from time to time. The gifts were all in a box in her closet. Sandy was muttering under her breath, which was something she always did when she was trying to keep her emotions in check. She didn't say anything, because good friends weren't a dime a dozen. Sandy was the kind of friend that came along once a lifetime. It wasn't often that your best friend got angry for you at someone's actions. She went into the bathroom and looked at herself in the mirror. She didn't know what it was about her that made him want other women when he had her. She stopped trying to understand that a long time ago. She stepped in the tub because she needed to take a quick shower. As the water ran over her body, her mind wandered back to those years when she and Jesse were together.

When she and Jesse got engaged to be married, things changed in her friendship with Sandy. Things were hard for a couple of months. Jesse and Sandy didn't get along. She always felt like she was defending one to the other. It left her drained at times. He always tried to keep her from spending time with Sandy. That was never an option for her, and she let him know that. One time it caused a huge blowout between them, and she decided to let them cool off a couple weeks before the wedding. She allowed some time to pass, and then she decided to surprise him and make up for the lost time. She ended up being the one surprised when she found him in bed — with not one but two women. He said that they were fans. It didn't matter to her, as he chased her down the street. Her hurt was deep. He was with those women in the same bed she had slept in with him. She came to town to visit him and didn't know how many other times that had happened. That was over two years ago. Every time he contacted her since, he always claimed he had changed. Yet, he seemed to stay in the tabloids. He was with a different woman every other month it seemed, and she started not to care one bit.

Shontell let the water wash her tear stained face, and she promised herself that was the last time she would shed a tear over Jesse Wright. She finished showering and came out of the bathroom to find Sandy fully dressed and waiting on her. She looked like she was sad, and that pained her.

Going over to where she was, Shontell took her hands in hers. They sat in silence for a few seconds.

"I am sorry. I don't know why I still get mad when he is brought up. He didn't deserve you, and he still has the balls to try and see how you are doing!" Sandy squeezed her hands and the two women embraced in a hug. They made their way out of the room and headed downstairs. They were having some coffee when Shontell felt she needed to tell Sandy something.

"Sandy, I want you to know that I appreciate you so much. You were there for me when others stayed away. Jesse is my past and, thanks to you and my parents, I now know my full worth. It has been hard...I won't lie...but I just wanted to say thank you."

"Girl, don't make me cry. Ugh, I am going to get you if my makeup starts running," she told her as they both dabbed at their eyes. Shontell didn't hear Nico, but she felt his presence behind her. Sandy had a huge sappy smile on her face, and she nodded for her to turn around. Turning, she was greeted by a huge bouquet of lilies. Nico handed them to her and kissed her cheek.

"They are beautiful...thank you," she told him as she stood to hug him. Shontell, Nico, and Sandy made small talk about the concert while the ladies finished off their coffee. Cleaning the space, they all walked over and joined the rest of the group. Their tour bus pulled up, and Martin's wife said it was time to go. The older woman came over and said goodbye to her, along with Felecia. They promised that they would get together in Miami.

Dennis walked up to them looking sheepish, and he addressed Sandy.

"It was nice meeting you. Shontell, it was nice seeing you again so soon." He was the only one who laughed at his bad joke.

"Thanks, I guess," she returned. They were about to step back on the curb to wait for her car when Sandy's friend from this morning called out her name. She excused herself and waved to the rest of the guys as she walked over to where he was. Shontell noticed the quick change in Dennis' facial expression as he watched Sandy walk over to him. She wanted to laugh out loud. *When the heck did he get smitten with Sandy? She would never give him the time of day.* Sandy had a strict rule not to date entertainers. Shontell stepped over to the side, and Nico walked back over to her after putting his luggage on the bus.

"Dennis, David is looking for you," he told him, looking in the direction where he still seemed to be looking.

"Oh, okay. See you," he said, and turned and walked away. Both Shontell and Nico looked after him. Nico lifted his eyebrow.

"What the heck was that about? I know he..." Shontell lifted her finger to his mouth to stop him.

"Whatever it is, she isn't going to have it. So let's not even think about it."

"Oh, yeah. Okay, I can get that. Now, back to you beautiful. Can I get another hug?" He pulled her into his arms. He held her tight and she exhaled.

"I won't embarrass you by kissing you in front of everyone. Please text me as soon as you and Sandy make it back to Detroit. Promise?" He barely whispered the words. She knew that he didn't want her to go as much as she didn't want him to go.

"I promise, and I will see you in a few days. We are still on for Miami, right? Dinner?" He slowly let go of her hand. She folded her arms to fill the void it caused her to feel.

"For sure, darling," he said, as he hugged her again. He ran to get on the bus and she waved as they pulled off. She stood holding herself as they pulled away. This time was worse than yesterday. She didn't understand how that was possible. She walked over to the valet booth and handed her ticket to the young gentleman. He ran off in search of her car. Shontell reached inside her purse to get some money for her tip. She looked around and wondered where Sandy had wandered off to. She knew her best friend, and figured that she was probably in the corner somewhere getting a quickie. She laughed at that thought, because she knew Sandy would. It wasn't that she was out there sexually; she just always seemed to get what she wanted when it came to men.

After she became a widow, she and her confidence seemed to have taken on a new life. Kareem had died in a work accident six years ago, and it took her a while to bounce back. He was her first love. Sandy had to bounce back quicker than anyone. Because of all of her drama, she was the first one she saw when she opened her eyes in that hospital. The valet driver pulled up just as Sandy walked out of the hotel doors. She shook her head at her friend, and she knew her assumption was correct.

Are you ready, hot mama?" she asked jokingly as she handed the couple of dollars she retrieved a few minutes before to the driver and got in her car. They both waved to her friend.

"Girl! I needed that fix. It's going to be a long while before this happens again." Sandy stepped around the valet guy and sat down in the passenger seat. "Oh really. I find that hard to believe!" "Girl Scout's honor. I do have to set an example for my child at some point," she told her, putting her fingers up to her chest as she grabbed her sunglasses.

"You do know that you are doing the sign for the Boy Scout's honor, and not Girl's. Besides, you are a great mother. Monica knows that." "Thank you. That means a lot to me, coming from you…especially with everything I put her through."

"Stop that! That's in the past and over with. I can't wait to see our baby walk across that stage this year."

"Me either. I am so proud of her. The party you are doing has her so excited."

"Well, she deserves it. She went from being an average student to salutatorian."

"Right. Are we still hitting that new outlet?"

"You know it."

"CHARGE!" They both shouted and began cracking up.

They spent the next four hours shopping. They were getting things they needed for the cruise and wanted to make it back to Detroit by nightfall. Shontell dropped off Sandy, waving to Monica who was sitting on the porch with friends.

Later that night, she texted Nico and told him she was home. He responded that he missed her already. She was smiling as she headed into the bathroom to run her water. She was testing the water temperature when she heard her doorbell. She looked at the clock in her kitchen. It was almost 10:30 p.m. She wondered who would be coming over this late without calling. She grabbed her Taser gun out of her purse and slowly walked toward the door. She was glad that her shoes were off, preventing her from making a sound. She stood up a little bit on her tiptoes as she looked through the peephole. She groaned and cursed to herself. This is not how she wanted to end her day.

What the heck was Jesse doing at her door? She stood there for a few minutes not knowing if she should open it. She started to walk away, but knew he would stay out there until she did open the door. She slowly cracked it open.

"What are you doing at my house, uninvited no less?" she asked him, not even trying to hold her annoyance in.

"Hello to you too, Shontell. I don't remember you ever being this rude before." Jesse stood there looking at her through the crack of the door.

"Shon, please tell me that you aren't going to make me stand out here." Jesse flashed his smile that she remembered all too well. She cringed when he called her Shon. Hesitantly, she opened the door. She wanted to get this over with sooner than later. She stepped back, and he stepped into her foyer. She folded her hands and tapped her foot. She looked him in the face for the first time in two years. He still looked the same...just older and more distinguished. He was still as fine as he could be. She could tell that he had been working out more. He was always a horrible eater. She almost told him what she was thinking, but then it hit her that she shouldn't even be thinking about that. He didn't mean anything to her. She berated herself. "What do you want, Jesse?" she repeated.

"I was in town, and I just came to see how you were since you never respond to my texts."

"Yeah, a normal person would have gotten a clue by now. I don't have a reason to answer your texts or even entertain this visit. You have exactly two minutes to tell me why you are really here, or I will be escorting you out," she said. She didn't even want to look at him anymore. She had always wondered what would happen if they had crossed paths. She thought that it would be in public, not him just showing up unannounced in her personal space. She thought looking at him would repulse her, knowing what she lost when he cheated on her. But she had been surprised. Her heart didn't betray her this time, like it always had in the past while she was trying to get over him. She used to hear a song by him, or his name, and it would nearly tear her in two. Right now, she didn't feel anything for the man in front of her. Did her seeing Nico have anything to do with this? She happened to look at Jesse, and noticed that he was staring at her. She rolled her eyes and unfolded her arms as she glared at him. "Jesse, I know that look, and you need to fix it now. You lost that right a long time ago. Your time is ticking away!"

"You look so beautiful when you are mad. Shontell, I am a little confused by your actions tonight. Why are you being like this? Doesn't our past warrant some kindness? I mean I...I miss you. I miss us." He spoke quickly, to fix the words he had just said. He began walking in her direction. Shontell backed up from him and held her hand up. She sort of laughed and began shaking her head. This could not be happening to her. She closed her eyes and said a silent prayer for strength. She hoped that she wouldn't be going to jail tonight. Her emotions quickly shifted when she noticed the flowers from Nico. She was getting lightheaded, and she needed to get him out of her space. She removed her hand from his chest and tried to contain her shaking voice. She didn't like being in this situation at all.

"Jesse, I think it's time for you to leave, NOW!" she said through clinched teeth, as she was trying to control her anger.

"Shon, please don't do this. We need to talk," he pleaded, as he stood his ground.

She looked at him incredulously. Was this fool serious? Talk? Did he just say that?

"I know you didn't just say we needed to talk. Please tell me I misunderstood what you said," she yelled at him. Jesse backed up from the force of her words. "We've talked, I've screamed, and I've gotten over you! That was something that I thought I couldn't do some days. But, you know what? I did. There isn't anything you can say that can make me change my mind. You cheated on me...maybe more than once, for all I know. I have forgiven you so that I could go on with my life. I will never be able to forget what I saw and how you hurt me, Jesse. Go run your game on someone that gives a damn. You interrupted my bath with your unexpected visit. I'm going back to take it, and when I get out, you better not be here." Shontell hoped her face didn't look as she was feeling right now. Her whole body was shaking. She had never been this angry in her life. She started to head to her bathroom, when she stopped dead in her tracks. She thought about the question that she had asked herself this morning. It was a question that only he could answer. She turned back around and faced him. "I do have one question. Why wasn't I enough for you?" she asked as she swung back around to face him.

LOVE IS A VERB

Jesse

Jesse stood there. He opened his mouth to respond to her question. He wasn't prepared for the hurt that he saw in her eyes when she asked him why she wasn't enough.

"Shontell, I thought I was going to die myself when I saw you hit that gate. I replayed that night over and over. As much as I would like, I can't change what happened. I can try and be better, and that's what I am working on. But you must know it never was about you not being enough. You were more than enough. I told you those women didn't mean anything to me. I know that may not be what you want to hear. My love for you is real. You are more than any of them, and that shit scared the hell out of me. I... I didn't know how to give back what you gave to me."

Jesse watched as Shontell stared at him emotionless. She threw up her hands and walked away. He observed her until she rounded the corner. He wanted to run after her and tell her that he had changed. He couldn't get himself to move, because he wasn't sure if he had really changed or if he had finally realized that there would never be another woman for him like Shontell. In the two plus years since their breakup, he tried to find someone that stood out like she did. He had failed miserably. After what he said, he questioned if he could ever be ready for her. His heart kept telling him that having her in his life was far better than not having her in it at all. He stood in the living room and didn't hear sounds coming from the bathroom. He started to get concerned, but he still couldn't make himself walk in that direction. He would always blame himself for her accident. Her parents forbid him to see her and, even as much as it hurt him, he couldn't blame them. It was his fault.

He slumped his shoulders, and he did the only thing he could do. He did what she asked. He walked over to the door and opened it. He walked out. He had three days in Detroit before he left for Divine Attraction's twenty-fifth anniversary cruise. He was a special guest. He wanted Shontell to accompany him, which was one of the reasons he came by her place. He knew how much she liked the group.

When Dennis called him a day ago and asked about her, he thought it was strange. He didn't think too much else about it. They had hung out that night, but he didn't mention her again. Shontell was known in Detroit for her catering and event planning, so it could have meant anything. Dennis was a cool guy and if it weren't for him, he wouldn't be on the cruise. He needed the exposure. He was trying to get his career going again. He may not have acted like it, but that accident shook him and losing Shon had affected him. He covered it up well, he had to admit. Lately, she had been all he thought of. He had to think about how he was going to do this. As long as he lived on this earth, he never wanted to see that look on her face again. The pain he saw was too much.

The metro car driver opened the door for him. He quickly grabbed the glass and poured a drink. He winced as it burned going down. He would normally relish a good bourbon burn, but tonight he felt he needed to feel that sting. He finished the glass and poured another one before they even left her cul-de-sac. He did like that she still looked beautiful. She was glowing. She let her hair grow, and she had dropped a little weight. He put the glass down, and he grabbed his phone as it began to ring. Dennis' name flashed across the screen. He answered it as the driver used the screen in front of him to ask what his destination was. He looked at the words as he listened to Dennis give him the info he'd asked about. He had set one meeting with a producer who he had wanted to work with. Jesse typed in an address quickly. He knew one person who would welcome him the way he wished Shontell would have.

Ebony tapped her man on the shoulder. He didn't respond. Well, she guessed he was her man, even though he hadn't made it official yet. She figured he may as well be. She did everything sexually a woman could possibly do for her man. She was still working on that domestic part though. That was her mama's fault, she concluded. Elena was always working to provide for her and her brothers. She didn't take out the time to teach her how to cook anything besides fried chicken, eggs, toast, and spaghetti. She could make a mean ass pot of spaghetti. Most men these days wouldn't even eat it because of that stupid old wives' tale about the period blood in the food to keep a man. She laughed to herself. There were a whole lot of ways to keep a man, and in her book, that wasn't one of them.

Ebony was pouting on the inside; she wanted some attention. When he got to her house, he was on a call. She made him his usual drink and then gave him some quick head while he finished his call. When she finished she wanted more, but he was too distracted. She watched him as she tried to read his mind. Her man always kept her guessing. That was a good thing, right? They never had a dull moment. She laughed to herself as she stood up, opening her robe for a dramatic effect to let him see what he was missing. She left him in the living room. Going into the bathroom, she used her mouthwash. Within seconds, she was done. Looking at herself in the mirror, she admired her own beauty. She could have any man but, for some reason, she only wanted HIM. Sighing, Ebony turned around to head to the kitchen and ran smack into her man's chest. He looked down at her with a mischievous smile. "Going somewhere?" his sexy voice came at her. "I…I," Ebony attempted to respond, but his mouth came down on hers so swiftly that she was caught off balance. He grabbed her waist to make sure she didn't fall. Why did his kiss feel different? Maybe it's because he normally didn't kiss her. She was surprised at how sweet and soft his kiss actually felt as their tongues danced. Ebony felt her juices start to pool as he untied her robe and pushed it off her shoulders. She was now naked. He deepened the kiss, and she fought with her emotions as she tried not to think. She knew what her man wanted…what he always wanted…and that was to fuck her. They never made love, and she used to be okay with that.

Ebony racked her fingers down his back. He flinched from the sensation but didn't stop kissing her. When he picked her up, she instantly wrapped her thighs around his waist. He walked a few feet and placed her back up against the wall.

Her dude lifted her up slightly higher and started blowing on her wet pussy. Ebony squirmed as she made her way up his body and put herself on his shoulders while he went to town on her pussy. Ebony could have sworn he was eating her like she was his last meal. Within seconds, she was cumming.

Damn, he always knows my hot spots, she thought.

Ebony was catching her breath when she felt him slowly letting her down. He handed her a condom, and she opened the packet with her teeth.

When he picked her up again, he opened her legs wider as he positioned her wet, still throbbing, pussy at the tip of his dick. Ebony gasped out loud when she felt the sharp pain of his size as he tried to enter her fast. She never got used to his size. He wasn't huge, but he was big enough. She had not been with any man other than him. When he noticed her cries, he pulled out. This time he entered her slower as he took her whole breast in his mouth. Ebony's juices lubricated the condom with each light stroke. After a few more strokes, she slid up and down his shaft more and more, filling her up to the core. Ebony came instantly. It was like his dick knew right where her g-spot was. Smiling, he knew he had her and could go all in. He leaned her back on the wall, holding on her waist, and fucked the shit out of her. With each orgasm, her head spun faster. She lost count after the third one. She felt like she was floating on cloud nine. She instantly thought how stupid Shontell was to let all this go. She held on to his shoulders as he pounded into her sweet pussy. When he called out her name gruffly, she knew what that meant. As he let her down and pulled the condom off, Ebony went to her knees. When she sucked his dick hard, she arched her neck as she felt his semen coating her throat. She swallowed some but let most of it exit out her mouth, using her tongue as she continued to suck his semi-hard dick. When he let go of her head, she stopped and he stepped backwards until he landed on her bed. She stood up and went to plant a kiss on his mouth. He was fast asleep. Shaking her head, she got back up — not even bothering to put her robe on — and headed into the kitchen that had been her original destination before the distraction.

She opened the fridge and grabbed the juice out, drinking it straight from the carton. She finished it off and threw the empty container in the garbage. She looked over to the wall clock and she saw that it was almost three in the morning. She knew she needed to go and wake Jesse up because he had a meeting in the morning. He told her he couldn't stay the night. When she was walking back to the room, she heard noises. She knew then he was up and she wouldn't have to wake him up.

She watched as Jesse got dressed. His body was molded with some muscles and tattoos. She loved watching him work out. She used to sit in that hot ass home gym of his, watching him flex. He turned her on with the slightest effort. She smiled, recalling them having sex a couple hours ago. The things he did to her body and mind weren't like anything she had ever experienced. She wished he would move here or take her with him permanently. She was tired of going days and weeks without him. Whenever she brought up the subject, he cleverly avoided it. It always pissed her off. Then he would start playing with her body, and she would easily forget about it for that moment.

Jesse must have sensed her watching him because he stopped buttoning his pants and turned around to look at her. He licked his lips as he scanned her naked body. His eyes traveled from her feet to her full breasts as she stood in the doorway. The look he gave her made her cream instantly. She walked seductively to where he was and kissed his chest. She circled his nipple, and he let out a low growl. She did the other side, and he grabbed her hair hard and pushed her head down toward his crotch. He unbuttoned his jeans the rest of the way, and she pulled his dick out. She wanted a round two, as she put his dick into her mouth with expertise. She worked her magic with her tongue until she felt him push her away. She stood and backed up to the bed, trying to take him with her. He stood still as she fell on the bed. She knew what that meant, and she and tried not to get into her feelings—even though she already knew he wasn't staying. She wanted him to do what she wanted for a night. He always had to be in control. It was one of the things that drew him to her. She decided to try her luck anyways.

"You do know that it's almost 4 a.m. Why do you have to go?" she asked him, this time reaching for her robe and tying it.

"My meeting is at the hotel and I need to prepare...that's why." He grabbed his jacket to get his phone. He called his driver while she walked around him into the living room. She tried hard not to act like a baby. She hated when he didn't stay the night. He was only going to be in town a few days, and she wanted as much of his time as she could get. He walked up behind her and kissed her neck. She closed her eyes and let the scent of his cologne fill her nose.

"Okay, so you need to stop doing that. You know that's my weak spot, especially if you are not staying the night. Will I see you later today?" She stepped out of his embrace.

"Um, I guess. But I am not sure what time," he said, heading toward the door.

"Oh, okay. So it's like that?" she said, sensing his hesitation in seeing her.

"Ebony, don't start this mess again. I said you would. What you need to be doing is focusing on the plan we have. We need to get this done before I leave. I've given you this lifestyle, and I can take it back…remember that!"

"Humph, how can I not? You make sure to remind me every chance you get." She sat on the edge of the couch. Jesse said nothing, but he kissed her forehead and gave her a look of a father scolding his child. He walked out the door without saying anything else. Ebony picked up the first thing she saw and threw it at the door. The coaster bounced off the door with a soft thud and landed on the floor. She flipped onto the couch and screamed into the pillow. She was being a little dramatic. She didn't care. Jesse treated her like a night whore sometimes instead of someone he had feelings for.

Shontell

Shontell wished she had something to throw, but she opted to not say anything to him. She threw her hands up, turned back around, and headed to the bathroom. She kept hearing his answer. What was she supposed to say to that? How could he tell her that she was more than enough but still think it was fine to have sex with someone else. She thought back to that night. She had been lucky. That's what doctors kept telling her and her parents. All she sustained was a broken arm and leg from hitting that gate. She didn't feel lucky. All she had felt that night and the weeks after was pain; inside and out. She never told Sandy or Jesse that she was pregnant. How could she? She didn't even know until they told her she had a miscarriage. That made her pain and heartache even more unbearable during that time. Her parents were the only ones who knew. She made them promise not to tell anyone. For her, it was something she would take to her grave.

Shontell hated to admit it, but Sandy had been right about Jesse. He did think she was supposed to pause her life and wait for him to be a man…be who she thought he was from the beginning. Jesse had a whole lot of balls to think that she would be so accepting. She caught that he said he was in love with her. He said it in the present, not past tense. *Whatever*, was her only thought? She couldn't care less. She felt cold all of a sudden. She blew out a breath that she didn't even know that she was holding.

Shontell quickly wiped the lone tear that managed to escape her eye before she knew it. The few steps she took from the door to the sink seemed so difficult. She reached out and grabbed ahold of the sink. She made sure that she locked the door just in case he was stupid enough to follow behind her. When she heard her front door open and close, she leaned over the sink. She turned the water on and willed the rest of her tears not to fall. She had hoped she wouldn't feel this way. She did. She literally felt like she had just relived the last three years all over again in a matter of minutes.

Shontell replayed the last fifteen minutes over in her head. She didn't know why she asked him that question, but it was like she just had to ask the question. She needed to know. His answer totally caught her off guard. She finally got her legs to hold her up. SAs he stood up, she avoided the mirror. She didn't want to see or feel the damage her question did to her soul. She touched her stomach and felt pain; fighting down the bile she felt in her mouth.

After a few seconds, she got herself together, taking her robe off and sliding into the lukewarm water. She turned the hot faucet on and saw the goose bumps forming on her arms and legs as the hot water cascaded over her. She closed her eyes, and different thoughts embarked in her mind. She needed to clear her mind. She reached for her wine glass and finished it like it was a glass of water. She refilled it and took another swallow before she put it on the edge of the tub. She didn't want to let the wine take her pain away. Suddenly she got upset all over again. What right did he have to show up and try and walk back into her life like everything was fine? Because of him, she could have been paralyzed for life. She didn't owe him anything. She wanted to feel hate for him, but she couldn't. It just wasn't in her nature. She wondered what the hell Jesse was drinking or taking? It had to be something powerful if he thought that having one conversation would make it all better. Did he really think that she was gullible enough to go running into his arms? Her parents didn't raise a fool. She was just getting her personal life back, and she wanted to see where this could go with Nico.

Shontell laid her head back and let the hot water soothe her body. All the thinking and reactions had taken a lot of energy out of her. She was tired physically and now mentally. She didn't want Jesse; that she knew for sure. She was done with this. She needed to regroup, and that would only happen if she did what relaxed her. She opened the panel on her bath cabinet, hitting the play button. The room quickly filled with music. She was going to redirect this energy, even if it took her the rest of the night.

She turned her thoughts away from Jesse and his uninvited visit. She began humming the music. She closed her eyes and the song changed. Nico's voice came over the speaker. She opened her eyes with a start as she looked around the room. She realized that it was the music, and she sat back. In her mind, she knew that this was what she needed. She allowed the lyrics to take her to the last couple of days. Her thoughts instantly turned to her passion-filled night with Nico. She loved him kissing her and the way his mustache tickled her lip. His lips alone were delectable. She still had to pinch herself to make sure this was all happening. She was with Nico.

Suddenly her phone vibrated. She hit the speaker button. She started to hit the pause button.

"Hey, I hear me singing," Nico laughed.

"Yes, I'm attempting to relax. Sorry it was so loud."

"It's okay, sweetness. We made it to Miami. I wanted to hear your voice. What are you doing?" Nico's semi-deep voice filled the room, and she instantly shivered.

"Taking a bath." Her voice was seductive as she was almost out of breath, listening to his voice.

Nico chuckled deeply, which sent another shiver to her core.

"You know that's not fair. Why are you answering the phone while you're in the tub?"

"Well, I didn't want to miss your call, but I needed to unwind some." She splashed the water as she shifted. Nico groaned aloud, and Shontell smiled. She knew he was thinking of her naked body. The thought made her feel sexy.

"Are you all right over there?" she asked playfully.

"Yeah, I'm good. But now I think I need a shower…a cold one. Call me when you are dry, woman," he told her.

"Okay, give me an hour. I need to fix dinner. Are you in for the night, or does the group have something to do?"

"Nope, we have tonight and tomorrow free. The day after we have a couple of promotional spots for the cruise and anniversary, then we are off. So you have me all night."

"Lucky me. Talk to you in a little bit, baby," she replied in a low voice, concluding their call. She took the loofah and poured the vanilla and honey body wash on it. Her bathroom smelled like pure vanilla as she washed her body. She closed her eyes and pretended it was Nico. The man was so different, and it felt good, real good.

Nico

He walked into the enclosed patio of his hotel suite after hanging up with Shontell. He looked at the chaise that set in the corner and immediately thought of the passion that he had shared with Shontell last night. He talked himself into believing he was doing the right thing by stopping them. He knew he wanted to make love to her, but it was too soon. Not many men would have had that much restraint. It was hard for, him but he knew he made the right decision.

He heard a knock at his door and he went to see who it was. He opened the door and Dennis stepped in.

"What's up man?" He started unbuttoning his shirt so he could change clothes and relax for the night.

"John called me, he has a few females at the bar and we were all about to go to this new club. You want to join us? It's three of them," he added for good measure.

"Nah, I will pass. I plan on chilling until we have the promos. I am still tired, and I want to catch up on my rest."

"Aw, man, you can rest anytime. We are in Miami. You aren't going to be cooped up in this room until we set sail, are you?"

He looked at his friend and said nothing. He walked over to his suitcase and unzipped it. Dennis followed him and took a seat at the desk. He could feel him watching him as he attempted to ignore him, hoping he would get the hint. He still had his back to him, when he heard Dennis sigh. "Really, come on man. It's just a club. It's been a while since the three of us hung out. We need to enjoy all this free time because it won't be like this later." Dennis was still trying to convince him. Nico was becoming agitated. Dennis always pushed his buttons when he didn't agree with what he wanted to do.

"Dennis, I said I would pass," he said sternly. He sat on the bed to take off his shoes.

"Guess Shontell got you on lock already, huh?" Dennis smirked, rubbing his chin. It was if he was testing him and Nico was trying to preserve his lifelong friendship. He suspected Dennis was trying to get a reaction out of him. Nico took a deep breath because he knew what this was all about. Dennis was jealous. He didn't understand why he was so afraid of them growing and changing as they got older. How long could they go from bed to bed and club hop? It was never his thing anyway because he knew that once he liked someone, he didn't do all the extras he normally would do.

"Man, you have really been going overboard lately. So I am going to cut you a break tonight. I'm going to pretend I didn't hear you say that. Shontell has nothing to do with this. I just need to relax. Is that okay with you?" He was no longer trying to hide his annoyance.

"Nico, you're my friend. I am looking out for you. I don't want you to fall too deep, too quick. You don't even know her like you think," he said.

A MESSY SITUATION

Dennis

Dennis wanted to kick himself for making that comment.

"What does that mean?" Nico responded as he balled up his fists. Dennis eyed him and involuntarily stepped back.

"I mean...well, it has been a while, right? It's been a long time since you've been in a relationship. It's nothing I haven't been saying since day one. What do you know about her past? Do you talk about that?" Nico looked at him like he was crazy.

"Do you ask the women you sleep with about their past?"

"No," he said quickly. Dennis lifted his hand to his neck, rubbing it. He shouldn't have said anything.

"I didn't think so. What Shontell and I talk about is *our* business, not yours. For the record, a person's past doesn't define them. You of all people should know that," he said, giving him a look of contempt. Dennis instantly felt like nothing he said was going to change this conversation. It was steadily going downhill.

"Look man, I didn't mean anything by it. Can you just do me a small favor?"

"What kind of favor could you possibly want me to do?"

"Just take it slow, and I will back off," Dennis said sincerely. Nico regarded him and cocked his head. Dennis knew he was thinking about what he'd said about Shontell. Dennis was glad he was able to cover up his mistake. He checked his watch and realized that he was late getting downstairs. He backed up toward the door.

"Well, enjoy your quiet time."

"Trust me, I will."

"If you change your mind, we will be at Waterfalls off the beach."

"Okay, I hear you. Thanks. Now go out and enjoy yourselves. Tell John not to hurt anybody, and I will see you all in the morning for breakfast." Dennis knew that was his way of letting him know that his decision was final. He ran toward the elevator when he heard it ding.

"Hold the elevator," he yelled out. When he stepped on, he was looking into the smiling face of Tina. He was caught off guard because they hadn't talked about her being in Miami.

"Hey there," she spoke. She was smiling but not really paying attention to him because she was looking at her phone screen. She then stopped, looked up at him, and then looked back again.

"Tina, I thought we agreed that you were going to be on the cruise and not on land."

"I know, I know. Robert had to meet a client down here, and I decided to tag along." She acted like it was nothing for her to be there. Maybe he was wrong to do this. Tina was messy. She didn't care about how this was going to end. At the end of the day, she would be going back to her husband. It was one thing to have her here, but for her to show up with her husband was a little much. She was taking a huge risk in the others finding out. It was not like she wasn't going to be noticeable.

"Tina, did I just hear you say that you're here with Robert?"

"Yes. What's the big deal, Dennis?"

"The big deal is that no one knows you're married but me. You are making it obvious. You know like I do that Robert is going to be under you like a rug."

"Let me handle Robert." She looked back down at her phone.

"Yeah, okay." Dennis remained quiet the last two floors down. He was calling this off. He looked over at her and he instantly knew why Nico had dated her. He could also see why he wasn't with her anymore, even if she was the one who ended it. She was so superficial, Dennis thought. He watched her apply makeup and touch up her hair on the ride down. She stepped off the elevator and Dennis called out her name. Tina turned around.

"I am having a complete change of mind on this. I think we need to abort these plans. Who am I to try to come in between them? Nico is happier than I have seen him in a long time. So yes, I am going to leave this alone," he told her, confirming for himself, yet saying it aloud.

"Really! So you think Ms. Thing is better than all this?" She motioned to her head and then pointed to her feet. He didn't answer her right away. She got irritated.

There were very few men who turned her down or said no to her.

"Do I still get the other half of my money?" she asked with attitude. Tina realized he was serious, and that was throwing a monkey wrench in her plans. She needed that money to fund a project. She wasn't about to let him ruin that for her. She was fuming inside.

"No, Tina, you don't." He started to walk past her. She paused and reached out for him. This wasn't going to end because he wanted it to. She still had the upper hand, and she needed him to know that. He came to her for this little game.

"Then I guess my work is not done. See you later." She proceeded to walk off in a dramatic way. The short dress she wore rode her thighs as she walked fast through the lobby. Tina caused more than one man in the lobby area to stop in his tracks. She knew the effects she had on men; they were eye pleasers. That was always her advantage. She didn't even bother to acknowledge Dennis as she heard him calling after her.

Dennis stood there dumbfounded. What was he going to do now? What if she went to Nico and told him about what he had hired her to do. He quickly snapped out of his frozen state and headed in the direction she went. He was pissed, seeing she wouldn't stop when he called out her name through his clenched teeth.

Dennis had forgotten that quickly why he was coming downstairs in the first place until John called out to him. Now he really couldn't do anything. He had to talk to her again. He needed to make sure that she understood what he said and didn't try any crazy stuff. He was seething at the whole situation, but he went to join John and the women.

Nico

Nico placed the room service menu down and called to place his order. He shook his head as he thought of this conversation with Dennis. He knew he meant well, but the line he continues to cross may backfire on him one day. He didn't like being so out of sorts with him. He needed to be able to live his own life. Martin always encouraged having a life outside of Divine Attraction. He never really took that to heart until now. His life had always been about music until now. The way Shontell had affected his life in a matter of days was still amazing to him. Nico decided to jump in the shower while he waited for room service to bring his dinner. The knock on his door came just as his cell phone rang. He answered his phone and headed to the door.

"Hey, baby, give me two seconds. Room service is knocking." He set the phone down and opened the door. He waited until the server was finished setting up his food and table for him. He gave him a tip and closed the door. He picked up the phone. "So how was the rest of your bath and dinner?" he asked her.

"It was what I needed. I had a lot of tension because of an uninvited guest before you called earlier. I was still trying to wrap my head around it."

"Really? Is everything okay?" he asked. Dennis' words came into his mind about knowing about her past.

"Yes, and I promise to tell you about it when we see each other. I don't want to spend our evening talking about that." She heard him clanging the dishes.

"So what did you get to eat?" she asked, changing the subject. She wrapped her towel around her still-damp body and grabbed her oils.

"A turkey burger, organic fries, and hot tea." He stirred his tea, blowing on it and taking a sip.

"Would you like to call me back after you eat?" She set the phone down and put it on speaker.

"Nope. I promise not to smack. I miss hearing your voice. I don't want to have to wait until I finish my food for us to talk. I'm sorry if it sounds selfish." He bit into his burger, licking his lips to savor the dripping juice.

She laughed and went on to tell him about the ride home. She told him about Sandy's new friend, Eric. He was going to be on the cruise as well to work security detail.

"See, now that wasn't so bad was it?"

"I guess not. I couldn't tell you were eating at all."
She rubbed the oil into her arms, balancing her phone.

"So why are you in for the night? What do you
normally do when you hit a city?" she inquired. Shontell
switched the phone to speaker, as she went over to her
lingerie drawer and pulled out a pair of panties and a night
tee.

"It all depends. John, Dennis, and I usually hit a
casino or club. David will hang out sometimes if Felecia
doesn't join us on the road. Tonight I declined. Remember,
I didn't get much sleep last night," he laughed. Shontell
smacked her lips.

"Ha, ha, that wasn't my fault. That was all on you,
Chocolate." She settled back onto the bed.

"Hmmm, is that a new pet name already?" Nico
wiped his hands on the last of his napkins. He scooted back
in the chair.

"Only if you are going to answer to it," Shontell told
him. Nico laughed heartily at her comment.

"Well, I have one condition." He got up, kicked his shoes off, and got into bed. His body sank into the mattress. He loved these heavenly mattresses.

"Okay. So what's that?"

"Only if you video chat with me. I want to see that smile."

"Okay, you got it," she told him. Nico sat back on the pillows and propped the phone up as he waited for her face to appear. He wiped his mouth again, to ensure there was no food residue. A second later, she was smiling at him.

Shontell was glad that she had decided on a night shirt. She looked down quickly when he came onto the screen. She missed him as she touched the screen as if it was his face. She could not believe that she and Nico video chatted until almost 3 a.m. Neither of them could keep their eyes open. She woke up that morning still tired but strangely excited. This was one time she was definitely glad she was her own boss. Her day didn't start until later. She had errands to run. Their conversations felt as though they had known each other forever. The only thing she hadn't talked to him about was Jesse...well not formally. She knew that she would have to eventually discuss her past. He knew that she had been hurt by her last boyfriend, but not that it was Jesse she was referring to. Shontell threw on a pair of jeans and Nico's shirt. She took a quick selfie and sent it to him. Nico made her feel that love was an option again. She had missed that feeling.

Shontell walked into her kitchen. She put water in her plants and the flowers that Nico had given her. The car service was right on time to pick up her car for its three-month maintenance service. She decided to look over the buyout contract her lawyer had drawn up for her. She had not decided exactly when she was going to do it. She knew that it was needed. Shontell sat down while her coffee was brewing. She was getting up to grab cream out the fridge when she heard a key in the front door. She hoped it wasn't Jesse. *Now where in the heck did that come from*, she thought. She knew she had changed her locks. She didn't know why she thought it was him. It must be one of her parents. She finished pouring the cream in her coffee. The door opened, and she watched Ebony walk in. She forgot she was supposed to be dropping off files and two new contracts. She almost got up to help her, but she stopped when she thought about their last face to face. She could handle it. Sitting back down, she put peanut butter on her bagel.

"Hey, Ebony," she greeted in a flat tone. She bit into her food. Ebony nearly dropped the box she was holding. Now why was she so caught off guard, she wondered?

"Hey, Shon. I didn't know you were here. I didn't see your car out front."

"Oh. Well, I sent it over to get serviced. Thanks for bringing over the files." She got up and walked over to where she set the boxes down and started reaching over into one of them. They had a client that they were preparing a presentation for right before she left for the cruise.

Ebony

Ebony set the box down, silently cursing to herself. How in the heck was she going to be able to look for the safe like Jesse had asked her to if Shontell was home? She looked at Shontell. She looked different for some reason. Her cell phone started to buzz, interrupting her inspection. She was trying not to show her attitude as she looked at the screen. She saw that it was a text from Jesse, asking if she'd located the safe. She quickly put the phone back in her pocket and walked over to where Shontell had made coffee.

"Mind if I have a cup of coffee?" she asked.

"Sure, help yourself." Shontell handed her the spare cup she kept on the counter.

"I wanted to apologize about my behavior Sunday. I shouldn't have reacted that way, especially when I was in the wrong." Ebony wasn't making eye contact, but she was sure Shontell was looking at her. Ebony leaned over the counter, taking a sip of the hot liquid. She felt the phone go off again. She didn't want to be here. She respected Shontell, but she had never liked her. She was doing all of this, including faking her desire on this business, because Jesse wanted her to. She loved Jesse, so she would do what he needed. "Shontell, you look different," she finally said.

"Do I?" She gave her a blank look.

"Yes. Did you do something exciting over the weekend?" She saw the look on Shontell's face. "I guess you could say I did. But we just saw one another a couple of days ago."

"Right. I know. I guess I didn't see it then. I see it now. Are you ready to go over this stuff?" she asked her. Ebony tried to concentrate as they spent the next forty-five minutes going over the contacts and notes for the presentation. Shontell had a knack for this business. Her ideas flowed easily. She was impressed. There was no sound in the house; therefore, every time her phone buzzed it could be heard. She never looked at her phone after the first time. What was the point? She didn't have anything good to tell him. Her phone went off three additional times, and Shontell stopped in mid-sentence and looked at her partner.

"Someone sure is trying to get hold of you. Why aren't you answering?"

"Yeah. It's my brother. I am sure he wants to borrow money. I will call him when we are done." She quickly lied, hoping her voice wasn't noticeably shaking. She instantly felt nervous, and her hands started to sweat. She wiped her hands on her jeans. If Shontell knew half the things she had lied to her about, their working relationship would be done, and she would deserve it. They were finishing up, and Shontell's phone rang. She excused herself to go get it out of her office. Unlike her, she made sure that they didn't have any distractions.

She heard her answer the phone, and Shontell's tone changed immediately.

"Jesse, what do you want?" Ebony's eyes got big when she heard Shontell say Jesse's name. *What the hell?* She thought. She strained her ear to listen in on the conversation. Shontell walked out of the room. Ebony was trying to put her cup down and missed the table. The cup shattered once it hit the floor, splattering coffee everywhere. Ebony tried to hold back her emotions as she quickly got up to get paper towels to clean up her mess. She didn't want

Shontell to see how her call had affected her. When she looked up, Shontell was looking at her strangely. She hadn't even heard her come back into the room.

"Are you okay?" Shontell asked her, as she bent down to pick up the broken pieces.

"I...I need to go. I need to get a little air. I am so sorry about the cup." Ebony grabbed her purse and quickly headed out of the door.

***

She sat in her car as she gripped the wheel. She went to grab her phone to find out why Jesse was calling Shontell. When did this start, she wondered. The jarring ring of her phone startled her. She answered the call.

"Hey, why aren't you replying to my texts?" Jesse shouted into the phone. Ebony took the phone from her ear because the volume was painful. She got on the defensive and put the phone back to her ear.

"Here's a better question for you...what the hell are you doing calling Shontell?" she retorted. Jesse didn't say anything, but she definitely heard him curse as she suspected he was probably trying to come up with a good ass lie for himself. She spoke before he even tried. She couldn't believe this. She was here risking everything…and for what?

"Yeah, just like I thought. You told me that you were over her. Guess I am the fool."

"Ebony, don't say that…I…" before he could finish, she hit the end button over and over again. She wished it was the 90's and she could slam the receiver down hard on his ass. Ebony wiped away the tears she didn't even know she had cried. She looked up and noticed Shontell was watching her from the window. She smiled weakly and hoped she hadn't been watching her that long. She waved and backed out of the driveway. She almost hit another car because she wasn't paying attention. The driver blew his horn and yelled expletives at her. She put her hand up to apologize.

"Sorry, sorry…my bad," she said. It wasn't even loud enough for him to hear. She started backing out again, cautiously looking both ways before continuing. She continued driving down the street, thinking about why men always hurt her. Was she that unworthy of love? Her mother had told her she wasn't worthy. Coming from her own mother, she believed it. Her mother never showed her and her brother love. It was all business for her. She never said she loved them or hugged them. She didn't have a good kind of relationship with her mom, like Shontell had with hers. She wished she did. She needed someone to guide her about men and all their ways. Wiping away the tears, she sat at the red light and looked at her reflection in the rearview mirror. When did she stop seeing herself? Because the woman she was looking at didn't look anything like her. She hated her mother for her lack of affection. It had to be the reason why she felt she needed it so bad.

SHE AIN'T THE ONE

Jesse

Jesse threw his phone on the bed and began pacing. He couldn't believe Ebony had hung up on him like that. He cursed aloud. He couldn't risk her being mad at him. He needed her. He was slipping again. It was like when he got caught cheating. That night changed him. He couldn't believe he had been so careless, not to mention that he had underestimated Shontell's love for him. He never thought she would come all the way to California to fix things. He didn't remember that she had a set of house keys. He hit his forehead with his hand. Jesse didn't want those nightmares to start again.

Jesse knew his heart still belonged to Shontell. It didn't matter that he had not been faithful to her most of their relationship; she didn't know that. She could only prove that one time. He used the fact that she didn't like public appearances to his advantage. His conscience ate at him sometimes. He knew what he was doing was low down. When he hooked up with Ebony, it was by pure accident. They met at one of the clubs in Detroit where he was doing an event. That's why his plan had worked so perfectly. If it ever came out, he would lose her for good, and he couldn't take that chance. He knew he could convince her to give them another chance. He wished he could get her on his album. That would really jump-start his career. That's why he sent Ebony over there — the songs. He needed those songs. His mind wandered back to when he and Shontell were engaged. They were hosting a karaoke fundraiser, and they did a song together. He had heard she could sing, but he didn't know she could *SANG*. They sang *If This World Were Mine,* and they wowed the crowd.

He convinced her to write songs for him. A few months later, he took her to the studio one night. He didn't tell her that he wanted her to record the songs. When she finally learned of his true intent, she was furious with him. Shontell didn't want the spotlight. No matter how many times she told him this, he thought he could convince her. He was wrong. She took the songs and left the studio. That was the last time he saw the music and songs, and he knew that his career needed a major resurrection. He had told his manager he had new material. They were expecting something different from him, and those songs were it.

Ebony was a means to an end. He strung her along this long because he knew she would become useful one day.

He picked up his phone and started to call her back, but he was interrupted by the knock on the door. He opened it to a tearful and angry Ebony.

Ebony

Ebony parked in a slot at the hotel and walked in without paying the valet any attention. She headed to Jesse's room. She needed to look into his eyes and ask him if he still loved Shontell. Ebony thought they were progressing, although she never really saw him unless he came to Detroit. He didn't make any extra effort to ask her on the road like he had with Shontell. She was sure that he would. Of course he would, she told herself. They were sleeping together and had been for the past four years.

Ebony knocked and waited for Jesse to open the door. She didn't even try and change the way her tear-stained face looked. She wanted him to know that he had hurt her.

"Do you still love her?" She threw the accusation at him. "That has to be why you called her. You want to be back with her!" She continued to rant while Jesse watched her. She began pacing the floor and biting her nails. That's what she did when she was upset or nervous. She stopped because she realized that he still hadn't said anything. She squinted her eyes in anger. Who the hell did he think he was? She ran up to him and started pounding on his chest. She wanted him to feel the deep ache — the gut-wrenching pain — she was feeling right now. She kept hitting him until he grabbed her wrists and she fell to the floor at his feet, crying. She lay there. What did she have to do for him to see that she loved him? She needed him to know that she would do it. She didn't care as long as he told her he wouldn't leave her. She felt him pick her up. She kept her eyes closed as he rocked her.

Jesse

Jesse felt like a heel. How did they get to this point? He must have really given her the impression that he wanted something outside of the sex they shared. He didn't take her out anywhere but here in Detroit. He didn't do half of the things for her that he did for Shontell. Why did women always have to read other things into sex, and then act like this when they finally realized the truth?

Jesse continued to rock her until he thought she had calmed down. He always wished that women would learn that most men, himself included, were simple creatures. It shouldn't take a book — or even a talk show — to tell women what they should expect from men. All they had to really do was pay attention. If men were interested in a woman they showed it. They had no gimmicks and no lies. The last thing they would want to do was hurt them intentionally if they truly loved them. They would make time for them without a second thought. When you really want to be with someone, you always have time for them without excuses. He always gave Ebony excuses. He used to move heaven and Earth to have Shontell next to him, although she was mostly reluctant to be seen in public. He sighed and got his mind right so he could continue this farce. He lifted her chin and made her look at him.

"Are you finished now?" he asked her, after he took the towel that was sitting next to him and wiped at her tear-stained face. She nodded, and he made her sit up. She scooted off his lap and sat next to him on the bed. He turned toward her and had her look at him. The look he saw on her face was almost the same as what he had seen on Shontell's the night he saw her. It made him close his mouth. He stood up and walked over to his desk to get the vision out of his head before continuing. When he got his words together, Ebony was leaning back on the bed. She was sitting there watching him. Jesse felt uneasy for a few moments, but when he got his focus back he started speaking.

"Ebony, if I wanted her, why would I still be messing around with you? That boat has sailed. Shontell has made it clear that she doesn't want to be bothered with me. I still like to make sure that she is doing fine." He had to clean up the situation and make sure that she understood. She needed to continue to trust him so that she could get what he needed. He smiled at her. When she finally smiled back, he saw that as his opportunity to seal the deal. He knew what always made her do the things he needed.

He pulled her into his arms and began kissing her. She moaned. He took this as his green light to continue. He laid her on the bed and kissed her even harder. He undressed her, giving her what he knew she wanted. All women seemed to want it, with the exception of Shontell. An hour later, they were finished and he was sure she was pacified. He sent her home with a new plan in motion. She also begged to go on the cruise. He reluctantly told her that he would take her. He hoped that he could find a way to get what he needed, and get rid of Ebony as well.

Shontell

Shontell closed the curtains because she didn't understand what the hell had happened with Ebony. She was acting weird again. It was the same strange behavior she had exhibited when they were having their phone meeting. She felt like she was hiding something. Shontell went over to the sink and washed the sticky coffee off of her hands.

She glanced at the clock on the stove. She was running behind. She needed to get dressed and finish her errands, and then come back and prepare for dinner. She hoped her car would be there by the time she finished getting ready.

She was glad she was making good time as she quickly checked on her cake and fruit pie that she had made for dessert. It was a new recipe, and she wanted to get her mom's opinion. She missed her mother being at the shop with her. They had started the event company together. But when her health started failing, she had to cut back her hours. Now she helped out on an as-needed basis. She always loved cooking in the kitchen with her mom. Shontell's mother was taught by her mother, whom Shontell never had the opportunity to meet. She had died two months before Shontell was born.

Shontell and her mother used to spend hours in the kitchen. Her dad always had to make them stop. He pretended to complain, telling them the house was too hot with all that cooking and baking. Yet, he never complained about how much food and dessert he ate from the taste testing.

When she pulled up to her parents' house, her mother was talking to their next door neighbor, Ms. Margaret. She had lived there almost as long as they had. Over the last ten years, the Detroit neighborhoods had gone down. But now — with the new revitalization Detroit was implementing, — the neighborhoods were slowly coming back. People were now given chances to buy up the old abandoned houses and make things beautiful again. She had always wanted her parents to move, but they wouldn't have it. She stopped trying, but she made sure they were safe and protected. She waved and spoke, but kept going inside so that she wouldn't drop the dessert boxes. Her father met her at the door, taking one of the boxes from her.

"Thanks, Daddy. How are you doing today?" she asked after kissing him. She followed him into the kitchen. She really liked the new design. It was her anniversary gift to them. She had it done when they went out of town. Her mother cried for joy for two days after she returned and found her surprise.

"Baby girl, I am doing with these knees of mine..." He limped over to the cabinet and began pulling out the plates.

"Are you still having the pain and swelling?" she asked him, concerned.

"No more than usual. Ain't nothing they can do anyways. It's nothing but old age." Shontell stopped and watched her father's movements.

"Dad, stop saying that. You need to get a consultation. Will you at least make an appointment for when I come back? I will go with you." She bent down to pick up a towel he'd dropped.

"Go where with him?" her mother asked before he could give her an answer. She walked into the kitchen and started turning off the pots. She pulled out the cups and silverware.

"Mom, let me help." Shontell grabbed the items from her mother, heading to the table.

"Young lady, I got this. Now one of you needs to be answering my question."

Her father looked at her and then at his wife. He knew what was about to come when she told her. He would be going because he was outnumbered. So he was quiet while Shon told her what they had been speaking about.

"Daddy...the issue of his knees and that they are still bothering him. I wanted him to at least go get it checked out, and I told him I would take him. He was about to give me a yes or no when you walked in and asked," she explained. She started taking the stuff out of her hand and shooing her as she finished setting the table. Lydia looked at her husband of thirty-five years and smiled. He was very stubborn, but she knew he wasn't going to tell them both no.

"Yes, he will go. Thank you for offering to take him. I will set up the appointment tomorrow," she said without a second thought. She heard him moan, and she laughed.

"One of these days I am going to win a debate in my own house." He was acting like he was mad. Shontell hugged her father, and he melted. This was his baby girl, and she would always be his darling.

"Where's that young fellow I met? He seemed very nice...not like that Jesse."

"Daddy, please. Don't start. You already embarrassed me enough that night with your comment." Shontell tapped him on the shoulder to show her displeasure.

"Darnell, what is she talking about?" her mother asked. Darnell told her about the night, but it seemed like he had forgotten something as usual. She looked at him with her arms folded. He looked sheepishly at the two of them.

"He basically threatened him if he hurt me," she told her mother.

"Darnell Banner, you didn't!" her mother scolded. She knew where his heart was. They both wanted their daughter to be happy. A husband and some grandkids wouldn't hurt either. She knew Shontell may not be ready, but she wasn't getting any younger. Lydia wouldn't say that out loud. She would never want to hurt her daughter's feelings and bring up the miscarriage. She wished she could have taken that pain from her only child. Shontell served her parents and sat down. Her father said grace, and then the questions started. Her mother wanted to know what he looked like. She pointed him out in one of the pictures she had taken with them that she had on her phone.

"Now that's a handsome young man," she told her daughter.

"I agree mama. I agree." She smiled, thinking about him. They continued to ask her questions, and she reassured them both that she and Nico were being careful and taking it slow. She also told them she liked him a lot. Having had only one child made her parents very protective. She didn't mind it much now. But when she was a teenager, it had driven her crazy.

They finished dinner. Shontell shooed her parents out of the dining room as she cleared the dishes. She went to grab her phone and check her messages. Nothing. Putting it back into her purse, she opened the boxes she brought in with her. Shontell placed the items on the tray, along with coffee for her dad and tea for her mother. Walking into the family room, she joined her parents. Setting the tray on the table, she handed her father his coffee. He reached for the sugar. She placed the fruit pie in front of him. She set the vanilla bean caramel cake in front of her mom. She sat down and waited anxiously for their responses. Lydia was the first one to speak, but she had an expression that couldn't be read.

"Shon, is this your grandmother's recipe?" she asked her. She could see her mother getting emotional, and tears instantly sprang into her eyes. The pie and cake Shontell made today were extra special. They were the final two things that she and her mother were trying to perfect.

"Yes mom, it is. Do you like it?"

"No," her mother paused and didn't look at her daughter.

"I love it. She would be so proud of you. I hope you will share with me what you did to it." Shontell breathed out hard. She scared her. She wiped the tears off her face. Her father handed her a Kleenex.

"Shon, this pie is so buttery. It tastes like Ma Bell made this. It was one of the reasons I married your mother: all the pie I wanted," Darnell said as he dodged the pillow that his wife threw at him. They all laughed. She loved seeing them so happy and playful after all their years together. She wanted what she saw with her parents' relationship. Checking her watch, she stood up. She still had a few things to do before she left tomorrow.

She kissed them both and told them she would let them know when she made it to Miami. She got into her car and heard her phone ringing. She grabbed her purse and saw it was Ebony. She had been concerned about her. She had not talked to her since that morning. She was hoping that she wasn't about to pull out of the meeting that they had scheduled for the morning before her flight. This was huge, and she needed to have it if she wanted to continue with her expansion and other plans. She rolled her window down some. She watched the kids playing outside as she mentally prepared herself for whatever this call was about.

"Hey, Ebony. What's going on?"

"Shontell, I am sorry to bother you. But my brother was in a bad accident early this morning. Because I didn't answer the calls, I didn't find out until now. I don't think I am going to make the meeting tomorrow," she lied. She continued talking before Shontell could respond. "I am going to have to take the rest of the week off." Shontell pulled the phone away from her ear. She wanted to jump through the phone and punch her. Shontell was glad that she didn't pull off away from the curb yet, because she was sure she would have had an accident. Why was she doing this? She was purposely trying to sabotage her. She worked too hard for this to let it get ruined. Thinking of her mom's emotions about her new desserts, she realized that this was for her mother and her grandmother even more than it was for her. She would not let her take that away.

"Ebony, are you serious? What is going on with you? What about the things we have booked for this week? I am not trying to be insensitive, but you knew I had my time planned for months. If I didn't know better, I would say you are doing this to spite me." She did not care that she was getting louder.

"Whoa, now that's a low blow. I may not have as much as you have invested in Precious Timeless Events, but I am a part of that company too. So if it fails, so do I. Besides, they are small events. I am sure the staff can handle them. I gotta go. The doctor is coming in. I will be in touch," she told her. She then hung up before Shontell could say anything else.

Shontell almost screamed, but she caught herself so that she didn't scare the kids. Something didn't feel right. She quickly thought back to when Ebony started doing things out of the ordinary. It was right when she announced the expansion. She was upset that she hadn't included her in the process. She felt like Shontell was being secretive. Well, now the tables were turned and Shontell felt that Ebony was being secretive. The expansion was funded in part by her and the rest by her parents. In her opinion, Ebony had no say so. Something told her she needed to watch her back.

The image of Ebony's face when she walked into her home and saw her gave her the shivers. She started her car and activated her speaker. She called her two assistants and told them of the changes for the week. She gave them a heads-up that more permanent changes would be coming when she returned from her vacation. As soon as she was done with that call, she called a locksmith. She was getting her locks changed and her alarm recoded today. Shontell finished her last-minute packing while the locksmith and the security company worked. Once they left, Shontell felt better. She wished she could talk to Nico; she knew they were out doing promotions all day, so she didn't want to bother him. She was surprised she hadn't heard from him all day…not even a text. She closed her suitcase and placed it near the door. She turned on the tea kettle and sat on the couch. She had way too much on her mind.

Shontell was getting antsy. She needed to talk. While making her tea, she called Sandy. When Sandy answered, she immediately took over the conversation.

"Girl, Eric called me. He wanted to know if I would be okay with him spending time with me on the cruise. His brother pulled out at the last minute and he was now going to be solo," Sandy told her. She could hear the excitement in her friend's voice.

"I thought it was just a sex thing?" Shontell asked. As she rolled down her window, a breeze immediately came through.

"I did too…but whatever happens…happens," she told her.

"Okay…well…as long as you're okay with it. I called to tell you that Ebony claims her brother is sick and she can't work while I am on vacation. That woman is driving me crazy!" Shontell sipped her tea, as she waited for Sandy to say something.

"Shontell, I have something to tell you." She could hear the hesitation in her friend's voice.

"What is it?"

"Monica said, when she and her classmate were coming from the competition last night, they saw Jesse and Ebony together. Monica said they were more than friendly. They were down there for the National Math and Science scrimmage matches at the Westin Hotel Downtown. "

"What!! What are you saying?" she yelled into the phone, almost dropping her phone in her hot tea. Shontell grabbed the edge of the counter and pressed down hard.

"I wasn't there. I am informing you of what she told me this morning. You may want to try and reach Ebony and find out what's going on."

"Maybe I will. Maybe I just don't care anymore." Her head was beginning to hurt. She suddenly didn't feel like talking right now.

"I will see you at the airport after my meeting."

"Are you going to be okay?"

"Yes, I just need some time to think. Love you and talk to you later."

"I love you too, and good night. Call me back if you still need to talk." They ended their call. Shontell's mind was racing. What were they doing together? Although they were both free to see whomever they wanted, she didn't even know they talked to each other outside of when she was with Jesse. Why would Ebony do that to her? She hit a button and Ebony's number auto-dialed. She answered on the second ring.

"Hey, Ebony. I wanted to check on you. How are you holding up? How's your brother?" she asked, sounding cooler than she felt. She didn't miss the hesitation in her voice.

"My brother? Oh...um...he is still recovering," she said, sounding confused. Shontell now knew for sure that Ebony was lying.

"Ebony, I have a question for you. Someone told me that they saw you and Jesse together last night. What's that about?"

THE LIES WE WEAVE

Ebony

Ebony was glad that she was alone. She almost fell on the floor as she missed the bed where she was trying to sit. She threw the bathing suit in her suitcase and thought fast. How did anyone see them? They always tried to be careful. She warned Jesse that staying at that hotel this week wasn't a good idea. There were too many activities going on. He got stopped almost every five steps with someone wanting a picture or autograph. She heard Shontell call her name on the phone. Damn, she didn't like being in this situation. She answered her nervously.

"Um...well...he called me and asked me to meet him. He was asking my help in trying to get you back."

"Really? Is that so?"

"Yeah, he asked for my opinion. That's all. It's nothing to worry about." Ebony rolled her eyes. She wanted to get off the phone with Shontell. She was never a very good liar, and she thought that she was very transparent when she tried to make up stories.

"Mm...hm...well, I will let you get back to your brother. Sorry I bothered you with this. You are my friend, and I know that I can trust you." Shontell wanted her to hear the sarcasm in her voice. Ebony didn't reply to what she said. But she thought it was pretty much a question to get a rise out of her. Before she could answer, all she heard was the dial tone. She hit the end button and pulled her knees up to her chest.

She started crying because she felt like the shit was about to come back to her. She wanted this over with. The plan was for her to go back to Shontell's after her flight left and look for the safe. She hoped to find whatever it was he was looking for so they could move on. She typed a text and hit send. Getting up to get the Kleenex, she heard her phone. She answered before she knew who it was. She groaned when she heard her mother's voice.

"Ebony, Ms. Elaine said she saw you kissing on that celebrity. What's his name? He used to be engaged to your partner, right?" Ebony could not believe this. Who the hell else saw them together?

"Since when do you care about my love life!" she said forcefully into the phone.

"Don't raise your voice at me, young lady," she told her daughter. Ebony set her phone down to get something off her dressing room table. She could hear her mother still talking. Picking the phone back up, she lit a cigarette. Thinking that Jesse would have a fit if he smelled the smoke on her clothes. She put the cigarette out.

"Mom, Jesse and I are friends. We were hanging out."

"Hanging out my ass, Ebony. I know you. You have an agenda," she said to her only daughter. Ebony couldn't believe her mother. "Mom back off. I don't tell you how to live your life. It's time you started keeping out of my business." There was silence. A few minutes later, her mother said something that took her breath away. "That man is going to destroy you. You deserve better than him. Didn't you learn anything from my mistakes? I know I may not have been the best mother to you and your brothers, but I tried to be the best mother I could. I really did." Her mother cried as she spoke to her daughter. Ebony started pacing her floor. What right did her mother have to tell her that she deserved better? To her, Jesse was her better, and she knew that for a fact. Ebony's hands started shaking with her over-emotional state.

"You are wrong! Jesse loves me," she said. Although her words were barely audible, her mother heard her clearly.

"I promise you that man doesn't love you. Leave him alone, child. But I know you won't do it because the warning is coming from me. So don't come running to me when he leaves you empty. Goodbye, Ebony," her mother told her before she ended their call. Ebony almost threw her phone at the wall. She flung herself on her bed and cried. What did her mother know that she didn't know? Why was she so adamant about her leaving Jesse alone? Lying in a fetal position, she grabbed her phone and typed her text.

Jesse

Jesse was having lunch with one of the best producers in the business. He was known as the comeback producer. This meant that anyone who worked with him had their career come back with a full vengeance. He was so glad that Dennis was able to make this happen for him. He saw the light flash on his phone and looked at the message: *people saw us last night and told Shontell.* Jesse almost knocked his glass over and quickly excused himself. He walked towards the bathroom and quickly dialed Ebony's number. She sent him to her voicemail. He cursed silently, and he stood there to get himself together before he walked back over to the table. He sat down and got through the rest of the meeting. By the end of the meeting, he was feeling like his career could be salvaged as the producer agreed to take on the project. Stepping into his town car, he tried Ebony again and was furious when she still didn't answer him. Leaning back in his seat, he tried to put her text out his mind. He was in a good mood, and he wanted to keep it that way.

Nico's whole body hurt. He dropped across his bed and laid there. They did so much today that he couldn't move. Even the rehearsals were brutal today. He kicked his shoes off and turned on his back. He was so mad at himself for rushing this morning and leaving his phone. He knew Shontell must be wondering why she hadn't heard anything from him. He saw that he had about six text messages and a couple missed calls. He opened his text messages, and he saw the three pictures of her in his shirt. He was glad that he let her keep it. The other texts were from his brother, telling him that he and his parents would be getting in around three tomorrow. He wanted to call Shontell, but it was after midnight. He did send her a text and was surprised when she replied back asking him if they could video chat.

"Hey, chocolate. How was your day?" she asked him. Nico blew her a kiss before he spoke.

"Hey, sweetness. It was hard. I am so sorry about not talking to you all day. I was rushing and left the phone on the night stand," he explained

"It's okay. I knew you were going to be busy. I spent the day preparing for this meeting and then had dinner with my parents. They told me to tell you hi."

"Aw, that was sweet of them. While we are speaking of sweets, how did the desserts go over with them?"

"They both loved them. Giving my mom such a nice surprise made my world. It got emotional, but it was a good time," she told him as she shifted on her bed. Nico smiled at her gesture as it made her breasts shift as well. Nico was about to comment about it when he heard a knock on the door. He looked at her in frustration, hunching his shoulders. Getting up, he walked over to his door. Sometimes he regretted giving up having a bodyguard. He put Shontell in view before he looked out.

"It must be one of the guys. I am not putting this phone down. I have already missed you too much today," he told her. He could see her blush, and that made him happy. He really did miss her.

Nico peeked out the viewer and silently cursed.

"You are not going to believe this. It's Tina," he whispered into the phone.

"Oh really? Are you going to let her in?" she asked him. Nico shook his head no. "Go ahead; let her in," she encouraged.

"Are you sure?"

"Yes love, as long as you keep me on here," she instructed. Nico nodded his head in agreement as he opened the door to Tina, who was holding a champagne bottle and two glasses. He stepped half way into the hallway and looked around. He was thinking that this had to be a joke. He was being punked! He wiped his face.

Nico heard shuffling and looked down at this phone. He was so glad she was on the phone with him. He saw the look on Shontell's face, and it mirrored his but for different reasons. He didn't let Tina see that he was on with Shontell. He made sure that Shontell could see what was going on. She remained silent. Nico was trying to make sense of all this. He didn't invite her in. Tina looked behind her and in the same direction that he had been looking. She turned back around with a look of confusion.

"Are you looking for someone?" she asked him with a sexy smile.

"Tina, you must have knocked on the wrong door. You know good and damn well I am not letting you in my room. So please stop…now!"

"When did you become so mean?"

"The day your ass decided someone else was the one for you. Now leave me alone, or you might get your wish and see how mean I am." Nico tried to close the door, but she put the bottle in it to keep it open. He looked at her like she had lost her mind.

"Tina, please don't test me," he told her through clenched teeth. He held his phone a little tighter. He decided not to do what his gut said. Shontell was watching, and he didn't want her to see him as less of a man because of his actions.

"Why is it that SHE can have your attention and I can't?"

"You can't be serious."

"But I am. I am a ten, and what is she?" Tina said, pouting as she stood in the door. Nico could smell that she had been drinking.

"A thousand, compared to you. She has more class, style, and grace than you can even hope to learn about." He glared at her as he again tried to close the door.

"Now I am going to ask you nicely one more time to leave me alone. My time is too valuable to waste it on you," he said. He yanked the bottle from inside his door and from her hand. He tossed it in the hallway and closed his door. He held the phone up and saw that Shontell was crying.

"Shontell, baby. What's wrong? Why are you crying? It's not about Tina, is it?" She nodded her head and then put a finger up as she placed her phone down for a second. The screen went black. He could hear Tina out in the hall yelling and cursing. She was drunk. Things like this didn't happen to him—Dennis, yes; him, no. Shontell still hadn't come back to the phone, and he was getting scared. He didn't understand her tears. He hoped that she didn't think anything was going on between them. He wouldn't jeopardize their beginning nor disrespect her in that way. He let out a sigh of relief when she came back into view. She had taken a minute to compose herself.

"Are you okay? Are you going to tell me why you are crying?" he asked in a small and desperate voice. When she didn't say anything, he started to panic.

"I hope you weren't thinking that I was doing anything with her. I promise I wasn't. I…" he tried to tell her. He sat on the edge of the table in his room, running his hand back and forth over his head.

"Nico, Nico. Stop and listen, please. No, I didn't think you were with her. I'm reacting to your actions. The way you wanted me to see that you were being truthful and honest with me was just different. I never had that experience. It wasn't as if you had to prove it to me otherwise. The act itself was heartwarming. Thank you for that," she told him when she interrupted what he was saying. He wished he could touch her. He needed to have her in his arms. He realized that God put them together for a reason. They both needed to learn some things and he was showing out lessons on their behalf.

"Shontell, I am sorry that your ex and the ones before him hurt you. I can't take away what they did. But I can show you how a real man can love and treat a good woman, like yourself. I would rather lose my voice than hurt you or mess up what I have found in you," he told her into the screen. He was about to say something else when the banging on his door got louder. He stood up and walked a little closer to his door. They could hear Tina being dramatic. He needed to diffuse this situation. He sighed and he reluctantly told Shontell that he needed to take care of the situation before it got ugly.

"Yeah, go handle that. I will try and stay up. I am more drained than I was when we got on here."

"Yes. I second that, beautiful." They ended their call. He opened his door and saw Dennis, Martin, and the two hotel security guards. He started to close his door, but thought better of it as he stepped into the hallway and joined the other men.

KARMA IS A BITCH

Shontell

Shontell went to put eye cream on her face. She was way too emotional lately, and her face was showing it. She held onto the sides of the sink, and she put her head down and said a silent prayer. Her mind went back to the last few days. On one side, she was exactly where she always wanted to be. She hoped she never had to see again what was on the other side. Why does it happen that way? When a person finally moves on and tries to have a real life, they can't because someone always wants to throw a monkey wrench in it. She wasn't going to let that happen. She was being given this chance by luck. She was over Jesse. The situation with Jesse and Ebony had nothing to do with her. She was going to stick with that until she saw otherwise.

Shontell finished her nightly regime and was headed to bed when she heard someone knocking on her door. She sighed because she felt that this was going to happen. She walked slowly to the door as she prepared herself for whatever it was that this man was bringing to her door at 1 a.m. She opened the door, and he was leaning on the pillar. She could smell the alcohol before he even said hello. She instantly regretted her decision.

"Jesse, why are you at my house at 1 a.m.?"

"I...I...just wanted to talk to you," he slurred as he tried to make his way into her house. She placed her hand on his chest and stopped him. He gave her a dejected look.

"You're drunk! So what makes you think I am stupid enough to let you in?"

"Because I love you. I have never stopped loving you."

"If you love me so much, then why are you hanging out with Ebony?" Jesse looked ashamed. He opened his mouth and then closed it. He looked down at his feet.

"That's exactly what I thought. You know what? You are a grown man. Do as you please," she told him as she got ready to close her door.

"Please...please...don't close the door. I need to be near you," he barely whispered into the night air. Shontell didn't want to care. She wanted to slam the door and go on with her life. Jesse was her monkey wrench, and he didn't even know it. She walked over to where he was and helped him to her couch. She took off his shoes, and then she went to grab a blanket. When she came back, Jesse was out cold. She spread the cover over him and went to lock her doors. Shontell got into her bed and tried to sleep. She looked at her phone and expelled a long breath. She had to be at her meeting in four hours. How in the heck was she going to be able to do this? She closed her eyes and was determined to fall asleep.

Shontell awoke with a start. Why did she smell coffee? Jesse! She recalled his unexpected appearance last night. She got up and dressed for her meeting. Walking into her kitchen, she didn't feel comfortable with what she saw. Jesse was making breakfast, and his back was turned to her. She cleared her throat to get his attention. He turned around and gave her a big smile. He handed her a cup of coffee and then placed the cream on the counter. She sat on the stool and didn't say anything. She wanted to see if he was going to say anything about earlier. The room remained silent. Shontell looked over her notes as she sipped her coffee. Jesse finished cooking and placed her breakfast in front of her. She took a forkful and put the rest of her things in her bag.

"When did you start cooking?" Shontell said to him as she tasted more of the food.

"Don't act like I didn't cook for you," he told her as he bit into his bacon.

"Whatever. Your meals were very few and far in between. But thanks."

"You're welcome, but I want to apologize about last night. I shouldn't have come here like that. That won't happen again," he told her.

"Oh, I know it won't happen again. Jesse, you have no claim to my life anymore. If you want a friendship from me, you need to let me get used to you being around. A friendship is all we will ever have. I am not going backwards with you."

"Shontell," he whined looking at her like she had just broken his heart.

"Don't Shontell me. If you can't abide by that, then all bets are off," she told him as she got off up the stool. She didn't care that he didn't like what she said, because that's the way it had to be.

"I have a meeting, so we need to get going," she told him as she started to straighten up. Shontell did her walk-through to make sure everything was in place since she was going straight to the airport after the meeting. She didn't want to leave anything. Shontell walked over to her door with her suitcases and her garment bag. She stood there waiting on Jesse. His driver pulled up, and they walked out seconds later. For a moment, it felt like old times, but it wasn't. There wouldn't be any sweet goodbyes. She gave him a light hug as he got into the waiting car. Then she got in her car and pulled off. Neither of them saw Ebony a few cars down the street.

Ebony

Ebony parked her rental car three houses down from Shontell. She was reading her magazine and looked up when she heard voices. She glanced towards Shontell's house and did a double take. What the hell?!! Jesse was coming out of Shontell's door. What was he doing there? She almost got out her car and confronted them. But if she did, she would lose Jesse for good. What's going on? Karma was a straight bitch, she thought. Should she have expected this? Was she losing Jesse? Had he spent the night there? There was a reasonable explanation, she told herself as she continued to try and make herself believe what she was saying.

Ebony could have had her pick of men, but yet she put up with the scraps that Jesse threw her because she broke her own cardinal rule. She fell in love with him. She knew that even though he didn't say it, he loved her too. He had to. He couldn't sex her body the way he did and not feel something for her. She reached over and grabbed a napkin and wiped her eyes and nose. Damn it. She hated it when she let him get her. She didn't like feeling weak. Her phone buzzed and she rolled her eyes at the sound. She wouldn't even pick the phone up.

Looking at her watch, she began to fidget. At this point, all she wanted to focus on was getting this over and done with. Shontell should just be finishing that meeting. Her flight was scheduled to leave at eleven. Every time she looked at her house, she saw Jesse coming out of that door. They didn't hug with passion, so maybe it was platonic. She shook her head because she was doing it again. She was excusing his behavior. She needed to divert her mind. She turned the radio up and began to hum the song absently. Ebony drummed her fingers on the wheel. She was too antsy. Ebony looked in front and in the back of her for activity. She was ready to do this and get it over with. She got out of her car and put on her sunglasses. She headed to the house. Ebony quickly made a detour, because she needed to make sure no one was watching her. Most of the neighbors knew her and her car. That's why she had on the glasses and the hood. She decided to walk the block and then come back around to the house. The morning's brisk air made her walk faster.

It took her about fifteen minutes to do the walk, and she was out of breath. She needed to get back in shape. She headed up Shontell's driveway. As she took her keys out of her pocket, she felt her phone buzz again. She looked at the screen and sucked her teeth. She looked around, trying not to look suspicious as she inserted her key. The key wouldn't turn. She took her key out and tried again. She shook her head in disbelief. Shontell had changed the locks! She thought back to the call she received from Shontell yesterday. She messed this up, and she didn't know how to fix it. Damn it, now what was she going to do? She started to leave the porch, but instead she looked around. She didn't know for sure what she was expecting to see. Could there be something of Jesse's out there? She needed to think. Her heart was pounding so loud that she couldn't even hear the birds chirping. She went to see if she had changed the extra key as well. Feeling for the key, she retrieved it. Trying the key in the side door, she was met with the same resistance. Ebony threw the key in her frustration, and then regretted it. She went to where she thought the key had landed, but she couldn't find anything. She heard a woman's voice close by and panicked, quickly forgetting about the key. She needed to get out of sight, and she cursed under her breath when she heard a woman's voice call her name. How did she see her? Her luck couldn't be this bad. She turned and looked at Shontell's mother.

"Ebony, what are you doing here?" the older woman asked her, looking like she knew she was up to no good.

"Um...well...I was hoping to catch Shontell before she left."

"Is that so? Then, why are you back there?" Ebony thought quickly as she didn't know what to say to her.

"I forgot my key, and when she didn't answer I was just going to put this paperwork on her counter," she lied with so much ease that even she believed her own lie for a minute. She waved the papers and started walking in Ms. Lydia's direction. She handed the generic documents to her, glad she had thought to bring them out the car.

"I guess since you are going in there you can take them."

"Yes, I guess I can. Say hello to your mother for me, will you?

"Yes, ma'am," she told her, waving as she high-tailed it back to her car. She knew that she was watching her. She waved to Lydia as she drove off, and the woman returned the wave but kept watching her. What was she going to tell Jesse? She couldn't go back to him empty handed. He told her that he didn't want to see her otherwise. She pulled over and laid her head on the steering wheel. She needed to get herself together. One thing was for sure — she wasn't going to tell him anything until she boarded that ship. She wanted to distract him until they left in a few hours, and she knew exactly how to accomplish that. She thought of the new lace and leather body suit she had just purchased.

PLAYING THE FOOL

Jesse

Jesse was still kicking himself for what he had done earlier. He didn't remember how many drinks he had. He knew his antics had cost him more than any record deal. Shontell made it clear that she was done. He couldn't blame her after he came over there drunk. He pulled out the only picture he had of her. It was one of them. It was their engagement portrait. He stared at the picture until he heard a knock on his room door. He stood up and felt dizzy. Bracing himself, he held on to the chair for a quick moment. It was very rare that he got that drunk. It seemed that everything that had happened in the last few days was slowly sneaking up on him. Maybe it was time for him to slow his life down. But could he? Especially with the resurrection of his career, he could make the changes that he needed. He had to face the fact that he might get all he wanted but Shontell. He wasn't ready for that. He looked through the peephole and instantly got pissed. Ebony was one of the most incorrigible, but sexiest women he had ever come across.

"Ebony, you are going to get enough of ignoring me. And what are you doing here anyways?" Jesse didn't care if she knew that he was irritated. He opened his hotel room door wider for her and walked back over to his bed. He flopped on it and grabbed the aspirin bottle from his bedside table. He swallowed two aspirins dry. His head was still hurting from his hangover, and he wasn't in the mood for her right now. He literally groaned when he remembered that she was going on the cruise with him. He knew that was a huge mistake. Jesse could get out of it. But he knew that, in the end, it wouldn't be in his favor. He needed to end this relationship with her. He watched her walk in and over to him. She was wearing a black trench coat.

"I thought we agreed not to see each other again until we boarded the ship, Ebony," he reminded her in a low voice. She smirked at him, while she did what she wanted to. She kneeled in front of him and placed both of her hands on his knees opening them so her sleek body could fit comfortably. He didn't want to look at her, but her aura made her impossible to resist.

"I know you said that we should lay low, but I needed to see you. I won't stay long. Besides, the lobby was empty," she told him in a voice he wasn't familiar with. It caught him off guard.

"What are you up to, Ebony?" he asked, as he observed her through slit eyes, while she pushed him back slightly. She hunched her shoulders and then licked her lips.

Jesse's eyes roamed Ebony's body as she stood and began to undo her buttons. She unfastened the coat belt. It fell to the floor, and he immediately got hard. The woman had a banging body. She always got mistaken for the singer Brandy, and she got a kick out of that. Jesse wished she had Brandy's mentality. She wasn't needy like Ebony was. He bit his lip, as she turned around and gave him a good view of her ass.

He never should have taken this thing with her so far. He thought about what Shontell said to him on the porch. He had a feeling that it wasn't going to turn out in a good way. He didn't know why he was thinking of Shontell when Ebony was so willing to please him in ways that Shontell would never have agreed to. He couldn't deny the sex was off the chain. Ebony did the things he had only seen in porno movies. The woman was skilled. Even with all that, she couldn't hold a candle to his Shontell. He loved Shontell, and he realized he probably always would. He needed to make her see that he loved her too, no matter how many times she refused to give them another chance. He didn't want to let go of Shontell.

He felt that Shontell still cared for him. She showed that care last night. She didn't let him stay out on the porch like she could have. He smiled at the thought.

Ebony leaned over him and kissed him...bringing him out of his thoughts ...sucking his tongue hard. He loved it rough, and she knew it. He pushed his thoughts of Shontell out of his mind, but he knew he still had work to do when it came to her. He flinched when she bit his chest. She pulled him up and bit him on his nipple and stomach, as he watched her slide down his body and land on her knees. She reached up and unbuckled his belt, as she used her teeth to unzip his zipper. She took him into her mouth in one smooth motion. He groaned, as he held onto the back of her head. He felt his legs turn to jelly.

Nico

Nico's night was long. He was with security, Martin and Tina until 4 a.m. He still didn't understand Tina's motives. Why would she have come to his room acting like that? He tried to watch Dennis' reaction to her. He didn't flinch. So either he was a good actor or he didn't have anything to do with last night. That made him sigh with relief. He wanted to believe that he wouldn't try the things he did with his brother. When he finally got to go to his room, it felt like all his energy was drained. He sent Shontell a quick text to let her know that he was back in the room. They took Tina down to the security office to let her sleep off whatever what was wrong with her. He was so glad Shontell's flight didn't get in until mid-afternoon. He somehow managed to get at least five hours of sleep.

Nico initially was going to have the car go and pick up Shontell and Sandy, but he couldn't wait to see her. Nico had the driver arrive at the airport early, in case their flight came in early as well. Nico called his brother to pass the time.

"Hey Nate, are you guys on schedule?" he asked him as he waved to two women who were walking past and were staring at him.

"Yes, we are. We should get to Miami later tonight. You know mom is looking forward to seeing you. Are you sending the car?" his brother asked him.

"Yes, and I will see you guys for dinner, right?"

"You know it. Dad said he wants to go check out that new fishing place before we hit the boat."

"I am sure he does," he told his brother. Their father was a huge fish enthusiast. Nico wrapped up a few last-minute details with Nate and ended his call. He looked down at his watch, as he leaned on the car. The driver was now inside with a sign waiting for them. He would text him once he got the women and they were heading back to the car. He was so excited to see Shontell.

He needed her next to him after all the drama from last night. This was not his usual style. He hoped Tina would back off. He didn't know when she got like that, but it was too much. She liked being the center of attention, and she was succeeding in that area at the moment. He wondered how he fell for two entirely different women. He figured that it happened like that sometimes. He wasn't perfect...not even close. He must have done something right for him to have Shontell in his life.

Nico saw the women out the corner of his eye. Sometimes this was both a blessing and a curse. As the women approached him and asked to take a picture with him, he obliged. He sighed once they walked off. He wondered how all the attention that they would be getting this weekend would go over with Shontell. She seemed adamant about not being in the spotlight, but he wasn't willing to hide her. He wanted everyone to see what he saw in her. He would have to talk to her again about it before they boarded the boat. He hoped he would be able to make her feel comfortable. The women fans could be a bit much. He recalled the one or two times that he found naked women in his room. He never knew how they got into his room, but those days were over. He usually had a security sweep of his room now, before he even went up. He learned his lesson.

He felt a vibration and read the text: They were here. He got back into the car, and he waited with the flowers in his hand. He couldn't wait to see her smile. It had only been three and a half days, but it seemed like longer. The boat was due to set sail tomorrow afternoon. Martin had given them all the rest of the land time off until they hit the boat. He was glad, because he had wanted to spend quality time with Shontell before they got busy. He remembered his surprise, and he made a quick call to make sure that their evening plans were still on track. He heard the ladies before he saw them. He sat back and waited for the door to open.

Shontell watched as her client signed his contract. She was so happy. This client would take her where she wanted to go. They shook hands and departed from her office. She dropped her buy-out papers on Ebony's desk in a sealed and confidential envelope. She hoped Ebony would read her letter and sign it. The check she enclosed was a good-enough offer. She wanted this working relationship over. She could never work with someone she couldn't trust. The town car she paid to take her and Sandy to the airport was waiting for her. She was leaving her car at her office. She texted Sandy to let her know she was on the way, as he put her bags in the trunk. She was getting excited.

Shontell was glad to see that she had a text from Nico; she must have missed it this morning when she texted her good morning to him. Her distraction with Jesse had her out of sorts. On her drive to her meeting, she wondered: did she make herself clear enough to Jesse that she had moved on?

The driver explained to her that the chilled mimosas she requested were in the refrigerator as she had instructed.

Within a few minutes, they were pulling up to Sandy's home. Monica ran out to the car to greet her god-mother.

"Hey, Auntie Shon, I am so glad you are making mommy take a vacation," her god-daughter told her. She was the spitting image of Sandy.

"Yes, we both know she needed it. Are you staying with Mona?" she asked her, referring to Sandy's mother.

"Yep, Grams is on her way now. I have finals this week. Then it's party time. You are still coming over to see me off for prom, right?" The teenager was standing on her tip-toes as she talked to her. She laughed and wrapped her arms around her. "Now you know I wouldn't miss that for anything. Don't forget to send me the list of food you want," she reminded her. She then remembered she had something for her. Reaching into her purse, she handed her a pre-paid Visa card. The young woman looked at her strangely. Sandy was walking in their direction.

"What's this for?" she asked her in confusion. Sandy handed her bags to the driver, watching her two favorite people. She stood with her mouth open when she heard Shontell's reply.

"This card is for you! It should cover all of your prom clothes, activities, and then some," she told her. Sandy and Monica both started to cry. Monica hugged her.

"Don't cry, Monica. Your dad had me start this fund when you were thirteen. I added to it. But this is from all of us," she told them. Monica looked at her and cried harder. They all dried their eyes as Mona pulled up. They didn't want her asking questions. She hugged Monica again and waved to Mona as she went to sit in the car. The driver handed her some Kleenex. When he spoke, she looked up.

"Ma'am I hope you don't mind my eavesdropping, but that was beautiful. Not many people would have done what you did. If you don't mind me doing this, I would like to refund your money for this ride. I'd also like to take her and her date to their prom. Because I am an independent driver, I can do my own scheduling," he told her as he watched her through the mirror.

"Thank you, but why would you do that?" she asked him.

"Because I believe in service. I try and be supportive whenever I see a need. Your generosity had brought mine out," he told her, as Sandy opened the door and sat down.

She nodded to him, and he looked ahead. They rode in silence for a minute, and Sandy turned to her with sad eyes.

"When...when did you and Kareem do this?" she asked her softly.

"He had me start the fund a week before he was killed. Initially, it was started for your ten-year vow renewal, but he told me if anything happened to him before that to switch it for Monica."

"Oh," was all she said before she fell into her best friend's arms and cried. All these years Sandy kept up this strong front when it came to Kareem. She never wanted Shontell or Monica to see her hurting. She thought that was the way it had to be. Monica was a daddy's girl in every sense of the word. Kareem had spoiled her. But he spoiled her too with his love and attention. He was a good husband. When Kareem died, she thought her world was crumbling. She resorted to taking Valium. That little pill took her to a painless place. But then the effects wore off, and she needed more. When did she get addicted to the pills? She couldn't remember. It took one huge episode to wake her up, though. One day she left Monica at school for hours, and the school had to call Shontell to come and get her. Monica stayed with

Shontell for six weeks, while Sandy checked into a clinic for treatment. Now she wouldn't take anything for pain, unless it was absolutely needed. Monica was the reason she fought so hard. They were lucky to have Shontell in their corner. She always looked out for her and Monica. Wiping her eyes, she sat up as the driver pulled up to the departure gate doors at Detroit Metro Airport. She hoped her eyes didn't look puffy. The driver handed their bags over to the check-in agent. Shontell gave him a fifty dollar tip, and he gave her his business card. It was so good to know that there were people out there who are still kind-hearted. Once they boarded the plane, Sandy grabbed Shontell's hands. "Thank you for everything…Monica…this vacation…thank you."

"We have each other's back always. You don't have to thank me. I love you."

"I know, I know. But I needed to tell you. We have both been in some dark areas, but because we stuck together we saw the light," she told her. Sandy laid her head on her shoulders and was out cold within a few minutes. Shontell looked out the window at the clouds. If she was a writer, she would have a best-seller on her hands if she were to describe the last few days. She sighed and was ready for this flight to be over. She wanted to be in Nico's arms. That would make her feel better. Putting her ear buds in her ear, she hit the button on her iPod. Before she knew it, they were landing. She had never been to Miami. It looked beautiful.

Shontell and Sandy headed towards the baggage claim and were surprised to see a chauffeur standing by the carousel with their names on a sign. They smiled, thinking that must have been Nico that set this up.

"Girl, I think I can get used to you dating Nico if it's going to be like this. Jesse never sent a driver for us...I mean you," Sandy said, trying to be funny. She swatted at her arm and then signaled to the driver. He immediately came over and grabbed their suitcases they had pulled off the belt.

"Yeah, you're right about that. See, that's what scares me about Nico. He is so different from Jesse and from all the other men I have dated before."

"Then you take that difference and add to it. If anyone deserves it, you do. Promise me you won't push him away because it's so new to you." Shontell didn't reply to her friend's comment, but she had said out loud what she had been trying not to worry about. She didn't think that she would deliberately push him away. She had to learn how to let go and let the situation blossom. Sandy continued chatting away as both ladies followed behind the driver.

While he was placing their bags in the trunk, the ladies took several pictures and selfies together. The Miami heat felt good on her skin. This was a climate that she could get used to. It was March, so the weather was going in like a lion and supposed to come out like a lamb. In Detroit that was always up for interpretation, but it was not unusual to see snow in April. Sandy squished her nose up at the guy who walked past as he tried to grab her hand. Sandy stepped back. They both started laughing. So it began — the crazy antics of Sandy. It was like she attracted the strangest behavior from strange men. The chauffeur put the last of their bags in the trunk, as they quickly snapped a few more pictures. The driver told them that he was ready. He opened the door for them. Shontell slid into the seat and was surprised to see Nico sitting in the back. He looked as handsome as ever in shorts and a tee. He smiled when he saw her.

"Hi, ladies. How was the flight?" He immediately grabbed Shontell's hand.

"Nico, what are you doing here?" she asked as she scooted closer to him.

"Meeting my girl," he said as he squeezed her hand and she winked at him.

"Your girl, huh?" Sandy asked as she watched them both blush. Sandy noticed how Shontell's face lit up when she saw him sitting there. He handed both of them flowers, as he then leaned over and kissed Shontell on the lips. She wanted to kiss him again, but then she remembered that Sandy was with them. She opted for holding his hand again instead, as she laced her fingers with his. They all talked comfortably as they rode to the hotel. They pulled up in front of the Westin in Miami about twenty minutes later. The hotel was beautiful. It was set right off the beach, and the sidewalks were filled with people walking and enjoying the beautiful day. They all got out, and the driver unloaded their luggage. He handed their bags to the bellhop. He, in turn, told the ladies they were already checked in and handed them their key cards.

"Wow, really?" she said, looking at Nico.

"Yes, y'all got it like that. Sandy, I want you to enjoy your birthday. As my gift, I have set you ladies up for a spa renewal for the next three hours. Felecia will be joining you two as well. She insisted. Hope that's okay," he said.

"Seriously?" Sandy began dancing. "It's my birthday...it's my birthday!" They all laughed.

"Oh, and yes, it's cool about Felecia. We enjoy her company. Where is she?"

"Great. She is up in the room. I told her I would call when we got back." He pulled out his phone and called Felecia. He watched Shontell. He loved seeing her smile. She looked radiant.

"Okay, sweetness. Please enjoy yourself. I have to get going. We were initially off, but we're called to do a last-minute rehearsal due to a couple of changes. Once you ladies come down, Brian will be out here waiting for you. He will bring you over to where we will be afterwards." Shontell hugged him and whispered, "Thank you." He winked at her and kissed her hand.

"Anything I can do to see that smile...I would do in a heartbeat." This time Shontell didn't care if Sandy was there. She kissed him on the lips again, and their kiss went on for a few seconds. Nico broke the kiss and stepped backwards to the car. Shontell waved goodbye to Nico, as he got back into the car with Brian. She looped her arm through her best friend's and they crossed the lobby. Shontell wasn't surprised to see that Tina was in the lounge area, sitting with an older man. Tina gave her a toxic smile and went back to her suitor. The women went to their room — which looked more like a suite — to get ready for their spa treatments. Shontell plopped onto the bed and fanned herself. She was counting down in her head when Sandy would ask the question — 4...3...2...she counted in her head.

"Okay, so who was that woman in the lobby that was glaring at you?

"I knew you didn't miss that. That was the infamous Tina — Nico's ex that I was telling you about."

"What?! What the heck is she doing here?" she asked, throwing her sandals to the floor and grabbing her waiting robe.

"Your guess is as good as mine. I am sure it's to cause waves between me and Nico," she told her.

"Well, I hope she ain't stupid enough to step your way. I didn't come here to fight, but you know I got your back." She was ready for a good showdown. It had been a long time since she gave somebody a "7 Mile and Meyers" ass whopping.

"I know you do. But I can handle her. I did notice something interesting. She had on a wedding ring, and so did the man she was sitting with," she told her, as she put her purse on the bed and started looking through it for makeup wipes.

"Really? I thought you said she wasn't married."

"It's the first I have seen it. It does give me an idea. You know how we do. Come on, let's finish getting ready," she told her, not giving Tina another thought.

"Okay, changing the subject. What are you going to do about Nico? You two look like more than just friends," she said, as she pinned her hair up.

"Yeah. That's a good question. I am going to listen to all the advice you and my parents gave me and see what it happens. I can't lie...it scares me," she admitted honestly. They put on their spa shoes and sat on the bed together.

"Shontell, you know I try not to give advice. I want you happy. And if you're happy with Nico, then go for it. Enjoy the ride you're going on with that man." Her best friend was being serious in a joking way. They heard Felecia knock on the door. They grabbed their bags, and the ladies went to get pampered for the next three hours.

Don't Mess With My Girl

Nico

Nico wiped the sweat off his face as they went over the new dance steps. They were also introducing unreleased music on the cruise. They wanted everyone to have a different concert experience than what they got at the usual concert venues. They were scheduled to perform six shows in the five days that they were cruising. They were all excited to be doing something different. Nico still wondered how he was going to bring up the limelight issue. He didn't see Shontell come in, but he felt her. The lights were bright on the stage, and he couldn't see the seats. He was glad that Felecia, Shontell, and Sandy were spending time together. She was always by herself when she came to the events, and David was always worried about that.

Martin clapped his hands loudly and they all stopped. Nico leaned over and had his hands on his knees. He was tired because the rehearsals were long, and he felt his clothes sticking to him. He grabbed a bottle of water and downed it. He grabbed a towel from the staff member and he wiped his face. He and the others went down the stairs towards the seats, and he smiled as he saw how beautiful Shontell looked. She wore little makeup, and she had her hair braided. She had it pinned up with a few braids hanging. He walked over to her and greeted her, being careful not to touch her with his sweaty clothes and body.

"How was the spa?"

"It was great. Thank you again for doing that; it was needed."

"Yeah, I figured as much. I had a massage before you got here, and it helped me. Let me go shower, and then we can head out. I have a surprise for you."

"Oh, do you?" He winked at her, as he left her standing there.

Shontell

Shontell filled Sandy and Felecia in on her plan about Tina while they were at the spa. Felecia agreed immediately.

She was tired of the woman and the way she was acting. Shontell couldn't understand why Tina would keep her being married from Nico. Shontell, Sandy, and Felecia talked excitedly about the massages and the other special treatment they had gotten. Shontell had not felt this relaxed in a long time. Riding the elevator, they went over the plan they put in place. Now all they needed was for them to see the man Tina was with earlier.

Shontell was switching shoes when the driver, Brian, called to say he was pulling up in about five minutes. Walking out of the room, they all headed to meet the waiting car. In the lobby, they scanned the area. Sandy tapped her shoulder when she spotted him. Looking out front, she saw Brian pull up, open the door, and look in their direction. "Can you guys stall Brian, while I see what I can find out?" Shontell asked her friends.

"Okay, go ahead. But don't be too long," Felecia told her as she and Sandy hurried out to the car. Looking around to make sure she didn't see Tina anywhere, she walked in his direction. The gentleman he was sitting with had gotten up; she pretended to drop her glasses. He reached down and picked them up before she could. Quickly turning on her recorder, she waited until he handed her glasses back.

"Thank you. That's an unusual diamond-cut ring you're wearing. I was thinking of getting my fiancé something like that. Where did you get it?" she asked him, as she stood straight up. She was making small talk with him, so he could get comfortable.

"Well, my wife, Tina, gave it to me on our third wedding anniversary last week. So I would have to ask her," he told her, as his face lit up when he mentioned her name. She instantly felt sorry for him, because she knew how low-down his wife was.

"Oh, okay. You must really love her. I couldn't help but notice how your face lit up." The man blushed, and Shontell extended her hand. "I am Shon, and you are?"

"Robert Forrester."

"Robert Forrester? That name sounds familiar; do you have any affiliation with the jewelry store, Forrester Jewels?" she asked him with her eyes wide.

"I am the owner," he told her proudly. Oh, this was getting better than she had anticipated.

"Wow, I love your pieces," she told him.

"Thank you. Here's my card. Come on in, and I will take good care of you," he told her. Shontell realized she was running out of time. He looked at his watch and at the elevator. Oh crap, was he expecting Tina? "Well, I don't want to take up too much of your time. But, oh…by the way…we are getting together this evening. Can I have my friend meet you in the bar? She is helping me with a ring selection for my fiancé, so if she could get a glimpse of your pieces, it would speed of the process."

"Young lady, you're actually in luck. I was down here for a showing, so I do have new pieces with me. I can bring them."

"Oh my goodness, that is awesome. Okay, I will have her meet you around 7:30 p.m. Is that a good time?"

"It is. What is her name?"

"Sandy. It was nice meeting you, Robert." Shontell told him. She was glad the plan was coming together as she waved and quickly walked to the car. Apologizing to Brian, she got into the car as he closed the door behind her. Both ladies were looking at her expectantly.

"What happened?" Felecia asked literally sitting on the edge of the seat. She laughed softly.

"He is a sweetheart. I feel so sorry for him," Shontell told them.

"Well, don't you think it's better if he finds out now?" Sandy said.

"True. But I did learn something interesting. She is married to Robert Forrester," Shontell said.

"OMG! I knew he looked familiar," Sandy yelled. Her wedding ring, which was a Forrester original, was in her safe at home.

"Speaking of that; Sandy, I need you to meet him in the bar at 7:30. He thinks you are helping me surprise my fiancé." Both ladies looked at her and smiled in response to her comment, which caused Shontell to blush. They finished discussing the plan, just as Brian pulled up to the rehearsal location. Getting out, Shontell and her friends headed inside. The music could be heard clearly when they opened the door. Felecia and Sandy walked up near the stage. Shontell decided to stay towards the back. She watched Nico dance. It was awesome. She never would have thought she would be in this place. Martin ended the rehearsal, and she got up and walked towards the stage. Nico walked in her direction, and she instantly smiled.

"You are sweaty," she told him, wrinkling her nose.

"I know. I will be back in a few after I shower and then we can head back to the hotel," he told her as John came over and wrapped his arm around Nico. He was also sweaty. She backed away from them, and they all laughed. She looked over at Sandy, who was having a sidebar conversation with Dennis. She looked like she was actually listening to what he had to say. Shontell wasn't comfortable with that. She sat down and waited on Sandy to finish. A few minutes later, she joined her.

"What was that about?" she asked her, nodding in Dennis' direction

"Oh nothing. He was being nosey and asking about Eric," she told her nonchalantly. Shontell wasn't sure she believed that. She hoped Sandy wasn't going to fall under his wretchedness. She was about to ask another question when she saw Nico and the rest of the group coming towards them. David grabbed Felecia's hand and Nico put his arms around her and Sandy, as they all headed towards the exit to return to the hotel.

The group all walked into the hospitality lounge together. Within minutes, the food was being served and the conversations and laughter were ongoing. Shontell watched as Sandy and Dennis talked. She tried not to be upset, but she was. Nico noticed her mood.

"What's wrong?" he asked her rubbing his hand along her bare arm. She instantly felt the little sparks his touch gave off. Shontell hesitated before responding, taking her eyes off her friend. Nico glanced where she was looking. He frowned.

"Now that's interesting. When did they get so chummy?"

"I don't know, and I am trying to not to think the worst," she told him as she sipped her water. The waiter was about to place a plate in front of her and Nico, when he asked him not to.

"We are heading out of here in a few," he told him. Shontell looked over at him, and her mood changed as she saw the mischievous sparkle in his eye.

"What's that look for?" she asked, nudging him.

"Nothing…nothing…" he said laughing. They were interrupted by Martin, who said he needed him for a second. Nico excused himself. She looked down at her watch, noting that it was 7:25 p.m.

"Sandy, can you grab Felecia so we can go to the ladies room?" she asked her friend, interrupting her conversation. Sandy stopped talking, looked at her, remembered what they needed to do, and nodded her head. Shontell stood up and stepped back from the table. Dennis was watching her. She smirked.

"I am not sure what you are up to, but remember your own words. Don't hurt her…because I won't be as nice as I have been," she told him softly. Dennis did a double take at her words, but said nothing. She walked out of the hospitality suite towards the restrooms. A couple of minutes later, she was joined by Felecia and Sandy. Felecia brought up what she was thinking.

"So I see you and Dennis are getting a little cozy," she commented as she applied her lipstick. Sandy turned the water on and washed her hands. She had not replied to Felecia's comment.

"Girl, I am cautiously checking him out. I don't have any real interest in him. Unlike you two, I don't and won't date industry men. They are too much for my blood," she finally told her as she went to dry her hands off. Shontell didn't comment. She straightened her hair.

"If you say so. But he is a smooth talker, so be careful."

"Yeah, I will. Eric will be here tomorrow, so no worries," she told her. "I am heading to the bar and will see you ladies in a few." Both women watched her walk out of the restroom. Felecia spoke first. "So what do you think about that?"

"I don't know. I will be glad when Eric gets here," she told her as she closed her lip gloss tube.

"Yeah, I have to agree. I love my brother-in-law, but I don't like him much. He has a way of getting under your skin...and not in a good way," she told her. They both laughed.

Shontell and Felecia walked out and saw Sandy talking to Robert. *Good. He showed. Now let's hope the rest of this goes according to plan*, she thought to herself. Walking back into the hospitality lounge, Shontell noticed that Tina was all in Nico's face. He didn't look happy. She looked around for Dennis, hoping he wasn't looking in her direction. But he was talking to one of the band members. She tapped Felecia and pointed in Nico and Tina's direction.

They walked over, and Tina's chipper facial expression changed. Shontell looped her arm through Nico's.

"Hey, Tina," Shontell said dryly. Tina didn't speak back, but her facial expression spoke volumes. She wanted to laugh out loud. Out the corner of her eye, she saw Sandy walk in with Robert. Dennis made a beeline in their direction. That movement caught her off guard for a moment. Felecia saw the same thing, gave her a look, and quickly went into plan motion.

"That's a beautiful dress you have on," Felecia complimented her, and Tina turned in her direction. Her smile was the first one since they walked over.

"Oh hey, Felecia. How have you been girl? It's been awhile," Tina stated as they gave each other a fake hug.

"That color looks good on you. Where did you get the dress?" Felecia inquired. Tina touched her dress. "I got this from a little boutique over in Paris," she bragged.

"Oh really. Did your husband buy it for you?" Shontell interrupted to ask Tina. The whole room suddenly fell quiet. Tina's eyes got big as she looked at Nico and then back at her.

"Husband? What are you talking about? I am not married," she said, with her shaking voice revealing that she was starting to get uncomfortable. Tina's emotions flashed on her face. She immediately got defensive. She pointed in Shontell's face as she spoke to her.

"You bitch...do you really think Nico is going to stay with you? He loves me and always will. You aren't me."

"Thank goodness for that," Shontell said to cut her off. She saw Sandy react. She shook her head to let her know she had it.

"Tina, I am going to give you that one. But I advise you not to disrespect me one more time."

"What are you going to do?" Tina laughed in her face. She still was in her personal space, and Shontell was trying to be calm. She felt Nico come up behind her.

"Tina, walk away."

"Nico, why are you doing this? Tell her what happened last night."

"Last night?" he said, confused.

"Yes...in your room...champagne...us," she stated matter-of-factly. Nico laughed because he realized that she was crazy. He was glad that he kept Shontell on the call last night. Tina didn't care who she hurt.

"That's funny, because if it was you and him last night, then it was a threesome. I was on the phone the entire time." Tina's mouth fell open. They all heard steps coming from behind them in the quietness of the room. Tina turned around, and her mouth fell open as she saw Sandy, Robert, and Dennis coming towards them. Nico took Shontell's hand and looked at her. Shontell squeezed his hand, and he pointed to Robert.

"Aren't you Robert Forrester? What are you doing here?" Nico asked. Before Robert could answer, Shontell spoke up.

"He is here because I asked him to show you his jewelry line. But what I actually wanted to do was expose Ms. Thing here. They are married!" she told Nico, and the room sounded with audible gasps. Robert's hurt expression was clear. He looked at his ring and turned to Tina. She shifted her weight under his stare.

"You told me that you were over Nico. Why did you lie? How could you stand here and say all those things like I don't even exist. I can't believe you have been using me...that the last three years of this marriage have been based on a lie," Robert spoke to her softly. Robert took his ring off, rolled it over in his hand, and then dropped the ring from his hand and walked out the room. Tina blinked, but was frozen in her spot. Dennis walked towards her and she glared at him hard.

"You did this! You ruined my marriage all because you didn't want them together. I am so stupid. I can't stand you!" Tina spat at him, as she bent down to pick up the ring that Robert dropped. Running towards the door, she called out to her husband as he walked out the door.

The room remained still, as everyone was now staring at Dennis. Shontell cocked her head to the side.

"What did I do to you?" Shontell asked him, trying to understand Tina's departing comment.

"Yes, what did she do to you? I was so hoping that you weren't the reason Tina came back around. Didn't you learn your lesson the last time?" Nico inquired, as he got in his face. Shontell wiped the tear on her face away. Sandy walked over to Dennis and slapped him across the face. "That's for what my best friend won't do. I can't believe I was stupid enough to think you were a decent guy," she told him.

"Shontell, I am going to the room." Grabbing her purse, she headed out. Martin walked in their direction. He had a deep frown on his face. "Okay, everybody, let's go on back to what we were doing. This is over." David took his wife's hand, and they went to sit back down. Within seconds, everyone else but the four of them remained where they were.

FORGIVE AND FORGET?

Nico

Nico looked at his friend, and for the first time he didn't know who he was. He laughed slightly to fight his building anger. He knew that if Shontell was not there, this would have turned out a lot worse.

"I can't believe you would rather see me alone and miserable than to see me with love and happiness. You truly need to seek some help," he told him.

"Come on, Shontell. I really need some air now."

"Nico, man," Dennis said. Nico didn't turn around. Shontell looked at Dennis and shook her head. She never would have thought he would have done something like this. Nico looked over to where David and Felecia were and saw that she was speaking softly to her husband. He wanted to grab him and choke him. Martin nodded in his direction, and he took Shontell's hand and led her toward the lobby.

Dennis

Dennis felt ashamed. Why did he do this? He didn't want to hurt Nico. Seeing the look on his, David, and John's faces, he knew this wasn't going to be a good thing. He had let himself and the others down. Dennis watched them walk away and wished he could say something to help make the situation go away.

Martin came up on the side of him, handing him a glass of water.

"Let's walk," he told him. He knew that he would not be let off so easily, and he deserved whatever else was coming his way. He followed behind Martin and knew that whatever this was, it wouldn't be good. But he deserved it. He hurt the people he loved; Nico, David, Martin. His face still felt the sting of the slap from Sandy. All chances he had with her are gone, he thought. Was it all worth it? Absolutely not. He wished he could turn back the hands of time to erase that look that he saw on Robert's face. He didn't deserve to be hurt. Even if Tina was a willing participant, he was an innocent bystander. This was all a huge mess…even worse than the last time. He sat down in the chair that Martin pointed to and waited.

Shontell tried to keep up with Nico, who was walking very fast. She knew that he was mad, so she let him have his moment. But she was too. She still never got her question answered. Why did Dennis dislike her? Was it all because he didn't want to see Nico in love? When she couldn't catch up to him, she called out to him. He stopped and waited for her to catch up.

"Wow, you can really walk," she said in an effort to lighten the mood.

"I am sorry. That was rude of me," he said, kissing her on the forehead.

"I am sorry for my part in all this. But Tina was trying me. She was getting under my skin." She looked at him with sad eyes. Robert's face came into her mind.

"I don't blame you. I am sorry you felt the need to intervene. I failed in my attempt to not make her an issue," he told her, kissing her hand.

"I don't care about that. I am a grown woman and can handle women like Tina. I don't understand Dennis though. Why would he do all this, and what did you mean about not learning from the last time?" she asked. Nico paused and looked like he was trying to decide how to answer.

"When David and Felecia were engaged. Dennis arranged for an ex-girlfriend to sneak in his room when he was sleeping...naked in his bed. Felecia came to the room and found them that way. It was awful. It caused a lot of stress and tension in the group. I just can't believe he did this again."

"Oh my goodness," she said as she placed her hand over mouth.

"Yes, I know. I guess he has a huge issue with us being involved. But that is his problem, not mine," he said with a seriousness she had never seen before. She squeezed his hand. They continued to walk in silence for a few minutes.

"Are you going to be able to forgive him?" she asked him gently.

"Eventually, I guess. I am so hurt. His actions were insane. What if...what if he caused me to lose you?" He stroked her chin.

"I know. But you didn't. So let's enjoy the rest of the evening, please," she told him. She didn't want to think about all the drama. Shontell stopped and held onto Nico. She unhooked her sandals and put them in her hand. They continued walking. It was early evening and getting dark. But her feet were enjoying the feel of the sand that was still hot. Nico laughed at her facial expression. Their focus shifted to enjoying the swinging of their hands and the sound of the water.

"I keep pinching myself to make sure that this is all real."

"Really? Why is that?"

"Well, being here with you is like saying dreams do come true. I didn't think that that was possible, even for me."

"You don't think you deserve it?" he asked her quizzically.

"Of course every person deserves to be happy. But being with a person doesn't define happiness. That should come from within."

"I agree. How about this? Let me enhance your happiness. I will give you my word I will never hurt you intentionally." He pulled her into her embrace, wrapping his arms around her while they continued walking.

"I hear you talking...I hear you talking," she told him, enjoying the feel of him next to her. Shontell looked up and saw a gazebo that was surrounded by candles inside and out. She looked up at him, and her eyes welled up.

"Wow," she whispered. The waiter ushered them in.

"Do you like it?" Nico asked her, as he held the chair out for her.

"I love it. So, is this my surprise?" she asked him as she sat down, and took her napkin and placed it in her lap. The waiter poured them a glasses of champagne.

"Part of it. The evening is only at its beginning, and I am returning the favor." Nico tasted the liquid and nodded his approval to the waiter. The waiter told them that dinner would be served in three courses.

"So, Nico, are you sure you can handle a relationship?" Shontell asked him as she sipped the cold champagne. The bubbles tickled her throat as she swallowed.

"It will be hard with my schedule, but if you're willing, then I am willing. I will take the steps to make this work for us," he told her, taking her hand across the small table.

"You make me feel so many emotions. I feel like I've known you my whole life, and it's only been a short time."

"I know exactly what you mean." They made a toast and began their dinner.

Shontell watched Nico as they were served dinner. She was very surprised to see the waiter place a plate of her favorite food in front of her. There was salmon, asparagus, and baked sweet potato. She watched as he ate. She loved that he always seemed to enjoy his food. Shontell closed her eyes as a breeze hit their table and she could smell his cologne. She meant what she told him, and she felt like he was making her wildest dreams come true. He was making her feel things that Jesse never did, and she had been engaged to marry him. She shivered a little as she took a bite of her food.

"Are you cold?" Nico asked. He reached for his jacket, but she shook her head.

"Just a little, but I will be okay." She finished off her glass, and the waiter immediately poured a refill. She smiled.

"Okay, you can have my jacket if you need it," Nico replied, as he finished off his plate. Shontell looked at the ocean. The waves hitting the beach made a beautiful sound. She always loved it.

"So how did the rest of your week go?" Nico sat back as the waiter cleared their plates.

Shontell chuckled some before replying, because she didn't even want to rethink all that drama.

"The night is not long enough for me to recount my week. All I can say is that this break came at the right time. My business partner, Ebony, has been acting very weird lately. I found out something about her that not only shocked me, but also hurt me. I will be looking to dissolve the partnership when we get back. I don't want to spend the night rehashing all that. It's my problem, not yours." Shontell wasn't ready to tell him about Jesse's visits…not yet anyway.

"Shontell, you can talk to me about anything. Please know that; if it's important to you, then it is important to me." He took her hand and squeezed it. His words meant a lot to her. She smiled, and they continued dinner. In the middle of their dessert, music came on from out of nowhere. It made her smile, because it was all her favorite music.

"How did you know?" she asked Nico, as he smiled back at her.

Nico

Nico didn't answer her right away, but he had done some research on Shontell from an interview she did. He made sure he knew what her favorite artists, scents, and food were. He wanted to make this time about her as much as he could. He needed her to understand that this was for real. Right before the waiter cleared their dessert, he slightly motioned to the waiter to indicate that the time was right for Shontell's next surprise. Soon music began to play louder than the original music, and he stood and bowed.

"Would you give me the honor of this dance?" Shontell blushed and took his hand. He loved the way she felt in his arms.

"I love this song," she said, as she hummed the intro to Tamia's *You Put a Move on My Heart*.

"She is one of my favorite female artists, but I guess you knew that."

"Yes, I did." As he was answering her, Shontell heard a female voice singing even louder, and her eyes got wide. She turned around and saw Tamia, walking on the beach towards them and bellowing the song out. She stood to the left of them as they continued to dance.

"I can't believe you did this. You are simply amazing." She was trying to hide her tears. They danced to another song, as Tamia continued to serenade them. When she finished, they stopped dancing and applauded. Tamia came over to them, giving a hug first to Shontell and then to Nico.

"You must be one special woman," Tamia told Shontell, as she winked at her. Nico laughed, and then he whispered something into Tamia's ear. She laughed back at him.

"I love it!" Tamia said to Nico. Tamia took pictures with them and then said her goodbyes.

"Are you ready to go back to the hotel?" he asked her as he hugged her hard. She loved the feeling he gave her. She wrapped her arms around his neck tighter, kissing him full on the lips.

"No, I am too excited. Do you mind if we walk the beach?" she finally asked him.

"Not at all. Let me finish up with the waiter, and we can go," he told her as he addressed the man who had served them all evening. Shontell rubbed her arms, easing her goose bumps.

Shontell turned around as Nico placed his jacket on her shoulders. The moon was so bright. They started walking, and she slowly exhaled. For the longest time, Shontell always felt that all she needed was her work. It helped with the pain. After the betrayal by Jesse, that is what she thought she needed. She purposely didn't date because she didn't want the heartache. As Sandy had tried to drill it into her, she knew that she couldn't fault the next man for Jesse's cheating. But it did make her feel inadequate...like she wasn't enough for him or any other man. Now she would find that out. She heard Nico's voice, and it cut into her thoughts.

"You okay? You're very quiet." She turned towards him and nodded her head to say "yes."

"What's that?" Shontell asked, as she pointed to the basket he was holding.

"Oh, this is a little end-of-the-night surprise," he said, holding it open and moving it back as Shontell tried to see inside. She wrinkled her nose.

"Seriously, haven't you surprised me enough today?" she said, getting off her tippy toes.

"If I have my way, every day with you would be filled with surprises. I want to find different ways to make you smile." She blushed and said nothing. What could she say? Is this what it felt like to be literally swept off your feet? They were holding hands as they walked past a group of partiers. They were both glad that for once, Nico wasn't recognized. They came across a small cove and stopped. He opened the basket, taking a blanket out and spreading it. He set the basket down and helped her sit. She held onto her knees as Nico emptied out the rest of the contents onto the blanket. He had a small radio, candles, wine, and fruit. She was impressed. She could not believe she was being courted. Nico laid back, and Shontell cuddled next to him. They watched the waves hitting the rocks as the music played softly. Nico dipped a strawberry in the chocolate and fed it to her. They spent the next couple of hours talking and laughing, as they finished off the bottle of wine. It was nearly 3 a.m. when they finally decided to head back to the hotel.

Nico

Nico held the door open to the hotel, as he and Shontell shared a laugh about the people they saw as they walked back to the hotel. Miami was in full swing. When they stepped on the elevator, he looked at Shontell. She was yawning slightly as she covered her mouth. She saw him watching her and smiled.

"I'm sorry. I guess that I am a little more tired than I thought. It seems that all this excitement now has me spent."

"Yes, I can definitely relate. Do you mind staying with me tonight?" he asked her, silently holding his breath.

"Sure, if you don't mind me going into my room first and changing." That seemed to have become a normal ritual with them. Nico figured that she wasn't ready yet to shower and dress with him, and he was fine with that. He wanted her to be comfortable.

"Not at all," he said as he handed her the extra room key. They got off the elevator and headed in opposite directions. He quickly showered and got into bed, waiting for her to return. Within a few minutes, he heard the door.

Shontell walked into the suite and then entered the bedroom area. She was wearing a peach nightie with a robe to match, and her hair was still pinned up. She turned around in model fashion.

"You like?"

He cleared his throat and looked at her with desire in his eyes. He quickly thought he had made a mistake by asking her to stay the night. She looked so sensual and sexy. He was reminded of how thick she was when he saw her in the nightgown. He made a sound that was only audible to himself and hoped that she didn't pull the covers back. He would be exposed. He was completely turned on. He finally spoke.

"You look beautiful," he told her, hoping she could see the desire in his eyes.

"Why, thank you," she told him. She stepped out of her shoes and started walking towards the bed. Nico pulled the covers back slightly.

Taking off her robe, she crawled into the bed with him. Nico pulled her closer to him and kissed her deeply, and he heard her moan as he ran his hands up her sides. The gown felt smooth in his hands, and it made his member grow. He wanted to touch her skin, but he reminded himself that they were taking baby steps.

He rolled her onto her side and broke their kiss. Her eyes were glazed with desire, and her body was slightly begging him to touch her. She touched his bare chest and ran her fingernails up and down his chest and stomach. She never broke eye contact with him, as she read his quiet turmoil of thoughts. She kissed him on the cheek, and he shifted so she could lay her head on his chest. He was glad she could read his thoughts. He wasn't sure he could voice what he was thinking. Having her this close was pure intoxication. Nico closed his eyes and once again told himself that he was doing the right thing. They both fell asleep.

Shontell

Shontell watched Nico sleep. She touched his face and smiled. Nico smiled and grabbed her hand that was still on his cheek and kissed it.

"How long have you been awake?"

"Not long. My internal clock never lets me sleep past 6 a.m., even on vacation. He pulled her into his arms and they spooned in silence for the next hour. Shontell had never experienced such mental lovemaking and intimacy in her entire life. Her cell phone beeped, and she knew it was probably Sandy.

"I guess it's time for me to go back to my room. I know Sandy wants to shop before we board."

"Okay, we have a breakfast meeting and I need to do something for my parents. They will be here around 5 p.m. (don't see anything wrong with five this evening). Actually, all of our parents are coming." Shontell looked at him a little terrified. Was he going to ask her to meet his parents? She was sure she would eventually have to, because the cruise was five days long.

"Shontell, don't worry. They will love you. If it makes you feel better, I can introduce you as a friend so you won't feel pressured."

"Okay. I guess when we decided on trying this friendship, meeting your parents never crossed my mind," she told him, as she propped herself up on her elbows.

"It's going to be okay, I promise. Come give me a kiss, so I can let you out this room before your best friend comes after me," he said as they both heard her phone beep for the third time. They shared a hug and a brief kiss before he walked her to the door.

TEST OF LOVE

Nico

Nico wondered if he should have mentioned his parents. He saw how her demeanor changed. He knew it was more than likely too soon. But, didn't he already meet her father? He was tough. He smiled and reassured himself that it would be fine. Then Nico's cell phone rang. He smiled as he answered.

"Good Morning, Mom. No, you didn't wake me. How are you? Dad? Are you at the airport?"

"We are good. Yes, we got here. Your father and Nate just went and got some coffee. So we should be getting into Miami on time. Nate said the driver's coming."

"Yes, Mom, he will be there. I will see you all when you get on the boat. Don't forget about the early dinner on the ship," he told her, as he pulled his clothes out of his suitcase. Nico talked to his mom for a few more minutes and then went to get dressed. He was getting excited about the cruise. He reached the meeting area. The breakfast food smell hit him, and his stomach growled. He headed towards the food line with the others. David walked up to him and spoke.

"So, how did Shontell like your surprise?"

"She loved it. Thanks for hooking me up with the gazebo idea."

"No problem. If she makes you happy, then you know I got your back. You know I am still tripping out on last night. I felt like he did that crap all over again to me last night. But at the end of the day, he is my blood," David told him, looking like he felt on the inside. He finished fixing his plate and then waited on David.

Nico looked at his brother, and he knew that what he said was right. Although Dennis wasn't his blood, he was still his brother. He didn't want to think about this anymore. David, on the other hand, had been such a strong influence and guidance for him lately. His love with Felecia encouraged him to pursue Shontell. They walked towards a table a couple of seats away from everyone else. Sitting down, they said grace and started to eat.

"Listen, David, I just wanted to say thank you for helping me with all this. I feel like a clueless teenager around Shontell."

"Sounds like someone is in love," he said, as he patted him on his arm.

"Wow, love?" he hadn't thought he would associate that word with himself again.

"Yeah, wow. That's what I was thinking too." They were laughing, talking, and joking around when Dennis walked over. David looked between the men and then nodded for him to have a seat. Neither man spoke.

"I owe you both an apology. I...I never thought any of this would happen," he started, but Nico interrupted him.

"What the hell did you think would happen when you play with fire, Dennis??? You get burned." Nico pushed his plate away. He had lost his appetite. He was about to get up and leave when David grabbed his wrist.

"Nico, sit down...please," David said softly. Nico sat back down, folding his arms and not looking at Dennis or David.

"Dennis, this time an apology won't solve this. You may have caused a marriage to end with your selfishness.

You also could have caused Nico to lose Shontell, like you almost caused me to lose Felecia. Don't you understand that, no matter what, we are a unit? All four of us are brothers. Our being in love won't take that away!" David told him, as he looked him straight in the face.

"I understand that now. Nico, I am not expecting you or Shontell to forgive me. But I am genuinely sorry," he told him, as he got up and walked away. Nico looked at David and knew they would not mention this again. It was done with.

"So where are Shontell and Sandy?" David asked as Felecia came over and joined them. She kissed her husband and took a bite of his sausage. David smiled at her while he started wiping her mouth with his napkin. Nico watched them in amusement.

"Shontell said something about Sandy wanting to go shopping before boarding. So, I assume they are getting ready for that."

Felecia pulled out her cell phone. "Nico, can you give me her number? I didn't save it in my phone yet. I'm going to see if I can join them." David groaned and slumped his shoulders. Nico gave her Shontell's number. She held her hand out for his credit card and kissed him again, telling them both goodbye. Nico could hear her talking to Shontell about meeting them in the lobby in fifteen minutes.

She looked back over her shoulder and she spoke to her husband. "Kiss your mother for me." She waved, and then she was gone. Both men looked at each other and then burst out laughing. Felecia loved to shop, but she spent his money and hers equally. Her design business was taking off, and her label was now becoming a household name on the east coast.

Shontell and the ladies spent the last three hours shopping. Now they were headed towards the cruise ship, laughing and talking. They had a ball shopping. Their instincts about Felecia were right, because she fit right in with Shontell and Sandy's quirkiness. Her excitement seemed to be boiling over. It was short lived, as she looked over the passengers and thought she saw a familiar face in the crowd. She had to be seeing things. Ebony couldn't be on this ship. She looked in the same direction again and didn't see her. Maybe her eyes were playing tricks on her. They say everyone has a twin. The ladies must have noticed her silence and asked her was she okay.

"Yeah, I am okay. I thought I saw someone I knew."

"Girl, on this cruise you probably will know someone. It seems to be packed."

"True, but the one person I wouldn't expect to see is Ebony," she told her as she continued to look at the passengers.

"Ebony!" Sandy shouted. Felecia looked at her friends in confusion and asked, "Who is Ebony?"

"Ebony is my business partner. She should be back in Detroit. Maybe I didn't see what I thought I did. When I looked again, I didn't see her in the same area."

"Well let's not worry about something we can't prove at the moment," Sandy told her. She saw her best friend visibly relax. She looked around again and hoped that she was right. It was probably someone who looked like Ebony. That woman was up to something, and she would end up in jail before she let another person hurt her friend. The steward gave them their room assignments, and the women headed in that direction. They were talking a mile a minute about the celebrities they had already spotted. Felecia hugged the ladies and agreed to meet them in a few hours for dinner. They were escorted to their room. The bellman opened the suite door, and the two women followed him in. They stood in awe at how it looked. After tipping the bellman, they walked around the huge room.

"Yeah…a girl can definitely get used to this," Sandy said, as she went to the table and admired the fruit, wine, and cheese. She picked up the note and read it out loud.

"Ladies, a complimentary gift. Enjoy your trip." It was signed by all the members of the group. The suite had two bedrooms, and it seemed they were already marked with luggage.

"Sandy, I didn't want to bring this up in front of Felecia, but how are you, about what happened last night with Dennis?" she asked, as Sandy began to hang up some of her dresses. She couldn't see her face, so she waited.

"At first, I was hurt. But then, I realized I didn't have a reason to be. Dennis had me fooled. I thought maybe...maybe we could start a friendship," she said, shaking her head.

"And now?" Shontell asked her. Sandy came and sat next to her on the couch.

"Now I will just have some fun with Eric. I knew there was a reason I didn't mess with entertainers. I will leave that up to you. You and Nico are good together," she told her, placing her hands over her friend's hands. Standing, she kicked her shoes off and went and got her sandals. Watching her friend, she said nothing. She needed to relax.

"If you are sure you are okay, I am about to soak in this jacuzzi before we go down. I need to get some of this tension off me," Shontell told Sandy.

"Okay, I'm going down to see the ship off and find Eric. I will catch you in a little bit," she told her, as they quickly hugged and Sandy walked out the room.

Shontell walked into her bedroom and immediately was assaulted by the smell of flowers. On her bed were two dozen purple roses, lilies, and orchids. She picked them up and inhaled. She found a vase in the bathroom and arranged the flowers. There was also a note on her bed. She opened it and smiled. *Shontell, if I forgot to say it, I will say it now: Thank you. Thank you for giving me the chance to be a part of your life. Nico.* Shontell pressed the note to her heart and held back the tears. How was this possible? How did she find this man that erased all the bad love she had, with just his sentiments? She exhaled and went to run her bath. She turned on the jets. She got in the hot water and closed her eyes. She was thinking over the last few weeks and shaking her head. She didn't even realize that she had fallen asleep until she heard a male's voice. She opened her eyes and she saw Nico kneeling over her. "Nico! What...what are you doing in here?" she asked. She sat up and then became aware that her breasts were in his view. She realized that she was naked, and she grabbed her towel.

"I'm sorry. I was worried about you. I tried calling and texting you, but I didn't get a reply. I saw Sandy downstairs, and she told me you were still in the room," he told her. He tried not to stare, but the sight of her wet body was compelling. Shontell looked down and then back at Nico.

"I didn't bring my phone in here, but I also didn't plan on falling asleep. I didn't mean to worry you."

"Can you meet me in the room? I will be out in a minute."

"Of course," he told her, as he left her in the bathroom.

Nico

Nico chided himself for just walking into her room. When she didn't respond, he naturally reacted since that wasn't her character. He shook his head, trying to get the vision of her wet, chocolate skin out of his mind. He willed his body not to react. He walked over to the balcony and watched as they began to set sail. Nico's parents were already down in the private dining area, eating the early dinner as were the rest of the group's family and friends. Everyone was there but Shontell, so he told his parents that he would be back, and he went to look for her.

"Nico, can you help me with this zipper?" Shontell asked, coming out the bathroom. She was fully dressed in a purple, strapless sundress that hugged her body. He zipped her up and then kissed her bare shoulder.

"Mm," she moaned slightly. "I see we aren't behaving," she said while giving him a wink.

"Actually, I am. Trust me, I am. Everyone's down in the private dining room eating dinner. Shall we join them?"

"Yes, but can you give me about five minutes to finish getting ready?"

"Indeed," he said as she turned on her Pandora and music filled the room. Nico began to hum, *Chill Tonight by Boyz II Men*. By the end of the song, Shontell came out of the room and joined him. She looked stunning. She came over to him and kissed him.

"Thank you for the flowers and the beautiful note. You sure know how to make a woman smile."

"As long as that woman is you, then I will completely oblige," he told her, grabbing her baby finger with his. He moved her to the door.

"Come on, I don't want a search party sent out for us," Nico said, as led them to the dining area. The room was abuzz, but it seemed everyone got quiet when they walked in. Shontell looked at Nico, and he knew she wanted to disappear.

"Hey, everyone...sorry for the delay," he told them all casually.

Nico and Shontell walked over and sat down. He saw her looking around nervously. He squeezed her hand, as the room once again began to come alive with laughing and conversation. Felecia was the first to say something.

"Shontell, you are working that dress. Where did you get it?" They both noticed how she relaxed as she answered Felecia's question.

"Sandy and I went to that new outlet mall when we were in Indiana last week."

"Oh, I am going to have to check that place out." They talked about a few other things as they were served their dinner plates like the rest. As they were finishing up, Nico noticed his mother and father getting up and coming over to their table. He whispered in Shontell's ear, "Here come my parents; just be you and it will be okay." Shontell nodded and smiled, as his mother approached her first. Shontell stood smiling at them both.

"You must be Shontell. I am Bethany, and this here is Nico Sr.," she said, gesturing towards her husband.

"Yes, I am, and it's a pleasure to meet you both." Shontell extended her hands to them both.

"Likewise, my dear. You're such a beautiful young lady." Shontell blushed and looked at Nico, who was smiling at all of them.

"Son, come walk us out. Your Mom wants to lie down for a bit. Shontell, it was nice meeting you. I am sure we will get to talk soon," Nico Sr. said to her. Nico excused himself, and Shontell sat back down as Nico walked his parents out the room.

"Nico, she seems lovely. Don't break her heart," his mother told him. He kissed her cheek.

"Mom, I won't break her heart," he told her as he let her go.

"We know you won't, son. We are proud of you. We're looking forward to relaxing and seeing you perform, and so we will see you later." Nico Sr. spoke for both of them, and he then guided his wife to their room. He watched them walk along the deck holding hands. He loved seeing his parents still so much in love. Turning back around, he walked back into the dining area. Nico watched Shontell talking to Felecia, Sandy, and the wife of one of the band members. Then he felt it...no, he knew it. David was right. He was in love.

The Girl With The Golden Pipes

Shontell

Shontell finished her glass of water and noticed Sandy was sitting with Eric. Dennis was watching them. He looked hurt. She felt bad for him. But he had only himself to blame, and now it was a lost cause. Catching Sandy's attention, she motioned for her to join her. Sandy got up and walked over to her in dramatic fashion. She instantly knew it was for show. She was letting Dennis know what he lost. Sandy sat down next to her.

"So, you met the parents. How was it?" she asked her, taking Shontell's wine glass and finishing off the liquid.

"Much better than I imagined," she told her as she watched Sandy with amusement.

"Yes, Mr. and Mrs. Baker are wonderful," Felecia interjected, as she and Gloria, the wife of the drummer, walked over and joined their conversation. The ladies' conversation quickly turned into their normal banter about men. Felecia suddenly stopped and looked in Eric's direction.

"So who is that fine man you are sitting with?" she asked Sandy. Sandy blushed, which was the first time she had done that since Kareem. "He is just a friend. We met in Indiana and hit it off. He is working security detail for the cruise," she said, answering her question.

"Serious?" Felecia asked.

"Not at the moment. I am just going to enjoy my birthday week. It officially starts in ten hours," she said, and the ladies all yelled and cheered as they made a quick toast. Nico and David came over to the ladies. "Hey, it's kind of noisy over here," David said playfully. "It's almost Sandy's birthday, and we are about to turn up in here!" Felecia said. The guys laughed. Shontell stood up and walked over to Nico. The men had about an hour before they had sound check. Martin interrupted their fun, telling the guys it was time to "pay the bills." By that he meant that they all had to do some mingling with the cruise guests. Nico told her he would see her that night. Felecia kissed her husband. Sandy excused herself to go say goodbye to Eric, and Shontell and Gloria went to walk on the deck.

Nico

Nico sat in the room with his friends and the band members. The opening concert was hot and the fans really came out and showed out. He loved seeing Shontell in the front row knowing that this time they were together. They also decided that tonight they would take a breather. She told him that she understood that he had to mingle with the fans and didn't want to interfere with that. He hoped he would be able to go long without her. He knew what missing her felt like. He tried to focus on what the guys were saying but was failing miserably. David noticed his distraction. He walked over to him and patted him on the back.

"Man, it gets easier. Remember how I used to be when Felecia and I first got together. I didn't want to be away from her," he reminded him. He poured a drink that he handed to Nico, and then he poured one for himself.

"Yes, and now I can see how you felt. I want to give her a little space so she can still get used to us. I think meeting my parents was huge for her. The last thing I want to do is scare her away," he told him.

"Right, I understand that. I mean this lifestyle is hard, but I am sure that you two will be okay," David replied trying to be reassuring. Nico sat with them for as long as he could and then called it a night. They still were having rehearsals. Tomorrow they had an afternoon show and then were free the rest of the day. Martin explained that they were expected to mingle during that time so the people who spent their money on the cruise could get to know them on a more personal level. It was what he referred to as "paying their bills." Any other time, it would not have been an issue. He just didn't want to take any chances on messing up with her. He was glad that she understood the obligation. He stood over the rail, watching the waves hit the ship, and got lost in his thoughts. He didn't hear the woman approach him but turned at hearing his name called.

"Um, Nico, I don't mean to bother you. But can I get a picture?" the young woman asked. She was strikingly beautiful, but he could also tell that she was young.

"Sure, no problem," he told her. He posed for a picture, and she stood close to him and took one of them.

The young woman kissed him on the cheek and went in search of her friends.

"So you give out kisses as well, huh?" He saw Shontell come out the shadow and walk towards him. "Only if it's to you," he told her with a serious expression on his face.

"Nico, it's cool. I know you have a job to do. Before these last few weeks, I would have been one of these women trying to get your attention. I trust...I trust you," she told him with a little hesitation in her voice.

"I know that had to be hard for you to say. I wish I knew what happened to make you leery of trusting me. But...yes...because I'm in this business, we are going to have to have trust if we are going to pull this off. Shontell, trust me when I tell you that I don't want any other woman. But I have to be frank with you. Our road won't be easy. We are constantly approached by very brazen women who don't care that David is married or that I am in a relationship." Shontell listened to Nico and knew what he said was true. She still didn't speak, but sat on the empty chaise lounge chair. Nico watched her before he went to sit next to her.

"You telling me you trust me means a lot. You have my word that I won't disappoint you. I am a good guy," he continued as he wrapped his arm around her waist.

"I know that. I know that you are. There is still some doubt in my heart. But I will work on that. It has to come from me. I didn't expect to be in a relationship like ours again. My ex put me through some things that I never thought were possible. I want to come to you eventually as baggage free as I can get. So patience is a must. But I won't push you away. I have overcome the hurt he caused me, and that door is closed in my life. You have given me the best thing a woman can ask for."

"And what's that?" he asked as he watched her swing her legs.

"Hope that real unconditional love still exists," she told him, leaning over and kissing him. After a few seconds, he broke the kiss, looking at her with a wanting that filled him. Clearing his throat, he said, "Yeah, you might want to stop that if I am supposed to be giving you some space." He took her by the hand and pulled her to her feet. She had changed into a different outfit for the night.

"Well let me go find Sandy. I think she is in the casino."

"Do you want me to walk with you?"

"Uh, no. I will be okay. Besides, I think you have company," she told him, motioning towards three women who were looking at him wide eyed. Nico smiled at the women and then waved at Shontell. He watched her until she was completely out of view, not even paying attention to the women who were asking him for autographs and pictures. Sighing, he gave them his attention. This is how his night ended.

Shontell and Sandy walked into the crowded club. It was karaoke night, and both ladies decided they were going to sing. Sandy decided that she was going to try and cheer her up, since her best friend was down about not being able to spend a lot of time with Nico. It didn't help that, after the concert this afternoon, they saw Nico, Dennis, and John all surrounded by women at the pool. Nico didn't even see her there, and she wanted to leave as soon as she saw the scene. Sandy suggested this in hopes it would lift her spirits. They signed up for two songs each before they could back out. They found an empty booth off to the side and ordered drinks. They listened to the other people go up and sing. Sandy was meeting Eric here, and they were surprised to see him on stage singing. Shontell hit her friend on the arm, as they sat down at their reserved table.

"Girl, he is good," Shontell told her, as the waitress came over and took their orders.

"Yes, he is. I am surprised. He never mentioned he could sing." They both clapped as he headed off the stage and in their direction. He scooted into the booth, kissed Sandy's cheek, and greeted Shontell.

"Maybe y'all should do a duet," Shontell said, smiling hard as she tipped the waitress who brought their drinks.

"Sure, we will if you do one," Sandy said, sipping her fruity drink. Eric was looking confused as they talked. The waitress set his beer down and he gulped it, intrigued by their conversation.

"And who would I do a song with, Ms. Smarty Pants?" Shontell said, glaring at her friend in a playful manner.

"Okay ladies, time out. What are you two talking about? Eric asked finally. He didn't like feeling clueless.

"Well, she wants you and me to sing. I want her to sing with Nico," Sandy told him, and he nodded. "Oh okay. That would be cool. But can you two sing?" he asked them both. Before they could answer, Sandy's name was called and she took to the stage in dramatic fashion. Shontell was surprised when she heard Sandy's song choice, as they both had kept their choices to themselves. Sandy belted out Mariah Carey's, "My All." The crowd was loving it. Sandy and Shontell had an all-girl group back in high school. They had won many competitions. They both loved singing. Sandy sat back down and they high-fived each other, laughing.

"Guess that answered my question. Your girl got a voice," Eric said to her.

"Yeah, I hope I don't have to sing behind her tail. I don't feel like competing," she told Eric, as she put her glass to her mouth. Eric looked at her, because he didn't know what that meant. Shontell had a much stronger voice than Sandy, and Shontell still sang on a regular basis in church. But Sandy only sang at karaoke and sometimes in church for special events. Shontell looked around, wondering if any celebrities were in the house. The group did a good job of having special guests do a concert. Sandy walked back over to the booth and sat down, gulping her glass of water until it was empty.

"That was hot, Sandy," Eric told her.

"Thank you, Eric," she responded, turning her attention to her friend who was smiling.

"So, did you decide if you two are going to do a duet?" Shontell asked her innocently.

"Yep, we got this."

Shontell took a long swig of her drink, as she heard her name being called by the emcee. She headed to the stage. "Hey everyone, I am dedicating this song to a special someone. I don't know if he is listening, but here goes." Then she nodded to the guy to cue her up.

Nico

Walking into the club, Nico felt Shontell's presence before he even saw her. When he came in, her friend Sandy was tearing up a Mariah Carey song. He was impressed. He went over to the bar, ordered two rounds of drinks, and told the bartender where to send them since he spotted them when he got to the bar. Before Nico could walk into the area he saw them. But then Shontell's voice made him stop in his tracks. He heard her dedication, but nearly dropped his drink at what he heard next.

"I know that when you look at me, there's so much that you just don't see, but if you would only take the time, I know in my heart you'd find; a girl who's scared sometimes, who isn't always strong, can't you see the hurt in me, I feel so alone. I want to run to you..." Nico stood there with his mouth open. He was stunned at how she commanded the audience and her voice. Her voice was awesome. He made it over to the table and greeted Sandy and her friend, but never took his attention off her. When she finished, he was the first to stand

up clapping and whistling. If he hadn't already, Nico knew he was falling for this woman.

He embraced her when she came to the table, and she was surprised to see him.

When did he get here? she thought, hugging him back.

"You were amazing," he whispered, as he let her go. She blushed. They sat down, and Nico signaled for the drinks.

"You seem to keep surprising me," he told her, handing her the glass of wine he brought over.

"Do I?" she said. Taking a sip, she noticed her hands were shaking. She quickly put the glass down and hid her hands under the table.

"Yes, but I love it. I now understand what Sheléa's comment meant." Shontell laughed as he tried to downplay his comment.

He turned to Sandy, "I heard you sing, too. You were also great."

"Thanks, Nico. Actually, your girl and I here were part of a girl group called Triple S back in the day."

"Really...now that's something. Was she the third person?" He asked as Shontell hid her face.

Shontell

Shontell wanted to sink into the floor. She kicked her friend under the table and gave her an evil eye. The conversation flowed, and she steered the topic away from her singing. When it was time for Sandy to sing again, she grabbed Eric's hand. They belted out Rachelle Ferrell and Will Downing with ease. Slightly embarrassed to ask, she turned to Nico.

"I have a favor to ask…"

"What's that?"

"Well, Sandy sort of challenged me. And since she and Eric just sang, I have to do my duet." Nico laughed, but said nothing.

"Um, so do you mind?"

"Not at all…in fact, it would be my pleasure."

He kissed her hand, and they greeted the couple when they came back to the table.

"Sandy, that was sweet. You and Eric sounded good together."

"Thanks, but don't be adding all the sugar; just do your part," her friend told her with a wink. She was looking sweetly at her and Nico. Nico watched the exchange between them, and he and Eric laughed.

Nico

Nico watched Shontell, and he could tell that she was nervous. He wondered why, because she seemed like a natural on the stage. He took her hand and guided her to the stage when her name was called again. He walked over to the guy and spoke to him. All the ladies were yelling with surprise to see him standing on stage.

"You trust me, right," he whispered to her and handed her the mic.

She nodded and prepared herself, not knowing what they were about to sing. The music began, and he began singing: "*I never knew such a day could come, and I never knew such a love could be inside of one. And I never knew what my life was for, but now that you're here I know for sure.*" Shontell came right in on cue: "*I never knew 'til I looked into your eyes, I was incomplete until the day you came into my life and I never knew that my heart could feel so precious and pure, one love so real...*" They sang as if they were the only ones in the room, oblivious to all the people that were watching them. When they finished, the club went into an uproar. They both had to regain their composure as they made their way back to the table. They were stopped by his group members.

"Damn, how long have they been in here?" he wondered. David was the first to speak, "Man you two were purely magical."

"Hey, Ms. Shontell. Where did you get those pipes from, girl?" Dennis asked.

Nico sensed how uncomfortable Shontell was by the attention they were getting, as people continuously came up to them to talk about the song. Then, to add more to the situation, a few women came up to the group for pictures and autographs. Nico felt Shontell let go of his hand. He wanted to comfort her, but he couldn't. He lost sight of her and sighed. Their conversation from the night before quickly came to mind, and he turned his attention back to the mass of women and men standing before him.

LOVE, LUST, LIES

Shontell

Is this what being with him is going to be like? Would they always be overtaken by his fans? Shontell made her way back to the table. Is it something she would be able to do or get used to? She needed to ask that question. She couldn't repeat what she went through with Jesse. She told Sandy that she was going to get some air and then maybe go back to the suite. She wasn't upset, but she needed some time alone to think. She could hear his voice from the conversation they had last night, and she knew what she was up against. She stood looking up at the moon, and she could faintly hear someone singing into the mic. Her thoughts went back to singing with Nico. The feeling it gave her made her excited. She was falling for him, and it had been barely a month. It just seemed so right because they had so much magic together, even with the situation of him being who he was. She stood at the rail and turned her attention to the water. It always soothed her. She shivered a little, but she began to shake even more when she heard his voice.

"Shon, the lady with the angelic voice," she didn't turn around because she was praying that she was hearing things. Jesse couldn't really be on this ship. She had not heard or spoken to him since they left out of the house that morning.

"So, you're going to ignore me?"

"I was hoping I was hearing things."

"Baby girl, it's me," he said as he staggered her way. He looked like he was drunk.

"You're kidding, right? Jesse, please leave me alone. I told you all I had to say when we had breakfast. We have nothing else to discuss, so why are you bothering me?" she rubbed her hands up and down her arms due to the chill.

"I just want to talk. But, I guess now I know why I can't get another chance," He said motioning back to the club. He saw her with Nico, she assumed. She didn't care.

"...as if I was going to give you one anyway. I told you that it was friendship or nothing. I see you won't even give me time for that to happen. I guess you think that I am the stupidest woman alive to even think..."

"Hey, there you are," Nico said, interrupting her. Walking in her direction, he had his jacket in his hand.

"Are you okay?" he asked, before he even saw who she was talking to. She was facing in his direction, and he could see that her face was frowning. Before Shontell could respond, Jesse turned around and addressed Nico.

"Hey, Nico. How you are doing?" he asked while extending his hand.

"Jesse? What's up, man? Do you two know each other?" he asked, as he shook the outstretched hand.

"I am going to let her answer that. I will see you tomorrow at rehearsal. Shontell, I will talk to you later. By the way, you two sounded great up there." He walked away and left Nico and Shontell where they were.

"Shontell, I'm sorry about earlier. I know that must have been too much for you."

She sighed and rubbed her temples.

"No, I understand. I mean this is your cruise. I knew that you would be overcome with fans. It just takes some getting used to. I am sorry for just running off. I was being unfair," she expressed to him.

"Come here," she said softly to him.

Nico walked closer to where Shontell was and saw her shiver.

"Are you cold?" he asked, as he rubbed her skin. It was ice cold.

"A little," she replied. Nico put his jacket around her, and she laid her head on his chest.

"Remember when we were talking last week and I told you I had an unexpected visitor?"

"Yes."

"Well, it was Jesse."

"Jesse?" Nico pulled her back some so he could look at her.

"Yes. I told you then I would tell you when I was ready. This seems like the best moment, if you have the time."

"For you, I have all the time. Come on," he said, guiding her towards the suite area.

Jesse

Jesse watched in the shadows as the couple walked away. He silently cursed under his breath. He was totally caught off guard when he, David, Dennis, and John walked into the club and heard Nico and Shontell singing. He would know her voice anywhere. He watched them on stage, and even a blind person could see their chemistry and sparks. Shontell finally got her wish: to meet the fellas on a more personal level. He casually asked how they met, and David told him about their album release party a week and a half ago. He half listened as he watched them, but he heard what he needed to hear. She looked stunning in a long, yellow maxi-dress and heels. He tried to keep his cool. All of his emotions came rushing toward him. How could he get her to just sit down and listen to him again? That's all he wanted. So much had happened in his life since that breakfast they shared. He walked back into the club and went to grab a drink. His phone went off, and he looked at the message. He acted like it didn't come through, as he took another long swig of the drink. He didn't know what made him bring Ebony on this cruise, because keeping her out of Shontell's view was going to be hard.

Shontell walked into Nico's room and sat on the bed. She hadn't said a word since they left the club area. She sat Nico's jacket on the side of her and exhaled.

"This conversation isn't an easy one for me, but here it goes."

"Wait, Shontell. You know you don't owe me an explanation about your past. If this makes you uncomfortable, then you don't have to tell me anything," Nico told her, as he took her hands in his and faced her. Shontell had been trying to keep the tears from falling and failed miserably.

"No, I have to tell you. We can't start a relationship with secrets and deception, which was what I had with Jesse. I won't have that with you," she told him, as she dabbed at her face.

"Okay, I'm listening."

"I met Jesse at the Detroit Sports Awards, and I fell instantly for his charm and wit. He treated me good. We didn't have arguments, except when it came to Sandy and my family. He didn't like sharing me much." Shontell played with a nonexistent lint ball on the bed. She didn't want to look at Nico. She felt him sit on the bed next to her. He lifted her chin, looking her in the eyes.

"Finish please," he urged her. She turned her head slightly, out of range of his touch.

"He used to complain about me not wanting cameras and media around me. It was our only other sour part...that I knew of, at least. I wouldn't attend many of his events. For some reason, his manager believed he needed to be out in the public's eye as much as possible. I disagreed. It left him open to have another woman on his arm. I dealt with that because I had to trust him." Pausing, Shontell leaned back a little and looked up at the ceiling. She didn't know why she wouldn't look at him. Maybe she was afraid...afraid that he would see how stupid she felt. Blowing air out her mouth, she continued. "When Jesse proposed, I said yes. But he had a stipulation. I had to start attending some of the events he went to. I fought him on it. But I did realize I would have to compromise on the whole thing. It was still hard for me. About six months before we were to be married, my parents asked us to do a fundraiser at the church. That was the first time he heard me sing. His reaction was similar to yours."

"I can imagine. You don't know how good of a range you have, do you?"

"I have been told that, but I sing in church and just for pleasure...not professionally. So after that event, Jesse begged me to write some songs and I did. So he invites me to the studio, and I am thinking it's just to see him record. When we got there, I heard the music I wrote playing. He was trying to coax me to record it with him. I was so furious with him. I wanted to shred the music, but I didn't. I just gave it to my mom for safe-keeping. I told Sandy, and she confronted him. That started even more drama. It got so bad, I told him we both needed some space."

"Wow. I can't believe he would do that," Nico said, as he clenched and unclenched his hands. He needed a diversion to hold his anger.

"Yeah, me either. I was really hurt that he betrayed my wishes. If he would have asked, I might have looked at the whole situation differently." Nico stood up and his face was hard to read.

"I know Jesse from the business, and we have worked together a few times. It was never a friendship. I heard recently that he was looking for a producer to do a new album. Most people in the industry believed he was a lost case. But, as I am sure you know, in this business things can change quickly. How long were you two together?" Nico asked, straddling the chair backwards.

"We were together for two and a half years. We've been broken up for a little over two years," she answered him, and then she finished her story.

"After the breather, I figured enough time had passed. I got on a plane to California to surprise him, in hopes that we could talk and get back on track. I was the one that got the surprise. I used my key to get in and walked in on him and two other women. I ran out, and he ran after me. I jumped in my car and hit his closed gate head-on, trying to get away. I escaped the accident with a broken leg and arm and..." She almost told him about the baby but stopped. Taking a deep breath, she got back on track. "Over the years, he tried to get me back. He called to explain and claim he had changed. I don't care, and I don't want him. I've spent the last two years wondering why I wasn't enough...why he couldn't love me and only me." Shontell was crying, and the tears fell on the bed sheet. She was mad that she still let him get to her. It wasn't him...it was just what he did to her. Nico went to her side and lifted her chin again, wiping her tears with his thumbs.

"Look at me. Don't ever think you aren't enough. Jesse didn't deserve you. You are more than enough, and you are more than enough for me. I am falling in love with you. I want to show you that love if you continue to let me," he told her, as he planted a soft kiss on her temple.

"Falling in love with me?" she pointed to herself, like she couldn't believe what he had just said.

"Yes, baby...falling in love with you," he repeated. Nico bent down so that he was face level with her. He bit his bottom lip, and the action caused Shontell's body temperature to rise. She reached out and pulled his face to hers. She kissed him hard. She wanted to feel him closer to her. She felt Nico could sense her need. He deepened their kiss, and he lowered her straps on her dress. He paused and looked at her for approval. Shontell gave it by taking the dress off completely. She laid back on the bed in only her panties. Nico laid on top of her, as he took her nipple in his mouth. Shontell moaned and grabbed his head. Nico kissed and licked down her body, until he got to her panties. He traced her honey spot with his tongue through her panties, and she nearly jumped out of her skin. Nico removed her panties and ran his tongue once again over her hot spot. Shontell screamed. He opened her legs wider and tasted deeper, as she moved up and down…locking his head with her knees as she came. Nico came up and kissed her, letting her taste her juices.

"Mm," she moaned. Her breathing was fast and heavy, as she tried to get her thoughts together. As her body came down from the high, she ran a hand over her wet face and hair.

"You tasted so good, baby." She smiled and lifted him from the bed.

"My turn," she said with her voice still dripping with passion, as she gently undressed him. She kissed his neck, licking down his chest. She kissed his stomach, watching him as she inched down more. Taking his shaft in her mouth, she ran her tongue up and down his shaft and deep throated him. Nico moaned loudly, as he tried to pull her up. She continued faster, almost bringing him to his orgasm more than once. "Where are your condoms?" she asked him in between her licks and sucks. Nico reached over to the table and pulled a condom from his drawer. He handed it to her. She opened it and rolled it on him. She pushed him back on the bed, looked him in the face, smiling seductively, and said, "Bébé, je veux te faire l'amour. Je t'aime aussi."

Nico looked up at Shontell. He recalled that she spoke French before, but this time he needed to know what she said.

"What does that mean?" he asked her in a husky voice. She lowered herself onto him slowly, and he drew in his breath.

"I said: Baby, make love to me. And I love you too," she told him, as he gripped her waist and she rode him. Nico felt himself losing control as Shontell bucked on top of him. He quickly grabbed her and switched their positions, as she wrapped her legs around his waist. He penetrated deep into her hot core and Shontell welcomed each thrust. They made love passionately and completely, speaking to one another in a way that only lovers could. She continued to speak French, and he answered her in his own language of love. He kissed her shoulder and tasted the salt from her sweat. She grabbed ahold of his fingers, locking them together as he thrust into her slowly. He then increased his tempo. Shontell pulled his face to her, as she sucked his tongue hard. He could feel her coming. Within seconds he was joining her, as they both called out the other's name. He collapsed on top of her and kissed her again. He noticed that she had tears on her face.

"Are you okay?" he asked with concern. She nodded and hugged him. After a few minutes, he rolled onto his back and she laid on his chest.

"I love you, Shontell."

"I love you back, Nico." They both fell into a comfortable sleep.

Shontell smiled when she woke up in the bed with Nico. Her mind went back to the night they shared. She laid everything on the line with him, and he still told her that he loved her. She had found her knight in shining armor. She got up and walked over to the balcony and stepped out. She watched the beauty of the sunrise. She felt the wetness on her face and wiped at her tears. She tried to keep her tears at bay, but they seemed to come more. She didn't want to wake Nico. She turned to look to make sure he was still in the bed and was startled to see him standing right next to her. She didn't even hear him get up. With concern on his face, he pulled up a chair and sat down next to her.

"Baby? What's wrong? Are you crying?" he inquired as he began wiping her face with his fingers. Shontell looked at him and knew that he was what she had been hoping for.

"Yes, I'm sorry I didn't mean to wake you up."

"Are you okay?" he asked still showing concern.

"Nico, I am okay. These are tears of joy. I was just thanking God for bringing us together, and remembering all the things that I went through with Jesse. I thought that was love. You have shown me more about love in the past couple of weeks than I could have ever imagined. I never planned on falling in love with you this quickly. You showed me patience and intimacy, and now it's my turn to show you how much all that means to me," she told him as she wiped the tears from her face.

Nico

Nico wiped away at the tear that was forming on his face. He didn't want her to see how her words got to him. He had never felt so strongly about a woman before in his life. He looked at her and saw how beautiful she was from the inside and out. It made him think of the video with her friend singing. He gave her what she wanted, and he was pleased. He pulled her onto his lap and lay his head on her stomach. They watched the rest of the sunset together. He looked up at her, and she rewarded him with a kiss. The kiss sent him into overdrive. Nico opened her robe and cupped her breasts. Shontell moaned from the touch. When the kissed ended, they were both breathless.

"Wow," Nico whispered. Shontell laughed lightly.

"Why did you say wow?"

"You don't even want to know why," he told her, shaking his head at himself. Shontell scooted off his lap and brought him down on the chaise with her. His thoughts quickly went to the first time they lay on a chaise together. He wondered if she was thinking the same thing, when she said, "Feeling DeJa Vu, huh?" He nodded his head yes. He lowered his head to her breast and let his tongue run over her areola. Shontell arched her body. She reached down and massaged Nico. He moaned as he bit her lower lip softly and then felt her sheath him and then guide him into her hot wetness. He felt like he was melting, with her gripping him repeatedly as he thrust in and out of her. He felt her about to climax and knew that he would be following. He sped up his movements and thrust deeper into her. He felt her tighten on him, and he clenched his teeth.

"Nico," she screamed, as they came together.

"I love you, Shontell. I will never hurt you," he told her between breaths as they lay together, coming down from the high. After a few minutes, Nico grabbed his watch. He had an hour before rehearsal. Getting up, he tried not to wake Shontell. He headed into the shower, turned on the water to just the right temperature, and stepped in. Letting the water cascade over his body, with his eyes closed he allowed the water to rinse his face and Shontell's scent from him. Hearing the door open, he smiled. He heard her shuffling around and wondered what she was doing. He almost looked, but didn't want to embarrass her. Soon after, he felt her hands on his back as she stepped into the shower with him.

"What are you doing?" Nico asked her, laughing.

"Shh," Shontell said to him, giving him a sultry smile as she placed her finger on his lips. He turned her around and pulled her body into his, spooning their bodies together. Nico grabbed the soap and began to lather her body, touching her in places that he thought he had missed in their lovemaking earlier.

"Open your legs," he said. Shontell moaned lightly as she did what he asked her. Nico placed his thick member in between her folds. Shontell gasped when it throbbed. Nico cupped her breasts, twisting her nipples hard. Shontell placed both hands on the shower wall. Nico kissed the back of her neck and trailed kisses down to her ass, as he raised her leg and placed it on the corner of the tub. Nico stepped back and let the now lukewarm water hit her skin. He positioned her body just the way he wanted to before he entered her wetness, which he knew it wasn't from the water. She squealed in pleasure as he pounded into her. Reaching back, Shontell pulled his face to hers and tongue-kissed him hard. Nico was trying to concentrate on their strokes and movements, but her kisses were making it hard. He extended his hand downward and started to play with her clit. Immediately her body began to tremble. He pulled out and re-entered her harder. She held onto the wall, as Nico took over the rhythm.

Nico felt Shontell come, and he bit the side of her neck. She pushed her ass out more, and Nico stroked her harder. Then he grabbed hold of her waist, and they made love in a way that he was unaccustomed to. He had never been so turned on by the way a woman sexed him. But he already knew she was different. Nico grunted and whispered Shontell's name. Nico felt himself about to explode. He stroked hard and then stayed still for a few seconds. When Shontell moved on his shaft, he tried to stop her. But he couldn't. Nico began pounding harder and harder. When he felt her tighten her sweet walls, he came hard. He knew she had to have felt his seed shoot into her, as she came again with him. He held onto her as he tried to turn the water off. After a few minutes, he stepped out the tub and held his hand out to her. Grabbing the towels, he wrapped up and then covered her up in the other. Picking her up, he carried her back into the room. He laid her on the bed, and they shared a deep kiss. Breaking the kiss, he shook his head at her. "What am I going to do with you!" he said, not expecting an answer. "Love me," she said softly, as she pulled him on top of her and they got back under the covers.

You Have Got To Be Kidding

Shontell

After they showered and dressed, Shontell walked with Nico to where they were rehearsing. They kissed, and he told her he would see her for lunch. As she turned to leave, she almost ran straight into Jesse.

"Hey, baby girl. I see you and your man are still on good terms."

"Why would you think we wouldn't be? You can't take away my joy; you didn't give it to me, you sorry bastard," she scowled at him. She quickly chided herself for her comment. She was doing what he wanted. She started taking a couple steps back from him. She didn't want to be near him.

"Whoa, such foul language coming out of such a pretty mouth," he said, holding both hands up in surrender. Shontell was about to turn and walk away. She wasn't aware that Nico saw her talking to Jesse until he was back at her side.

"Is everything okay over here?" He gave Jesse a stern look that he wasn't prepared for.

"Yep, it is; me and the lady here were just having a conversation," Jesse told him, as he put his hands in his pockets. Nico continued to regard Jesse, but said nothing to his comment. He turned to her and mouthed, "Are you okay?" She nodded, as she took her sunglasses off her dress. Putting them on her face, she smiled at Nico. Looking over at Jesse, she said, "Our conversation is over. I will see you later Nico." She waved to Nico and started off in the opposite direction, leaving both men standing there watching her.

Jesse wanted to go and snatch her to make her come back and talk to him. He knew he had better not press his luck. He needed this gig and the exposure. He looked back at Nico and watched him as he watched Shontell walk out of sight. There it was; he saw the look...the look that he wore when he fell in love with Shontell...the same look he still tried to cover up from everyone but himself when he looked in the mirror. Jesse was pissed because he would never get her back now. He walked into the auditorium and headed towards the stage. He heard his name being called and turned around. Looking at Nico, he stood and waited to see what he was going to say. He wasn't in the mood.

"I am going to say this as nicely as I can. Back off of Shontell. She doesn't want to talk to you," Nico told him through clenched teeth.

"So, now you are speaking for her. Let her tell me that Shontell and I have unfinished business."

"Unfinished business? I doubt that. Don't make me have to repeat myself," Nico told him. Jesse huffed and then continued walking to the stage. The game just changed. Nico couldn't even begin to understand his connection with Shontell. They would see who Shontell left the cruise with — him or Nico.

Ebony

Ebony peeked out of the door before opening it all the way. She was getting antsy because she had too much time to think. There was no way in hell that she was going to spend one more day cooped up in that room. Jesse was treating her like some kind of prisoner. They were supposed to be here together. That's what he had told her. But instead, he now said he couldn't have her seen by Shontell. She was so tired of hearing Shontell's name: Shontell this; Shontell that. If Shontell knew half of what she knew, her head would spin. Her thoughts were dark, as she ventured down the gallery walk.

Ebony looked behind her like she expected to get caught by the crew. She was a guest. Relaxing, she walked normal. She wondered what Jesse would do if he found out that Shontell had already seen her. She laughed some to herself. When she boarded, she took her sunglasses off to admire the ship and looked over and saw Shontell staring straight at her. She hurried through to get from the deck to the room. She had been in the room for two days, and enough was enough. She was missing all the fun. The ship was huge. What were the chances of her seeing Shontell again? She walked on deck and went straight to the buffet to make a plate. One of the big concerts was tonight, and she wanted to make sure that she would be able to see it...even if it was from afar. She sat down to eat her food. She never even saw Shontell, Sandy, and another woman walk into the dining area.

Shontell went straight to the bar and ordered a hurricane. She was still so mad at how she reacted to Jesse's comment and the way Jesse came at her. Sandy grabbed their table, while she and Felecia got the drinks. The ladies sat down.

"I can't believe you were engaged to Jesse Wright," Felecia said, as they made light talk. Shontell had filled Felecia in the last hour about her past. Sandy tried not to listen. But she did well in not responding or getting mad. They were killing time; the conversation was what she needed. Shontell wished she could share with them about last night with Nico. But that wasn't her style. She never kissed and told. They decided to make a small plate of fruit and appetizers, while they were waiting on the men to end their rehearsal. Biting into a strawberry, she addressed Felecia's comment.

"Sometimes neither can I. That was a long time ago," she told her, wiping the juice from her mouth. Sandy decided to change the topic. Talking about Jesse was making her head hurt. Turning to them both, she asked them excitedly, "Have you ladies decided what you're wearing tonight?"

"Yes, I have this hot strapless jumper I am sporting," Felecia told them.

"I think I am wearing my tangerine dress. I need to get my hair tightened," Shontell told them. They continued about their outfits, hair, and makeup over the next thirty minutes. When their conversation paused, Felecia turned her head, looking around and made a comment that made both of the other women stop drinking their fruity drinks.

"Hey, isn't that the woman you showed me the picture of? Ebony, I think that's her name," Shontell turned and saw Ebony sitting over about five tables.

Shontell did a double-take. What the hell, she thought to herself. What is going on here? Standing up, she headed in her direction. She ignored Sandy calling her. "Ebony?" The woman looked up with large eyes. Shontell saw her moving to run and grabbed her wrist.

"So, I wasn't crazy when I thought I saw you the other day. What the hell are you doing here when you are supposed to be in Detroit working?"

"I can explain," Ebony stuttered. "Shon, you're hurting my wrist. Let me go!" she yelled. People started looking at them. Shontell glared at her, and Ebony closed her mouth.

"I'm not letting you go until you start explaining, and you can start by telling me the truth," Shontell told her, as she gripped her wrist even tighter.

"Shon, stop!" she heard from behind her. She was still holding onto her wrist when Jesse stepped to the side of her and Ebony.

"I said let her go," Jesse said, as he pulled her away from Ebony.

"So it's true. You are with Ebony. Why?" Looking back and forth between the two of them, she could feel her anger bubbling. Shontell's question was directed at Ebony, more so than Jesse.

"You just had to have my scraps. Well, you two deserve each other. Don't think he loves you. He isn't capable of love. He reserves that all for himself," she spat at her partner. Then she looked Jesse up and down. They both looked like strangers to her.

"He does love me," Ebony yelled, pouting and stomping her foot for emphasis.

"Tell her; tell her you love me, Jesse. Tell her how long we have been together." She looked at Jesse; he had a blank look on his face, but didn't confirm or deny what she was saying. Ebony continued talking.

"I never knew what he saw in you. You never deserved him. I could please him so much better than you ever could. You should be thanking me."

"Thanking you. And what the hell am I thanking your trifling ass for? Saving my business? Yeah, I was grateful for that. But, I don't need you," Shontell told her, inches from her face. Shontell could feel how warm her skin was. The anger was getting deeper by the moment.

Ebony laughed in her face. "You don't even know, do you?" Shontell looked at her wide-eyed. *Now what, what was this woman talking about she thought.*

"What are you talking about? Know what?" Shontell asked. She watched Ebony look at Jesse, and the look he gave her terrified them both. She kept her eyes on Jesse, looking at his now-unkempt appearance. Jesse took a few steps in Shontell's direction. He clearly was ignoring what

377

Ebony said. She could see he was avoiding her on purpose. That made her even madder.

"Look, we need to hash out all this nonsense. Shontell, let's go somewhere and talk in private," he told her as he grabbed her by the elbow. She snatched away from him and she stood her ground.

"No. You or Ebony better tell me now what she meant by that comment. What is it that I don't know?" she asked, looking from Ebony to Jesse. "A lot," she heard Ebony mumble. Before she realized it, she had put her hand across the side of Ebony's face. The smack sound seemed to bounce off the waves. There was a collective gasp from the people who were watching them. Ebony was holding her face. She didn't even realize Nico had come over to where she was. "Jesse are you going to do something?" she asked with embarrassment on her face. Jesse took a step up and so did Nico.

Shontell saw the jaw line of Jesse tense and knew that he was getting mad from Nico's protection of her. She didn't care. That is what her man was supposed to do. She looked back to Ebony.

"Now, unless you want a repeat, I would suggest you spill it now, Ebony," she told her, getting her anger in check. Folding her arms, she waited.

"The money I gave you to save your business came from Jesse. He gave me the money and told me to say it came from me," she whispered. But everyone in the room heard her. Jesse went to hit her, but his hand was grabbed by Dennis. Ebony's eyes were huge as she cowered under the threat.

Jesse yanked away from Dennis and headed back in Ebony's direction. The bitch talked too much, and she needed to be taught a lesson. He was glad Shontell slapped her. She deserved it. What the hell was she thinking? "You really think I could have loved you? Look at yourself. Now look at Shontell. She is what class means, and you are nothing but a freak and a slut. I used you. I don't love you. I never want to see you again." He gave her the most evil look she had ever seen on him. Ebony broke down in tears harder, and Jesse turned his back. In his mind, he was calculating how much he would save by not supporting her anymore.

He needed to get Shontell alone so he could explain. He was just about to walk over to the bar, when he heard Ebony's words. He stopped dead where he was.

"Jesse, I guess since you don't want me, I can tell Shontell everything," she spat at his back. Shontell looked at her with distaste.

"Tell me what else? What could be worse than what you have already told me?" she asked her, looking defeated because she couldn't handle the betrayal too much longer.

"Well, for starters, the night you caught him cheating...it was me and Annette in the bed with him." Jesse's eyes got huge. He spun around on his heels. And with lightning speed, he headed back to where she was standing. He couldn't believe that she had just ratted him out. He caught the look on Shontell's face, and his heart sunk.

"Wh... what did you just say, Ebony?" Shontell stuttered. She was looking at her with so much hurt. Jesse was heated. He felt so much rage and should have known he couldn't trust Ebony. She was going to ruin everything he had been working on to get his career back. He couldn't allow Ebony to tell her about the songs. He panicked and grabbed the knife off the buffet. Before he knew it, he was stabbing Ebony and everyone was screaming. He felt himself being pulled off of her lifeless body, as she slumped to the floor with a thud. There was blood everywhere—on him, Shontell, and the ship's floor. Shontell was across from where he was standing. In between them, lay Ebony. She started screaming. The room moved in a fast pace within minutes. He wanted to reach out for her, but someone was holding him. He saw Shontell fall to the floor.

Jesse struggled with the hands that were holding him. Eric and several security guards were around him within minutes, and he was forced to lay still on the floor. His vision was clouded from the tears that were forming in his eyes. Jesse stopped struggling. He was suddenly tired. He watched as the guards covered Ebony's body. The ship's doctor was kneeling next to her body soon after.

Eric looked over to Shontell and then to where Sandy stood, nodding to them but staying focused on the task at hand. He lifted him up once the body was removed. Jesse looked around for Shontell. Nico was kneeling next to her whispering to her, as she kept her head down. He didn't want Nico next to her. He called out to Shontell. Her head snapped up. He could see the tears flowing down her face.

"Shontell, Shontell. I love you. I did all this for you. I love you. You hear me?" he was shouting towards her direction. The guards led him out of the dining area. He looked back, trying to see Shontell. Nico was now holding her, and he couldn't see her face. What right did he have to be with her? She belonged with him.

Everyone was looking at him. He had to protect his career. This may still help to resurrect it. At least that's what he was telling himself.

ALL FOR LOVE

Shontell

Shontell refused to look at Jesse, although she could hear him calling her name repeatedly. Nico held her tight and kept whispering, "Everything is going to be okay." But was it? Sandy ran over to her best friend, and Shontell collapsed into her arms. Sandy patted her hair and let her cry her heavy sobs. Sandy's tears flowed as well. Everyone in the room was visibly upset. Nico stood with John, as they all had to remain in the room to be questioned. Shontell and Sandy both dried their eyes. The ship's captain came into the room and called them over one-by-one to get their details. When it was her turn, Nico asked her if she needed him. Nodding her head, he joined her in the private room where they conducted the interviews.

"Nico, please don't leave me," she whispered during one of the breaks the captain allowed her to take. Her interview was much more extensive.

"I am not going anywhere!" he told her with sincerity in his eyes. The captain returned and questioned her for twenty more minutes. When he released her to go, they went straight to his room. Opening the cabin door, he ushered her in and had her sit on the couch. He had room service bring her some tea, and he gave her the sedative the doctor gave him for her. Within minutes, she felt her body starting to get relaxed. She gave Nico a half smile, as she closed her eyes.

Shontell woke up from her sleep with a start. She was sweating. The room was dark, and she figured she was in her room. She could hear voices in the other room. Her head hurt, so she just laid back down. She heard a faint knock on the door, and then the room flooded with light. Sandy walked in and put a cool towel on her forehead. Shontell opened her eyes and tried to sit up. "Are you okay?" Sandy asked her. Shontell nodded, asking her what happened. She only remembered coming into the room with Nico. Sandy filled her in with as much detail as she knew. Nico left to do the concert, and the captain asked him to keep the incident quiet since it happened in the private dining area. They still didn't know how Ebony had managed to get into that area.

Sandy told her that her family would notify Ebony's parents that evening. Her parents had already called a few times to check up on her, after Sandy called them to let them know what happened. They wanted to talk to Shontell, but said they would wait until she was up from resting.

Sandy told her that Jesse was being held in a guarded room. She had just finished giving her the last of the details when Nico opened her door and walked into the room. Shontell sat all the way up. Sandy got up and excused herself, as she grabbed the towel she brought in and quietly left them alone. Shontell wanted to go straight into his arms. But instead she patted the bed next to her and Nico sat down, gently folding her in his arms.

Nico

Nico took his shoes off and got into the bed with her, pulling her closer to his body. All through the concert, he felt like he was on automatic. They all did. They prayed for Ebony and her family before they went on stage. Dennis felt the worst, as he was the closest to Jesse but even he didn't know all his secrets. He was the one who was so adamant that he be included as one of the celebrity guests. He was in shock. Nico worried that Shontell would blame herself for all this. He wanted her to know that she couldn't blame herself. Jesse was responsible for his own actions.

"Shontell, please don't think any of this is your fault. As bad as this whole situation is, Jesse and Ebony are both adults. You can't control their actions. I am sorry this happened. Baby, please talk about this. Don't shut me out," he pleaded with her, as he tipped her chin towards him. Shontell didn't reply to his words. Nico felt her slipping from him, and he needed to hold on. He knew that he would need to give her some space. He also wanted to be there for her. He was thinking about asking Martin about cancelling the overseas tour. He didn't think that he could be without her for the six weeks that they were scheduled to be there. Maybe he could get her to go with him. Nico and Shontell had somehow fallen asleep in each other's arms. He was awakened by the sound of his cell phone going off. He answered in a whisper, but what the caller said made him sit straight up. He looked over at Shontell as he got out of bed so he wouldn't wake her.

"You can't be serious! She can't handle that now," he spoke into the phone in a hushed yell. He listened to the caller and sighed, as he saw Shontell watching him out the corner of his eye. He ended the call and walked back to the bed. How in the hell was he supposed to tell her this? He looked at her, and she knew something was wrong.

"Who was that on the phone?" she asked him. Nico ran a hand over his face and looked at Shontell. He took a deep breath before answering her.

"That was Martin. He said that the captain contacted him and said that Jesse is being irrational. He is refusing to sign his statement and cooperate unless he talks to you first. He said that he only wants ten minutes. Then they can do whatever to him. But not until he sees you first." Shontell looked at Nico with an open mouth. She sat there for a moment or two. She wanted Jesse out of her life. If this was how to do it, then she would do it. Sighing, she swung her feet out of the bed, putting her shoes on. Holding her hand out to Nico, she said, "I will go, if you will come with me."

Standing outside of the door where Jesse was being held, she became scared. She wasn't scared of him literally. But she was scared that she wouldn't be able to handle the situation.

"Okay, I am ready," she told him, as she squeezed his hand hard.

"You sure?" he asked her, not even caring about the pain in his hand.

"No, but I don't see much of a choice. I know that you are nearby, and that will help," she replied. An officer walked up and was about to get them in, when the captain held up his hand to Nico. "Son, I can't let you go in there. He will go off the handle if he sees you two together."

"I am not letting her in that room with him alone," Nico told him.

"You don't have a choice. I'm sorry." Nico looked over at Shontell

"It's okay. I will be okay. Come get me one second pass ten minutes," she told him, giving him a weak smile.

He let go of her hand, and Shontell instantly felt cold. The captain nodded, the officer opened the door, and she walked in. Jesse had his back to her. She walked around the table, after the officer who was watching him acknowledged her. Jesse looked a mess. His usually curly hair was wild, and his eyes were bloodshot red. He looked tired. When he heard her footsteps, he looked up and his whole face changed.

"I...I didn't think you would come," he told her. Shontell didn't say anything, but took a seat. Jesse was handcuffed at his hands and feet, which made her feel a little better.

"Why did you want me to come is the better question? Why did you ask to see me?" she asked, not breaking the stare they shared.

Jesse looked at the woman he had been in love with for the past five years and knew his life was over. When they told him what he did, he went crazy. He didn't even remember stabbing Ebony. He just remembered that he had to make her stop talking. He could see the sadness in her eyes and how tired she looked. It broke him even more to realize that he was the cause of it all.

"I needed to see you. I wanted to tell you that I am sorry for all this. I didn't love Ebony. She was just my way of staying close to you. She always keeps me updated on what you were doing when you left me." Shontell looked at him with shocked eyes and an open mouth.

"You're kidding, right? You were keeping tabs on me?" she asked him.

"Don't look at it that way. I just thought of it as keeping an eye on my investment. I did save your company. Plus, you wrote those songs for me. I wanted them. I needed them for my career revival," he confessed to her. He touched the cold steel that encased his wrists.

"You know, you are a sick man. I am not your investment. You needed the songs? You can't be telling me you think I have those songs. I wrote those when we were together. But those songs are history—just like we are."

"What?" he yelled. This made her jump, and the guard moved forward.

"What do you mean the songs are history? I need those songs. I need those songs," he continued to yell at her. Shontell could not believe that this is what it was all about. She felt sick.

Eric stepped closer and his voice filled the small room, taking them both by surprise, "Sir, lower your voice or we will end this conversation," he said to him, as he placed his hand sternly on his shoulder. Jesse's eyes looked wild. He was angry at her. How could she do this to him? Those songs were going to bring him back on the scene. She was bluffing. She still had them and was probably going to use them with her new man. "Shontell, I better not hear my songs on the radio. If you record those songs with Nico, I swear I'm going to..."

"Going to what? Kill me like you did Ebony?" she yelled at him.

"Aren't you even sorry you killed her? Why did she die? Because she was about to tell on you? I can't believe I ever loved you. You aren't a man. You're a coward. I hope you rot in jail," she told him, as she stood up. She slapped him across the face. "That's for Ebony's family," she told him, as she headed to the door.

"Wait, I'm sorry. I'm sorry I overreacted. I...I love you. Shon, please...don't walk out yet." He quickly calmed down.

The officer called her name, motioning to the paper. Shontell slowly sat back down. She looked at him, and he thought he saw a glimmer of love in her eyes. He needed her, and he needed her to believe in him.

"Shontell, please tell me you will support me through this," he begged. Shontell just looked at the guard and then back at him.

"I will do anything for you, Shontell. I just need to know you will be there. I am sorry I used Ebony. I needed you back in my life, but I thought you wouldn't give me the time of day unless I was back on top again." He continued to plead his case to her. This was his chance to make her see how much he loved her. It was his last chance, as he went to touch her face and felt the cuff biting into his skin.

Shontell watched Jesse and was glad that he was handcuffed. She remembered what Eric just told her about needing to have him sign the admission sheet. It was similar to a confession. But, because they were on the water, it was a different protocol. It would be just a formality, since he was definitely guilty. "If I agree to support you, will you sign this paper?" she asked him. She unfolded the sheet, and Jesse looked at her for a moment. He smiled a small crooked smile and turned to the guard.

"Give me the paper. Shontell, I would do anything for you. If this means you're going to leave Nico and be by my side, I will do this." Shontell tried to keep a straight face, but it was hard to not show any emotion. She watched as the guard pushed the paper closer to him. Jesse started signing the paper they needed and slid it over to her. She looked at it and then nodded. Standing, the guard took the paper and she backed to the door. She looked at Jesse. What she saw wasn't the Jesse whom she had loved. She needed to get out of there. She had enough and walked to the door. She turned the knob and looked over her shoulder.

"Jesse, God knew what he was doing when he took our baby away! I hope you rot in hell," she told him quietly, wiping the tears away as she closed the door. She heard him yelling and screaming once he realized what she said to him. She didn't know why she told him. She wanted him to hurt like she did. She also did it for Ebony. No matter what she did, she didn't deserve this. She went straight into Nico's arms and cried. Nico held her, as he took the confession from the officer. The captain thanked her, and they exited his quarters.

Nico heard what she said, but he didn't want to ask her about it. Baby? He put all that aside and held onto her. She needed him now more than anything else that was going on. He, along with the captain, Martin, Eric, and one other officer who served as witnesses, listened in on the whole conversation. He wanted to go in there and rip his heart out for the things he told Shontell. He knew that being an entertainer could be hard and finding love could be even harder. He saw that in Shontell immediately; he couldn't hurt her. He saw just how much of a fool Jesse was for doing so. Jesse was wise enough, at some point, to know how good of a woman Shontell was. They walked back towards his suite, but ran into his parents who were coming to see him. They heard what had happened, and they wanted to check on his friend.

"Son, there you are. We have been looking for you two. Are you all right, young lady?" Nico's mother asked her. Shontell wiped her face and nodded yes. She was still too upset to talk.

"Nico, go inside and make some tea for Shontell. I am going to take her to clean up," his mother told him. She gave him a look when she noticed he was about to protest.

Shontell

Shontell let Mrs. Baker lead her to her suite a few doors down. She sat down while his mother went into the bathroom. She came back into the room with a warm cloth and handed it to her.

"Shontell, my son told us what happened earlier today. I'm sorry about your friend. I wanted to take a moment to talk to you. I have never seen my son so happy with a woman until we met you. I know he said that you were friends, but I think it's more than that." Shontell was about to say something when Nico's mother placed her hand up.

"Let me finish, dear. Your friend, Sandy, gave me some details about your past. And don't be mad at her. She just wanted to look out for you. But even though your past was bad, don't let it control how you will do things in the future. One of the things that has kept me and Nico Sr. together was communication. That word means a lot to people in love. If you talk about everything…and I mean everything…you two will work out just fine. My son loves you. I can see it all over his face. I can tell you are good for him. This business can bring out the evil in people, which you know about first hand. Child, it can also bring out the best…if you let it. What I am trying to tell you is: even through the storm, you still need an umbrella. Let Nico be that umbrella for you. He can shield you from that storm, if you let him. Take what happened today and learn from it. All apples aren't bad," Mrs. Baker told her. Shontell listened to her, and knew she was right. She closed her chapter with Jesse when she closed that door. She would let Nico help her get through this storm.

"Thank you, ma'am. I appreciate your words of wisdom. I know my mother would have said something similar if she was here."

"I know she would have. Nico called your parents earlier because he saw they called you. He told them what happened, and my husband and I spoke to them as well. They raised a beautiful daughter." She blushed and hugged her.

"Thank you again. I guess I need to call my parents. Can you tell Nico I went to get my phone?"

"Sure, baby, I will tell him. See you in the morning," Mrs. Baker told her, as she headed back to Nico's room and she went to her room to get her phone.

She walked into the room, and Sandy and Eric were in the sitting area.

"Hey, you guys. I will be out of here in a hot second. I just need my phone," she told them. Sandy came over to her and hugged her, and she felt her best friend's pain.

"How did it go?"

"Well, it went bad. We have a lot to talk about later. I am going to stay in Nico's room. I will see you at breakfast in the morning, okay?" They agreed and she told Eric goodbye, as she grabbed some clothes and her phone. She decided to go into their private rehearsal area and make her call. Her mother cried throughout the entire call. Since her mother and Ebony's mother were good friends, she had been with her since she had received the news. It didn't matter what Ebony had done; she didn't deserve to lose her life over it. She ended the call with her parents and sat at the piano bench. She tapped on the keys and sighed. It was so true that everything was a lesson. We were always being tested. Jesse tried to control her life, even when he wasn't a part of it. Even when he didn't realize he had that control, she had given it to him by not allowing herself to heal and move on from the hurt he had caused her. She sat up straight and began to play the piano. Before she knew it, she was singing. *"Listen, to the song here in my heart, a melody I start but can't complete. Listen, to the sound from deep within, it's only beginning. To find release..."* She belted out the song with all the emotion she had left. She never even heard Nico come in, as he sat there and let her sing. When she finished, she sat there and was startled by his clapping.

ON BENDED KNEE

Nico

After his parents left his room, he went to look for Shontell. He went to her room and was surprised when Sandy said that she had been there and left. He didn't know where she could have gone. He was walking towards Felecia and David's room when he heard music. It was just after midnight. He opened the door and heard Shontell singing and playing. He didn't want to startle her, so he sat down and just listened as the lyrics requested. Her voice was so beautiful and strong. He wondered why she had never pursued singing professionally. When she was done, he wiped the tears that he hadn't known fell and clapped. He walked towards the front, and he got himself together before he reached her. "That was beautiful," he told her

"I didn't know you came in here. Thank you," she told him, as she felt nervous.

"I was looking for you and heard the music. I came in here to see what it was and saw you. I didn't want to startle you, so I just let you finish. I know sometimes that music is just what is needed," he told her. Nico sat next to her on the piano bench, and she scooted over.

"Yeah, when I was younger...whenever I was mad, hurt, or upset...I would just go in my room. I would light some candles and just sing until my throat hurt. It was my way of gaining my sanity back."

"Yes, so I see. You know, you have a gift." Shontell hunched her shoulders at his comment.

"No, I know I have a voice. I never considered my voice or singing a gift. It always caused me more trouble than help with other people."

"But Shontell, you do things with your voice just like you do with your heart. You make people feel something."

"Nico, I like singing. That's why I sing mostly in church and for fun. I couldn't do what you do. I respect your talent and your career. But that business isn't for me." Nico understood what she meant, so he let it go.

"Come on, your tea is getting cold," he told her, reaching out for her hand. She took his hand, and they walked back to the room together.

Shontell and Nico came into the dining area. The captain closed off the area where the stabbing had happened, and she was glad. She wouldn't be able to eat there. They only had six more hours of cruise time remaining. The group had one more concert left, and it was a private show for some contest winners. Felecia came over and gave her a hug.

"How you holding up?" she asked her.

"Thanks to Nico, a lot better than I could be."

"Yes, he does care a whole lot about you. So what are you going to do when they go overseas next week?"

"Heal the best way I can. I think Ebony's funeral will be at the end of the week. After that, I will just try to continue with as much normalcy as possible," she told her.

"Well, please make sure you keep in touch. I won't be joining them."

"Really, and why is that?"

"Doctor's orders," she said, smiling.

"Doctor's orders? Does that mean what I think it means?" she asked her, excited about the news.

"Yeah, it does. We found out last night. I was so upset about what happened, I got sick. The doctor came and then he told us. We were both caught off guard. But, we are happy and, outside of our parents, you're the only other person that knows." The ladies hugged again, as she promised to keep the secret. They talked all morning until Sandy joined them, and she filled them both in on what happened with Jesse and the conversation she had with Nico's mother. They all spent the rest of the day together. She needed their company, and they were all smiling by the end of the day. It was the first time she felt normal since Ebony's death.

Nico

Nico and the rest of the members said goodbye to every last cruise guest. After three hours, the ship was empty. He went back to his room. He opened his bedroom door and, on his bed, lay a dozen roses. He smiled. He had never been given flowers by a woman. There also was a framed picture of him and Shontell and a note: *A small token to thank you for loving me, and for being by my side through my storms. Loving you, Shontell*

Shontell, Sandy, and Felecia had all gone to an early dinner with his parents and David's mother. He would see her before they left for the airport in the morning. He gathered his things, and he heard a knock on the door.

He opened it, and Dennis walked into his room. "Hey man, are you ready?"

"Yeah, I was just gathering my small bag," he told him, as Dennis eyed the roses. "Those for Shontell?" he asked.

"Nope. In fact, they are *from* Shontell. They were on my bed when I got back, with this and a note," he said showing him the framed picture. Dennis was quiet, and he just sat in the chair waiting for Nico.

"Dennis, I think it's a good idea if you see a professional in regards to your personal issues dealing with women and these separation issues," Nico told him, giving him a soft but serious look. He waited for him to explode on the comment, but he didn't. He thought maybe he was growing.

"A therapist?" he asked finally, with a shocked, sad look on his face.

"Yes, a therapist. It's not a bad thing. In fact, I think it would help more than hurt. Just think about it," he told his friend. Checking the suite to make sure nothing was left behind, they walked out. Nico was upset to learn that the media had caught wind of what happened on the boat. Someone leaked the story, and Shontell was hysterical. She didn't want the media in her face. Martin found a way to get them to the car unnoticed. Nico, Shontell, and his parents rode in the town car in silence. Shontell sat next to his mother, and he couldn't see her eyes through the sunglasses she had on. Arriving at the airport, she stepped out of the car and helped Bethany out. Nico watched the interaction between his mother and Shontell. Shaking his dad's hand, he waited for them to finish. Nate, who wasn't joining them, had gone ahead with the band members.

"Remember what I told you, dear, sunshine is coming," she told her, as they hugged. She turned to her son and hugged him. "Take care of her and you," she told him. They both waved as they entered the airport. Seated back inside of the car, Shontell lay her head on his shoulder. They were supposed to be heading to the cruise wrap-up party. Nico kissed her hair.

"Do you mind if we go back to the hotel? I don't think I am up for the party this evening," Shontell said, as she glanced up at him,

"Of course. I am sure everyone will understand our absence," Nico told her, as he redirected Brian. He then texted Martin and also Sandy for Shontell.

Dennis

Dennis overheard John say that Nico and Shontell wouldn't be coming to the wrap-up. He went and grabbed a drink from the bartender, as he tried not to watch Sandy dancing with the man she had been with during the cruise and Indiana. He sat in the corner and wanted to be mad at Sandy, but he knew he had lost her fairly. He got what he deserved. He thought back to what Nico said in his room. He envied his friend. He had found love. No one deserved it more than he did. He thought about Jesse and all that had happened. What had happened to him to make him snap? None of them would ever know. The captain let him speak to him before he was taken off the boat that morning. Jesse looked like he had aged ten years overnight. Jesse wouldn't say much, outside of apologizing for his actions. "You know, I still don't understand what happened with Jesse," Dennis said.

"Love can make you do the craziest thing. So when you find it, bro, don't do what I did. Treasure it, if she is what you want," he told him, as he kept shaking his head.

He didn't reply to his words. Jesse was going to be tried in Miami. They said the case was simple. He closed his eyes as he felt his heart tighten when Sandy kissed that guy. David walked back up to him and looked in the direction his brother was looking. "Man you can't touch her with a ten-foot pole. You messed that up. You may as well get over it," he told him. David pulled out a business card from his suit pocket. "Nico mentioned you might not be ready for this, but here's a referral just in case," he said. Dennis took the card from his hand and read it. Was he ready to work on his problems? Setting his glass down, he knew he was. He pulled his phone out and dialed the number. Walking into a room, he waited for the call to be answered.

The week went by quickly. Shontell was getting dressed. Today was going to be one of the hardest events she would ever have to attend. "Are you ready?" Nico asked her, interrupting her thoughts. "As ready as I can be," she told him. She took his hand, as they headed to the waiting funeral home car. When they arrived at the church, Shontell sat there and let the tears fall. She blew out a hard breath and wiped her face with the hanky that Nico had just handed her. He took her by the hand; getting out, they were joined by the rest of the group: Sandy, Eric, and Martin. They all entered the church, and she was greeted by Ebony's mother. She had only seen her a few times, and she still greeted her warmly even under the circumstances. "Shontell, I am glad you agreed to sing today. Even with all that happened, my daughter looked up to you. I hope that you have forgiven her indiscretions."

"Ms. Walker, I forgave her. Don't you worry about that now. And we will talk later," she told her. Elana sat in the first pew, and looked at her daughter's body in the casket. She knew that man wasn't going to bring her happiness, but she didn't think this would have happened. She did wish their relationship could have been better. Elana did the best she could with what she had for her kids, but her daughter never saw it that way and didn't appreciate the things she sacrificed so they could have a roof over their head and clothes on their back. She was glad those young men offered to pay for the service. It was a life saver for her and her sons, because she never thought to have life insurance on them or herself.

Shontell sat between her parents and Nico. She tried not to look over in the casket. She bounced her knee in nervousness, trying to get herself together. When it was time for her to sing, Nico squeezed her hand. She took to the podium, and the music began.

"Here we are again, that old familiar place where the winds will blow, no one ever knows the time nor place, don't cry for me. Don't shed a tear. The time I shared with you will always be and when I am gone, please carry on. Don't cry for me..." Shontell belted it out. There was not a dry eye in the church, including hers. She didn't even remember the rest of the service. After the service, they all went out for dinner. The

table was mostly quiet throughout. They needed a distraction so she spoke. "So guys, tell me about your overseas tour." It wasn't directed at any one person, but David began to tell her the cities they would be visiting. The room's atmosphere changed, and it was just what she needed. The laughter and the talking helped keep her mind off seeing Ebony in that casket. She noticed Nico watching her throughout the night. She tried not to think about the fact that he would be leaving her tomorrow evening.

When they got back to her house, she brought him to her laying her head on his chest, "I just wanted to say thank you."

"Thank you?"

"Yes, thank you. I wouldn't have gotten through the last few weeks without you. You were with me through all this—the hounding press and today, the funeral. A lot of men would have bailed a long time ago."

"Shontell, I love you. Being with you is the only place I want to be," he told her, as he kissed her tears from her face.

"I love you, too," she told him. They spent the rest of the night talking. In the morning, her parents came over for breakfast. Shontell's dad asked to speak to Nico alone.

Nico and Mr. Banner went out onto Shontell's back patio. The men took a seat, and her father began talking to him.

"You know me and my wife were so afraid things were going to go bad with Shontell and Jesse. I could never pinpoint what it was about him that made me so uneasy. It is sad to see I was proven right. We can't thank you enough for being there for Shon. She is our only child and the highlight of our lives. We could have lost her to that maniac. We are just glad that it's over."

"Yes, sir. I agree. If I would have lost her, I can't imagine what state I would be in. I love Shontell."

"You love her. That's a deep statement and responsibility. I am sure you already know that. I don't think she can handle being hurt any more, if you get the meaning of my words, son." Nico understood what he was saying clearly. Before he could respond, Shontell and her mother joined them with the breakfast. "So, Nico, Shontell told us that you are headed overseas for a few weeks," Mrs. Banner said to him.

"Yes, ma'am, we are. It is a nine-city tour, but we will be mostly in Japan. It's one of our biggest tours. I was hoping that maybe your daughter would join me for part of it."

"Excuse me! When were you going to discuss this with me?" a shocked Shontell asked, looking at Nico and then her parents.

"Before I left this evening. We can talk about it more later. It is just a thought. I just thought you could use a change of scenery with all that has happened."

"Well, sweetie, he does have a point. You've never been to Japan before, and it could be good for you," Mrs. Banner said in defense of Nico's comment. The look on Shontell's face said she wasn't pleased with his comment. They ate in silence for a little while. Nico realized he may have really put his foot in his mouth this time. Nico's phone vibrated in his pocket. He ignored it because, at this moment, what was going on at the table was more important — or so he thought.

Shontell managed to get through dinner. She tried not to be so mad at Nico. But it was hard for her to act like she wasn't. She walked her parents to the door and kissed them both. Why did everyone feel the need to have to protect her?

"Are you upset with me?"

"Why do you feel the need to protect me? What else can happen that hasn't happened already?" Shontell was voicing the thoughts she had been thinking. Before he could answer her, his cell phone went off again. He looked at it, frowning. Looking up at her, he told her, "I have to take this."

"Go ahead. I need a little air anyway." Nico stepped into the kitchen foyer, and she headed to the patio. Turning and watching him as his body language changed as he listened to the caller. He spoke softly, so she wasn't able to hear what he was saying. But she knew it was about her, because he looked at her a couple of times. Throwing her arms up in frustration, she walked to the banister and looked out over her yard.

Shontell had been outside for a few minutes when she heard a sound behind her. She turned around and called out to Nico. When he didn't respond, she walked back into the room and saw him lying on the floor. She went over to him, but was caught off guard by the voice behind her. "Miss me, sweetness?" Jesse said from the side of where Shontell was kneeling.

"Oh my god, what are you doing? How did you get out of jail?" she asked Jesse, her face full of alarm.

"It's called escaping. Guess you haven't watched the news today. I fled during the transport."

"But why, why are you here? Haven't you hurt me enough? Why can't you just leave me alone?" she asked him, as her tears spilled down her face.

"I told you on the ship that I love you. If I can't be with you, then you damn sure are not going to be with him," Jesse told her, as he was motioning towards a still-unconscious Nico. Shontell tried to jar Nico lightly to get him to wake up. She jumped when Jesse yelled at her.

"GET AWAY FROM HIM!" he told her, as he pulled out a gun and pointed it at Nico. Shontell's whole body began to shake, and she began to cry even harder. She needed to figure out how to make Jesse focus on her. She stood up and headed towards the couch. "Jesse, please don't do this. I will do whatever it is that you want. Just leave him alone," she told him. She saw Nico stirring out the corner of her eye. She racked her brain for something to do. All she could think about was just to divert him with talking.

"Come on, let's...let's go talk," she stammered, motioning towards the patio. Jesse looked at her and then back at Nico. He needed to make sure he wasn't moving. He looked back at Shontell as she headed towards the patio. She stood at the railing waiting for him, and he didn't see her push the panic button that she had installed out there. All she had to do was stall him until they got there.

Nico

Nico was still looking at Shontell; he could only see her back. Martin had just informed him that Jesse escaped. They had not watched the news. Because of all the media attention, he wanted to shield Shontell from it as much as he could. So they didn't even touch the television. Ending his call, he decided they needed to go to the hotel and not stay there tonight as originally planned. He tucked his phone in his pocket and was about to head out to the balcony when he felt a sharp pain in the back of his head.

Nico didn't know how long he had been knocked out, but he could feel the throbbing. He opened his eyes and saw Jesse and Shontell. He quickly closed his eyes when saw Jesse pointing a gun in his direction. He knew they were talking, but he couldn't understand their words. As they pain subsided some, he was soon able to make out their conversation. He heard Shontell reasoning with him and caught on quickly to do what she was trying to do. He saw Jesse follow her to the patio, and he slowly made his way over to the door. He made a mistake and hit the chair. Jesse heard him. He came running back into the room. "Going somewhere, man?" he asked him with a sneer on his face. "Why don't you just leave before the police get here?" Nico said to him. He didn't even know if the police were actually coming. Jesse grabbed Shontell by the elbow. "Hell, it doesn't matter if they come or not. I don't have anything else to lose. I damn sure ain't going to prison. So, if I kill you both and myself that will be the end of it. I can't leave here without having another sweet piece of Shontell," he said, as he ran his tongue down the side of her face. Shontell flinched and cried out, as he tightened his grip on her and held the gun to her side. Nico wanted to lunge at him, but didn't want to take the chance of Shontell getting hurt.

"Man, I am going to ask you to let my woman go," Jesse said, waving the gun back and forth with a glazed over look in his eyes.

"Your woman?" Nico eyes widened with his statement. He didn't realize Jesse was this unstable.

"She was mine before you even came into the picture," he stated, scratching his head like he was suddenly confused. But he still didn't take his eyes off Nico.

"Was she?" Nico said, baiting him to divert his attention.

"YES!" Jesse yelled, stepping towards him. "And to prove it, I'm going to let you watch as I make love to my woman."

"Nico?" Shontell whispered. She was looking frightened, as Jesse turned his attention to her.

"Get undressed," he told her. Nico gave Shontell a look that said he was going to make a move. Shontell cried as she did as he asked. She had no choice, as he had the gun pointed at her forehead. Jesse watched her unbutton her shirt and Nico made his move, grabbing him from behind. They wrestled, and he was able to knock the gun out of his hand. He punched Jesse in the jaw, and he stumbled. Just as he was getting up, the front door was busted open and then four police officers came charging into the house with their guns pointed on Jesse. They all stopped frozen.

"Hands up Jesse, NOW!!" The police yelled at him. Nico went over to Shontell and pulled her into his embrace. They both were shaking, and her body heaved. One of the officers came over to them, asking if they were okay. They both nodded, as Shontell turned to fix her clothing.

"I never meant to hurt her. I love her," Jesse said as he looked at the police officers. Nico and Shontell were ushered back from where Jesse was, as they watched the officers subdue him.

Jesse

Jesse got down on the floor as instructed, all the while keeping his eyes on Shontell. He looked from Shontell and then to Nico, who was holding her. He could see their love. Jesse bowed his head, as the officers pulled him up from the floor. Shontell had never looked at him the way she was looking at Nico. It was right then that he knew he deserved whatever he got for hurting Ebony. She had loved him, despite how he treated her. Jesse didn't deserve the love of either Ebony or Shontell. As he was being led out the room, he stopped in his tracks. Jesse tried to look back, and gave the officer a pleading look. They turned him back around toward the couple. "Shontell and Nico, I am sorry for all this." He then looked at Nico. "Love her right, because I know I sure didn't know how. You two look good together." Jesse was then led out the door into the awaiting cruise car. The officer covered his head, as the news media started running in their direction firing questions at him. As they were pulling off, he saw both Shontell and Nico on the porch watching. The media was being contained by the police. He immediately thought how he knew that Shontell was hating all this media attention. He faced forward and remained silent the rest of the ride.

Epilogue

One year later

Shontell was standing backstage waiting for her cue. Martin walked over to her and gave her a warm hug. "I told you that you two were meant for each other," he said, winking. Soon after, the rest of the guys walked over to where she was standing. Each one touched her slightly protruding stomach. She turned as she heard Nico speak. "We have added a special performance to our show tonight. We have a hometown girl with us, and what better way to introduce her to you than in her beautiful hometown of Detroit. We did a duet which is on our current CD, and we will be sharing it with you tonight." The crowd went wild, the music began to play, and Nico began to sing.

"*I used to search for a love that was never there, waking up from a nightmare in a cold sweat, then I met you, and all my dreams came true…*" Hearing her cue, she began to sing as she walked out on the stage: "*I never believed in fairy tales, thought they were for those other girls, but one night I dreamed of a man, and it was you, you became my dream come true…*"

Holding hands, they sang to each other as if there was no one else there. After they finished, the crowd stood on their feet. Nico kissed her, and then kissed her stomach.

"This is the love of my life, the mother of my child, Ms. Shontell Banner. Hopefully, soon she will be my bride." Nico got down on one knee and pulled a ring box from his pocket. Shontell looked surprised, as her eyes filled with tears. She looked at him. No one could have ever told her that they would be here. The day that Jesse almost killed them was harder than she thought she could recover from. She was so afraid he was going to break out of jail and come after her again. She sold her house and moved near Sandy. Under her parent's and Nico's advisement, she started therapy and fought hard to get back to where she is now. Nico supported her through it all. Her family and friends were the strength she needed. Their pregnancy was a surprise, but they took it in stride like they did everything else this past year. How could she not marry him? He never left her side. Not just once but twice, he always stood by her through all her drama. She looked over at him and smiled, nodding yes. He placed the 1.2 carat diamond on her finger. He stood up, and they shared a kiss. The Fox Theater erupted. The rest of the group came back on stage, and she bowed. She was excited, but focused enough to wave to Sandy. She was with her fiancé, Eric. Her parents were also there, and they were all sitting in the front row. Like their song said, sometimes *dreams do come true.*

Epilogue

One year later

Shontell was standing backstage waiting for her cue. Martin walked over to her and gave her a warm hug. "I told you that you two were meant for each other," he said, winking. Soon after, the rest of the guys walked over to where she was standing. Each one touched her slightly protruding stomach. She turned as she heard Nico speak. "We have added a special performance to our show tonight. We have a hometown girl with us, and what better way to introduce her to you than in her beautiful hometown of Detroit. We did a duet which is on our current CD, and we will be sharing it with you tonight." The crowd went wild, the music began to play, and Nico began to sing.

"I used to search for a love that was never there, waking up from a nightmare in a cold sweat, then I met you, and all my dreams came true..." Hearing her cue, she began to sing as

she walked out on the stage: *"I never believed in fairy tales, thought they were for those other girls, but one night I dreamed of a man, and it was you, you became my dream come true..."* Holding hands, they sang to each other as if there was no one else there. After they finished, the crowd stood on their feet. Nico kissed her, and then kissed her stomach.

"This is the love of my life, the mother of my child, Ms. Shontell Banner. Hopefully, soon she will be my bride." Nico got down on one knee and pulled a ring box from his pocket. Shontell looked surprised, as her eyes filled with tears. She looked at him. No one could have ever told her that they would be here. The day that Jesse almost killed them was harder than she thought she could recover from. She was so afraid he was going to break out of jail and come after her again. She sold her house and moved near Sandy. Under her parent's and Nico's advisement, she started therapy and fought hard to get back to where she is now. Nico supported her through it all. Her family and friends were the strength she needed. Their pregnancy was a surprise, but they took it in stride like they did everything else this past year. How could she not marry him? He never left her side. Not just once but twice, he always stood by her through all her drama. She looked over at him and smiled, nodding yes. He placed the 1.2 carat diamond on her finger. He stood up, and they shared a kiss. The Fox Theater erupted. The rest of the group came back on stage, and she bowed. She was excited, but focused enough to wave to Sandy. She was with her fiancé, Eric. Her parents were also there, and they were all sitting in the front row. Like their song said, sometimes *dreams do come true.*

The End

Contact Jada Pearl:

Twitter, FB and Instagram: @authorjadapearl

Email: authorjadapearl@gmail.com

Blog site: www.jadapearl.wordpress.com

Website coming soon: www.authorjadapearl.com

Check out other romance novels from Jessica Watkins Presents:

Good Girls Ain't No Fun boxed set by Jessica Watkins

Good Girls Ain't No Fun finale by Jessica Watkins

Beautiful Prey by Phoenix Daniels

Beautiful Prey 2 by Phoenix Daniels

If Your Girl Only Knew by Kenya Moss

The Game of Love by K. Alex Walker

The Right Kind of Wrong by Chantria Taylor

Become a published author:

Jessica Watkins Presents is currently accepting submissions for the following genres: African American Romance, Urban Fiction, Women's Fiction and BWWM Romance.

If you have a complete manuscript, send the synopsis and the first three chapters to jwp.submissions@gmail.com.